Final Flock

Book Five of Feathered Dreams

By: Brittany Putzer

Final Flock

Editing by: Kat Pagan

Formatting by: Frankie Page

Cover design by: Rae Lumpkins

ISBN: 979-8-218-29419-9

Published in the United States.

Dedication

Thank you for your love and support during Ann's journey. This world I created is even greater than the dreams that first manifested it when I began writing *Feathered Dreams* in October 2019. Now here it is, 2023, and Ann's story is coming to an end. I hope the finale is everything you expected (with, of course, some twists along the way).

This book concludes Ann's feathered dreams.

Contents

Drifting

"Jeremy?" I toss the down comforter. "What the...?" My palm glides over a silk nightgown instead of my usual t-shirt.

"Did you have another nightmare, Ann?"

"*Christian*?" So many thoughts tangle together in my head. But when he wraps his arms around me, I melt. I breathe him in.

His lips graze my forehead. "Don't fret. I'll always be near to clear the cobwebs of your dreams."

His suit is pristine. Not a hair is out of place. I pluck a royal-blue feather from his pocket square and twirl it between my fingertips. Many words have been left unsaid between us.

"Did I do this to you?"

"Do what exactly? *Steal* my heart? Sneak chickens into my home?"

"*Destroy* everything you hold dear."

He tips my chin so I'm forced to look him in the eye. "You're the light in my dark world. Why on earth would you say that?"

My reply tumbles out. "Your family was perfect before I showed up. I'm a curse."

Christian's lips brush mine. "You are our curse *breaker*. Don't you see it?"

I shake my head as I bury my face into his chest.

"Before long, I promise everything will make sense. Oh, my sweet Ann, you're worth everything to me."

"Why did you have to die?"

"So that the truth could be revealed and transform

1

the world."

"Why didn't you tell me what was really happening? You killed innocent people..."

"I served my country as its sovereign and did what had to be done. Yes, my hands are covered in the blood of the innocent but also that of the guilty. It's a balancing act, the scale of justice. In the end, the safety of the citizens was always my highest priority. I worked tirelessly for peace, stability, and unity." He strokes my cheek. "I wouldn't change a thing I did, especially if it meant I'd never have the chance to love you."

I rub my pregnant belly. "Did you know about this?"

"Yes," he admits without missing a beat.

"This whole time, you knew what happened in the safe room?"

Christian arches a brow, and his regal grin makes me want to punch him in the face. "*Nothing* slips past me."

My vision blurs. I clutch his shirt, and the feather glides to my feet. "Christian!" His face is hazy. "I'm sorry," I sob. "For everything."

"Oh, Ann." Christian's sympathetic voice caresses my cheek until his features morph into Jeremy's tender gaze.

"Ann?" Jeremy swipes at my tears. "Are you okay?"

I touch my dingy t-shirt, lean back, and rub the dream from my eyes. "Yes. It's just my conscience getting the best of me."

"Anything you want to talk about?"

I snuggle into his chest. "Hold me. Tell me everything will be okay."

"Everything will be okay."

"Do you promise?"

"I'll protect you until my dying breath." He kisses the top of my head. "Now go back to sleep."

I can't shut off my brain. Images of Christian swirl in my mind. Does he know about the baby? Can we actually forgive each other? Or is it something I want so desperately that I'm *willing* it into existence?

I rest my palm on Jeremy's chest. It rises and falls while his heart beats strong. Whatever happens, I'm grateful I met the rebels. They've changed the way I view the world. I peck Jeremy's cheek. He works hard to keep everyone safe. He shouldn't have to add me to that list, but I'm glad he did.

I slip out of bed and into the common area in the compound. The quietness of night reminds me of everything they've been fighting for. The ability to own land, get married, and live their lives to the fullest.

"Get back here, you little terror!" Sally stirs up a breeze as she runs past me, and I clutch my chest. The older woman leaps, tackles her target, straightens her spine, and holds up her prize. "This will make you think twice before stealing my food."

The red hen blinks, as if to show how unbothered she is by the threat. I stroke Scarlett's plumage and turn to Sally. "You can't blame her for taking your crumbs."

She sighs. "With all the extra mouths to feed, it's getting harder to give *anyone* enough to eat." May attempts to scurry past us unnoticed, and Sally clears her throat. "Young lady. Stop right there."

The eight-year-old presents us with her best puppy-dog eyes. "What's wrong, Sally? You sound mad."

The older woman shoves the hen into the girl's arms. "We've talked about this. The chickens belong *outside*."

May sneaks a peek at me and I know I'll be the one in trouble next. "But Snowball gets to live inside the Palace. Why can't Scarlett live here with us?"

Sally gives me a pointed glare before returning her attention to the sweet-talker. "Snowball is a *special* breed. They are born to be domestic animals, trained to wear a diaper and walk on a leash."

"I can teach Scarlett to do that too!" May beams. "I'll take care of her and love her forever." The girl kisses Sally on the cheek. "Like you love and care for me."

Sally falters as May returns to her room with the red hen in tow. Then the older woman swipes at her cheek and stands. "That child doesn't fight fair."

I rub her arm. "Well, she learned from the *best*."

"Maybe I should let her play house with the hen. It's better than having her sleep outside every night."

I follow Sally as she returns to the living quarters. When the extra rebels were forced from their homes and moved in here, the compound filled to the brim. Most of the small bedrooms now sleep four to six adults. Sally volunteered to stay with the orphaned children to keep watch over them, and now that tiny space includes a feathered renegade too. When we crack the door, soft snores flutter through the opening. Sally smiles into the darkness before grabbing her boots, then she tiptoes out again. She sits on a bench and unlaces them.

"There's space in my room if you need to place someone somewhere," I offer.

Sally waves me off. "No, you are growing a child. You need proper rest and less stress." She shoves her foot into her shoe, and a loud crunch has her eyes bulging. "What in the devil?" She lifts her leg and watches as yolk and shell drip off the tip of her sock.

I cringe, holding in my giggle, while Sally turns fifty shades of red. I locate a towel and pass it to her. "Don't. Say. A word," she grinds out. "Not *one.*" I meet her gaze and her scowl melts into a smirk. "This is *your* fault. May never would have brought that bird into our room if you hadn't fed her stories of chicken queens living lavish lives."

"I guess today you are literally walking on eggshells." I elbow her in the ribs.

"Is that all you've got?" Sally raises a challenging brow. "Seeing as you're AnnaBelle's daughter, I would have expected more, but omelettin' it slide this time."

"Well, I know how you can't take a yolk."

"You're egg-hausting."

"I've got a dozen of them." I lean my head on her shoulder. As much as I wanted to hate Sally when I arrived, she has become an amazing adoptive parent. Filling a space in my heart I never realized was missing.

"What am I going to do with Scarlett and May?" She huffs while removing her moist sock and tossing it aside. "I'm glad that she's sleeping inside, but is it healthy for her to have a hen as a best friend?"

"I did and look how I turned out."

"Oh, you mean *pregnant* with your fiancé's brother's child," Tammy answers with a smug look as she joins us.

"That's a mouthful, even for you Tam-Tam."

"Don't call me that."

"What are you going to do about it?"

Even though Tammy apologized for her recent behavior and her obvious distrust of me, we still bicker. But now it feels as though we are sisters, because no

5

matter how much we fight, we are stuck with one another.

"Ladies, enough," Sally chastises with that motherly tone of hers.

Tammy narrows her eyes at me and passes Sally a folder. "I've set up the meeting like you asked and everyone is waiting in the office." Then she stomps off.

"Bye, Tam-Tam!" I call out to her back. She doesn't even bother to turn around as she waves a certain finger in response.

"Why do you instigate her?"

"Because I'm bored, and you won't let me have a feathered princess inside the compound," I reply with a pout.

Sally's laughter reverberates off the cement walls. "Come on, we've got work to do."

A few minutes later, we're all positioned around the conference table, shuffling through documents. Jeremy joins us, yawning and grumbling about me not waking him up. Once he settles at my side, he rubs my leg under the table.

I warm his wrist with my hand and address the group. "I understand how important this mission is to everyone. The Black Rose has been discriminated against, its members murdered, and your names slandered by the Royals." I tap the paper in front of me. "But you've tried *violence* and didn't get the results you wanted." Tammy's scowl makes me purse my lips. "Remember, *you* asked me to plan the next move… a more peaceful approach." My little boy does gymnastics at the sound of my voice, and I massage my belly to soothe him.

"I never suggested we use *weapons*, but we do need

to be forceful if we want results with these ignorant politicians," Sally answers.

"I never said we should not be forceful. But your plan of traveling to the Palace with *guns* resting against our thighs is not going to work."

She rubs her temples. "Jeremy, what do you think?"

All of our attention rests on the muscular man talking gibberish to my belly. He straightens his back and clears his throat. "There must be a compromise between your two proposals. I *cannot* allow anyone to walk into the Palace unarmed. But I don't want to threaten the Royals into acting irrationally. I mean, I did shoot and unintentionally kill King Christian. Who knows what they might have in store for us when we stride through the halls asking for peace?"

"What if we don't *go* to the Palace at first?" I suggest.

"You mean like send them a candygram with hearts embroidered on it?" Tammy scoffs.

"We've already sent them your hair, blood, ultrasound picture, and even your old engagement ring." Sally taps her fingers on the table. "What more can we do to get their attention, without *storming* the gates?"

I stand, using the table for support. I was hoping she'd ask this question. I stretch my stiff back before handing Sally a sheet of paper. As she reads it, I explain to the group, "I would like to take this essay to the newspaper's main office. It explains the Black Rose's history, attacks on them by the Palace, and also the retaliation raids. Plus, I'll add pictures for evidence. If they'll publish it, the Palace will have no choice but to respond publicly."

"That's the dumbest idea yet." Tammy shakes her head.

"Tammy," Jeremy warns between clenched teeth.

"The Palace has the media in *their* back pocket. There's no way we'll be able to get a butt-kissing reporter to print this. They value their comfortable accommodations too much."

"The enforcers are close to our compound, and we are running out of time," Sally interjects. "It could take months to locate a sympathetic reporter to print it."

"I have a friend on the inside. He runs the main office and I'm sure he'll do this for me." I look around the table. "Come on, guys. This article could educate the people about who you really are and gain sympathy for the cause."

"But then what? A *word* war with the Palace? That won't help us." Tammy groans. "You are starting to sound like Dan."

"It wouldn't be a word war," I mumble. "Once the story is printed, I'll let my contact know that, when the Palace reaches out demanding details, we'll set up a video conference to speak to the Royals face to face."

"Is that a safe option?" Sally questions.

I nod at our tech genius, Xander, and he takes over. "We can choose a remote location, away from the compound, and pick a specific date and time. Then make it short so we can't be traced."

Sally glances at her son. "And are *you* certain this is safe?"

Jeremy's muscles ripple as he shrugs. "Safer than attacking the Palace. Plus, the chat can be made public so even if the Palace won't acknowledge the video conference, the newspaper can report on it and gain us sympathy."

The team digests the proposition. It's been a rough

road for them. I've only been living at the compound for a few months, but the others have been here for the majority of their lives. They are itching for results, so that the death toll will cease and their freedoms will be restored. All they want is to return to a more normal existence.

"I say we give it a try." Sally turns to me. "When are you planning on delivering these documents to the newspaper?"

"As soon as I can." I sigh. "My energy level hasn't been the greatest and I feel like a potbellied pig."

Sally eyes my enlarging frame. I can only imagine what she's thinking about. My mom? Her children? "I can arrange for transport as early as tomorrow afternoon."

"Thank you and I will speak to Brad about escorting me to the office." I help clear the table before walking out.

Jeremy offers me his bicep. "You are out of your mind if you think I'm going to sit on the sidelines for this mission. We don't know that your source is safe and the location is in enemy territory."

"*You* told me that Brad is one of your top soldiers."

"But he is also young and still learning."

"You specifically said that he was trustworthy, strong, and intelligent."

"I never said he was strong." Jeremy tugs open my door and leads me inside.

I look around the small studio-sized apartment. I spot my water bottle from this morning and take a swig before lowering myself onto the couch.

"Why didn't *you* tell me you wanted to take someone else on this mission?" Jeremy stands with his hands firmly planted on his hips.

"Because I had a feeling you would act like a two-year-old. Thank goodness I was wrong." I roll my eyes.

"I only trust one person to watch over you."

I grab his scarred hand and kiss it gently on the center of the 'R' in hopes of easing him into my next statement. "Brad is not *marked*. I do not want to attract unwanted attention." I try not to recall the botched bank job from a few months ago.

"But you striding into the building *pregnant* won't do that?"

"I'm counting on their curiosity. The newspaper staff will ask questions. Questions that will hopefully be directed at the Palace once we leave."

Jeremy sits next to me. "This operation will be dangerous no matter how we go about it."

I lean my head on his shoulder. "I know. But now's the time to get the *people* to ask the questions and insist on receiving answers. If we can get this mandate signed and change the country's view of the Black Rose, *everyone* here will have a real future. No more hiding or fighting."

"I want you safe." His palms warm my jaw. "There's no doubt in my mind you can handle this mission, but I want to be by your side just in case."

I love that he's protective but also believes in my abilities.

"I know." I peck him on the cheek. "But this is my call. Brad is escorting me and that is final." I rise to my feet, stabbing my point further.

"I need to go have a *chat* with him before he escorts you." Jeremy meets my stubbornness head-on.

"Listen, I know we have a thing going on between us. But please don't scare him off because you are *jealous*."

He tugs my hips, bringing me to him. "A *thing*?"

I coil my arms around his neck. "What would you like to call it?"

"How about boyfriend?" He kisses my neck.

"You can try to butter me up all you want, mister. But I am still taking Brad."

"I'm losing my effect on you." Jeremy chuckles in response. "Fine. I'm leaving now to have an extra *training* session with your escort. Let's just hope I don't kill him before he has to depart. But if I do, I guess I'll have no choice but to fill his shoes."

My fingertips trail his arm. "If you *promise* me you won't kill him, I'll be very pleased."

"Oh? How pleased?"

I lean in, whispering sweet promises in his ear, and he groans.

"What if I beat him up a little?" he counters.

"Not a hair on his head will be hurt."

"No promises."

More to Lose

The mission triggers dread to settle like a brick in my stomach.

"Everything will be fine." Jeremy yawns from beside me. "Now stop worrying. Your nervous energy is making our child kick me." His warm lips tickle my belly button. "It's okay, buddy."

"I'm sorry," I groan. "I'm having second thoughts."

"Do you want to go in guns blazing?"

"No."

"Then stop. Because that's our other option."

"Jeremy?"

"Yeah?"

"What are you looking forward to the most when you're free?"

His body stiffens but he loosens the tension with a sigh. "My own *bathroom* would be wonderful."

"Really?"

"Yes. I share one with a ton of men and they are disgusting."

"Ew." I run my fingertips through his hair. "Tell me another thing you're looking forward to. Something different. One that's not for hygiene but fun too."

"I want a dog."

"Huh?"

He pivots and his eyes sparkle when he says, "I want a furry beast to sleep on my bed with me every night and to run beside me as I train."

"You know, a *child* is a lot like a dog."

His chuckle warms the air. "No, they're not."

"Kids are large and loud, and ours will probably sleep in our bed so I can breastfeed it without moving far. The main difference is that a child is smarter and sheds less."

"Breastfeed, huh?" Jeremy reaches for the milkers in question. "Why do I get the feeling that you do *not* like furry companions?"

I smack his wrist. "I'd rather have feathers under the covers."

He burrows his face into my neck. "Any way I can change your mind?"

"Nope. Anything with four legs is gross."

"What about five *legs*?" His grin resting on my cheek reminds me how immature he is.

"Good night, Jeremy."

"Would you consider having a dog… for *me*?"

My breath catches. This pillow talk is just that, a *fantasy*. I swallow my negativity. "As long as the beast sleeps on your side of the bed." He pulls me into a hug. "And *you* clean up its messes, all of them. I mean it," I'm quick to add.

I stare at my disheveled mess in the bathroom mirror. Jeremy pops his head in, as he tucks his shirt into his tactical pants. "What's the matter?"

I motion to my abdomen. "Nothing fits this melon-sized bulge! It's getting cold outside and the only things I can fit into around here are dresses."

"You are beautiful no matter what you wear, and you won't be pregnant forever." He rubs my back. "Besides, I love this dress." He meets my gaze in the mirror.

"It shows too much cleavage."

His laugh tugs at my frown. "It's another *gift* of pregnancy. Enjoy it." He runs a palm up my thigh. "Because I know I am."

"Stop being flirty." My hip bumps him back a step. I return my attention to the mirror as my fingers comb through my hair. "I guess it'll have to do for now."

Jeremy guides me towards the garage of the compound. I divert my attention away from the fact that we'll be separated and poke the bear instead. "Where did we leave off on our relationship status? Are we still calling it an *intimate* friendship?"

"You know as well as I do that we have no idea what the future holds for either of us. I cherish *every* moment I have with you, and I don't want to be with any other woman. Because, trust me, you are trouble enough. So let's enjoy each other's company while we have it."

A tinted SUV looms in front of us and Jeremy helps me inside. A tall, lanky man steps in behind us.

"Hey, Brad," I welcome the newcomer.

"Lady Ann." He dips his head to me, then to Jeremy. "Sir."

The two rebel soldiers stare at one another until Jeremy breaks the silence. "Brad, remember what we discussed. Stay close, be alert, and if one of her hairs is out of place…"

Brad nods. "I guarantee the mission will be a success."

14

"It better be."

My newly appointed bodyguard leaves a seat between us, while I eye his stoic expression before turning my glare on Mr. Troublemaker. "You are being way too hard on him."

Jeremy arches a brow at me but addresses the other man. "Brad, am I being too hard on you?"

"No, sir."

He smirks. "See?"

"Go and beat something up," I grumble under my breath.

"I'll see you guys soon." Jeremy kneels and rubs my belly. "Son, you better keep her in line—do you hear me?"

"Hey, you are not turning this child against me."

Tammy interjects as she shoves an earpiece into my ear. "Sally wants you to take this with you. Remember you need to get in and out within twenty, thirty minutes tops."

"If you never let us leave, we'll never return." I rub my sore lobe.

Tammy hands Jeremy a black blindfold with a smirk. "You also need to wear this for the ride there and back."

"She still doesn't *trust* me with the location of the compound?"

"Oh, come on, it'll be fun." Jeremy ties the fabric around my head before placing a kiss on my neck. "Maybe we can use it tonight?"

"In your dreams."

His soft, woodsy scent and warmth evaporate before Jeremy calls out, "Brad, make sure this gets replaced on the trip back."

I don't hear a response, but the door clicks shut and the driver starts the engine. I take a few deep breaths.

"Are you okay, Lady Ann?"

I swallow my uncertainties. "I need you to remember that I'm leading this mission. Meaning that I expect you to go along with or remain neutral when it comes to whatever I say or do inside that newsroom. Is that understood?"

"I understand." Brad clears his throat. "I respect you, Ann, but remember who I have to report to."

"I'll do my best to keep you out of trouble."

We're quiet again as we bounce along the bumpy road. My mind wanders to what I must do when we arrive. I'll have to hone in on my well-practiced Mary persona. I know Jeremy is going to be mad, but it's the only way to get quick results.

"Are you and Jeremy dating?"

Brad's question startles me out of my thoughts. "That's a complicated question." I smirk, wondering where this conversation is going.

"I was curious how... never mind."

"Go on, I'm listening."

"I was wondering how he made himself... *available* to you."

"Well, my being locked up with him helped a lot."

"Forget I asked."

He obviously isn't a fan of sarcasm. Brad and my dad would have gotten along great.

"It was an attraction built over time, through friendship and sacrifice. Then, one day, we each realized we didn't want to live without the other, no matter what the future held for us."

"Do you *love* each other?"

His question catches me off guard. Is what we have love?

"We would give our lives for each other. In a sense, it's a form of love. But, you know, I was engaged to King Christian before he died. I was also with Prince— now King—Ryan too. I told them both I loved them… and you see the aftermath. I want things to be different between me and Jeremy."

"So, your plan of action is to develop a strong companionship first?"

"Who are you developing a plan of action for, Brad?"

"I'd rather not say."

"Can I offer you a small piece of advice?"

"Sure."

My heart clenches as images of my parents have my lashes moistening. "Enjoy the time you have and don't wait too long to pursue something because life is too short."

"Especially for us rebels." He sighs.

I hate how defeated he sounds. I wish I could ease his burdens. The rebels are so misunderstood.

"That's why what we are doing is essential. We are hoping to change the way things are. Don't lose hope."

I lean into the seat. Brad's parents were killed by the same enforcers I'd always thought were here to protect and serve. He's an orphan and making the most of his borrowed time. But he dreams of having more, including a family of his own.

The SUV slows and pulls to a stop. Brad unties my blindfold. I fluff my hair. "Now, remember what I told you: go along with what happens next and please refer to me as Lady Ann until we leave."

I tug my jacket closer as the cold air smacks against my chest. A shiver zips up my spine. *Get it together, Ann.*

"Are you ready to change the world, *Lady* Ann?" Brad asks while he adjusts his sidearm.

I brush fuzz off the sleeves of his stolen Palace uniform and plaster on a smile. I pivot and scan the large marble pillars of the building looming in front of us. *Please don't let me throw up.*

I take a steadying breath. "Let's get this over with."

We walk up the steps to the double doors. Brad bows as he holds them open for me. The smell of paper lingers in the air while the hustle and bustle eases my nerves. Nobody is even batting a lash at our presence. I turn to the receptionist. "Good afternoon, I'm here to see Mr. Richard Olsen, please?"

The plump woman side-glances us from her computer screen. She blinks and drops the pen dangling from her lips. "Oh. Lady Ann. Yes, of course. Right this way." She leads us through the many cubicles to the back of the office space. "Here we are."

"Thank you. We can take it from here." I nod in her direction, politely dismissing her.

"Not a problem. Let me know if you need anything else." Once she turns the corner, I knock on the doorframe.

"It's open. Come on in."

"Showtime," I whisper as I square my shoulders and command my feet to move forward.

A tall man glances up from a pile of papers. He grins and arches a brow. "Look what the Palace dropped off." He opens his arms. "Anna Banana!"

I cringe at the nickname but hug him. "Dick. It's good to see you again"

He pulls back from our embrace. "You are the *only* woman in the world who is allowed to call me that."

"Look who's talking? How many times have I told you not to call me Anna Banana?" I push him back a step.

"School was never boring with you around. I miss your spunk."

I tug off my bulky jacket and hang it on his coatrack. His eyes trail up my body. "Well, someone's been *busy*."

I bite my cheek to hide my smirk as he takes my bait. *Curiosity may kill the cat after all.* I sit across from him. Allowing my cleavage to pour out of my dress.

"The last time I saw you, we were drinking and dancing at the charity ball. What happened since then?"

I reach behind my shoulder and Brad hands me a folder. Inside are the article and pictures I've collected for this exact moment. Richard practically drools as I offer him the evidence. "*Before* you open this, remember that I came to you because of our history together. And because, let's be honest, you owe me."

"Well, you certainly have my undivided attention." Richard winks at me, as I release the folder into his grasp. "You have always made sure we were in front of the line at the Palace press conferences. I am sure whatever this is…" His complexion pales. He rubs his hands over his face. "What the hell have you gotten yourself into?" Richard leans into his leather chair as he finishes skimming the materials. "I can't publish this."

He closes the folder on his desk with finality.

Game on.

I push to my feet, move around the desk to stand next to him, and collect the papers while brushing my leg against his. "That's okay. I can go to *another* newspaper—one that's more willing to help me."

He grabs my wrist. Brad steps forward but I lift a palm to stop him. "This is *dangerous*," Richard warns. "Once it's out there, there's no turning back for either of us. Are you sure you want to do this?"

I sit on the edge of the desk with my arms crossed. "Dick, come on. *Where* is the rebellious teenager I grew up with? The one who went behind enemy lines to get that scoop on the lunch lady's *dirty* secrets?"

"I tried to forget about that."

"That old lady was pretty fond of you."

He shakes his head. "I still can't believe I kissed her to get out of trouble."

"Those were the good old days." I grin and flick my eyes to the ceiling while soaking in the nostalgia.

"But we were *kids* then. Now, we're adults with more responsibilities."

"And more to *lose* too," I add. When our stare-off becomes too much, I huff out, "Are *you* going to publish the article for me or am I going somewhere else?"

"What if the Palace wants to reply to it?"

"I will be available for a video conference tomorrow night." I pull out a slip of paper listing the specifics. "Again, more information that could further *your* career."

His fingertips linger on my hand as he collects it. "You are always looking out for me." Richard tilts his head. "I'll do it, but under one condition." His palm warms my cheek before his lips brush mine. "Let me snap a picture of us." He grins into my eyes. "For the front page."

I let out a breath, glad that's all he wants. Poor Richard has been obsessed with me since grade school. He reminds me of Max, but at least Richard is more mentally stable. I hope.

"Tell me where you want me." I smirk.

"You are such a delectable tease." Richard smooths a wrinkle out of his suit. He turns to Brad, then me. "Can Mr. Smiley take a photo?"

"Yes, he's extremely intelligent."

Richard hands Brad the camera. "I wouldn't expect anything less from you, Anna Banana," he says as I wrap my arm around his waist, and he does the same. We both smile into the lens. "Now, I need a side shot of this." He motions to my belly.

"Is that really necessary?"

"A deal is a deal, little lady. May I?" Richard moves his hands to my belly as Brad clicks a few more shots. "I must be *crazy* for agreeing to print this."

"If the Royals question you, tell them I came in here all sweet and innocent, *demanding* that it be published as soon as possible."

"You, *innocent*? Ha!" We embrace once more. "No matter your intentions, I'm glad to see you again," Richard adds as he rubs his hands along my spine. Then trails them to my backside. "If you need *anything* else, you know where to find me." He squeezes to nail his point across.

I tip my chin to meet his gaze. "How long have you known about the Palace's mistreatment of the Black

Rose?"

He falters. "What makes you think I knew anything about that?"

"When you read through the documents, you didn't look surprised. You didn't even ask any follow-up questions." His silence speaks volumes. "How could you sit around while innocent people were being treated like dirt? That's not the man I knew."

"A lot has changed." Richard nods to my growing figure. "We do things we aren't *proud* of, but that doesn't mean we don't care."

"Well, you have a weird way of showing that you *care* for the citizens you swore to keep informed." I grab my coat and flip my loose locks over the collar as I button it.

"I like your hair short." His smile makes his eyes twinkle. "It reminds me of your mom."

I pause on the third button. "Thank you."

Richard grabs the doorknob. "I'll be watching your video conference too. Make sure you send me a smile."

My stomach sours at the thought of the road ahead, but I steel my spine. "You know, Richard, it's never too late to do the *right* thing."

"Then I guess I'll have to take a page from *your* book and begin that journey today. Goodbye, Anna. Be safe."

Brad and I stride to the waiting car, each lost in our own thoughts. I climb in, glance at my watch, and tap the earpiece. "Mission accomplished. We're on our way."

"10-4. See you soon," Sally chimes in.

I gulp in oxygen as bile rises in my throat. Will Richard follow through? Or back out?

I feel Brad's eyes burning into me. "Yes, Brad," I prompt him to speak his mind.

"What happened inside there..." He tugs a thumb behind him. "...is a lot to report back about."

"I did what I had to do to get the ball rolling. I've known Richard most of my childhood and I'm familiar with his weaknesses."

"You used your *body* to get results," he grinds out. "That's not what you were supposed to do."

I close my eyes and lean back. "I did what any spy would have done. Plus, I didn't shed a drop of blood to get the results we needed."

"What will Jeremy say about your tactics?"

"I will handle Jeremy."

"Oh, I bet you will."

My neck snaps in Brad's direction. "What's that supposed to mean?"

"You know exactly what that means."

"I am not *using* Jeremy!" I hiss.

"Are you trying to convince me or *yourself?*"

Paint the Town Red

After a few hours of strained silence, we arrive at the compound. Brad removes my blindfold.

"Brad, listen…"

But the words flutter around us as Jeremy offers me a hand out of the vehicle. "How did the mission go?"

I pivot to locate Brad, but like a ninja chicken, he disappears into the shadows.

"I need to eat, then we can discuss the trip."

"Was it successful?"

I force a smile. "I sure hope so."

I change into less-restrictive clothing while Jeremy grabs some fruit out of the mini-fridge. As I sit on the couch, he hands me the goods.

"Thank you." I munch, attempting to push the brick farther down my throat.

"Why do I get the feeling I'm not going to like your report?" Jeremy's frame rests against the counter. "Ann, talk to me."

"I did what I had to do and, well… sometimes peace involves other *forms* of sacrifice." I lift my eyes slowly to meet his gaze. "And Brad is upset with my methods." Jeremy arches a brow. But before he can pull the information out of me, I shove the food into my mouth and stand. "Let's go brief everyone."

I scurry past him. He snatches my wrist and squeezes me into a hug. "I missed you."

I snuggle into his warm neck. The world is right when I'm in his arms. We are two imperfect people supporting each other through thick and thin. "I missed you too."

"Come on, troublemaker. No more stalling." Jeremy takes my hand, and we meet Sally in the conference room.

She looks up when we enter. "There you are." Then she motions towards Tammy and Brad. "We've been waiting."

There's an edge to her voice. I take in the large circles under her eyes and sigh. "I'm sorry."

Jeremy closes the office door and sits next to me. "Mom, she's eating for two. Give her a break."

"I apologize." Sally flops into her chair and rubs her temples. "Now that we're all here, how about one of you tells us what happened." She turns to me, then Brad. "Or do I have to play charades and figure it out for myself?"

Brad clears his throat and stands. He explains every tiny detail. I'm amazed, and a tad envious, at his memory. Once he concludes the mission brief, he shoots me a look. I imagine it's the same look siblings throw at each other after one's done something naughty, and the other just snitched on them.

I cower in my chair in the silent room. Everyone wears an expression of shock and anger, or both. Jeremy sets his jaw and stares at a chip in the table, while Sally leans back with her arms crossed.

"Instead of using guns, we are using our bodies?" Tammy rolls her eyes as she speaks first.

"I did the job, didn't I?" I grumble.

Jeremy slams a fist on the desk, and I jump. "But at *what* cost?"

"One that's far better than our lives." I frown at him as my eyes water.

"This isn't *who* you are, Ann, and it isn't what we

25

trained to do. Dishonesty and manipulative tactics are what the *Royals* rely on, not us. I need some air." The door slams behind him.

Is he right? Did I cross a line? I thought the mission was critical. I was only trying to help. Why isn't he happy that, for all intents and purposes, the operation was a success?

"As a leader, we do what we must to get the job done. Even at the cost of our own self-respect." Sally rubs my palm and turns to Brad. "Is that all?" When he nods, she stands. "I'm going to get something to eat. Are you going to be all right?" She strokes my hair. "I can grab a hen for you to pet."

"I don't deserve it," I mutter under my breath.

"Give Jeremy some time. I think you may have stirred up some old Mary vibes with him. But he'll come around." Sally exits with an encouraging dip of her chin.

Tammy starts picking up her notes, and when she bends to grab a tumbled pen, Brad drools. Until he looks up, meets my grin, and blushes. I nod towards Tammy, but he shakes his head from side to side a little too frantically. I'm surprised his neck is still attached after all that. Then, as I stride to her, he gives me a death glare.

"Can I help you clean up?"

Her eyebrow shoots up and her red hair bounces behind her. "No thanks. I've got it."

"You know, Tammy, Brad was just asking me about this earpiece you helped Xander rewire." I hand her the item in question. "But you know how clueless I am. Can you explain to him how it works?"

"I might have some time to explain it to you,

soldier." She eyes Brad.

He waves her off. "I'm sure you are busy doing other things."

"How about you lend me some muscle and carry these to my quarters, and I'll explain how the equipment works on the way there." She hands him some papers, then walks out the door without a backward glance at either of us.

He turns to me and mouths, *"Thank you."*

"I don't have all day!" Tammy shouts over her shoulder.

I giggle as he falls in step with the female rebel.

"Ann, look!"

I startle as May holds up a disgruntled Scarlett. I bite my lip as I readjust the hen's dress. "She looks... uh..."

"I know it's not perfect." May glides a hand over her new bestie. "I had to sew scraps of clothes together." She shoves a finger into my face. "I'm not great with the sharp stick thingy."

I kiss the tiny prick marks. "That dress is one of a kind. You should be very proud of it."

May's smile brightens her dirt-smudged cheeks. "You really think so?" Scarlett wiggles and screams, clearly done with the little girl's antics. "I don't think she likes it though."

I tug off the fabric and the hen relaxes. "You know what?"

"Huh?"

"The last time Jeremy left the compound, he brought me back some beautiful red nail polish."

"What's that?" May's eyes twinkle.

"It's nail paint and I think it'd look perfect on Scarlett."

"Really?" She examines the hen's plain yellow talons while Scarlett narrows her eyes at my betrayal.

"Yes, and I think she would be the talk of the coop."

"May!" a woman yells from the back of the room.

She cringes. "I need to do my chores. Maybe tonight we can paint them together?"

"Sounds perfect."

The girl dashes off with the hen bouncing in her arms while I glance around the compound, trying to spot Jeremy. I hope my *rooster* doesn't stay mad for too long. When I can't find him, I return to my room to sneak in a quick nap. I slip under the cool covers, rest my hand on my son, and hum a sweet lullaby full of a promising future.

Front-Page News

I pat the mattress. Jeremy's normal spot is cold and vacant. There's no evidence that he came into our room at all. I tap the wristwatch that once belonged to his father. It's still early enough that Mr. Grumpy-Pants could have crept out of the room to start his morning exercises. I slip on my shoes and tug the door open and, sure enough, his familiar grunting sounds echo from the training area.

In the corner of my eye, I zero in on Brad. He's resting outside of the arena, holding an ice pack to his face. "Are you okay?" When he meets my gaze, I cringe at the black eye he's presently sporting.

"Jeremy's in a mood," Tammy answers for him, as she leans against the wall.

I can't help but take in Jeremy's less-than-perfect form. He's obviously fueled by rage, rather than looking to actually train. His normal swings are more intense. His dodges are more aggressive. Even though blood drips from his chin, he still bounces on his toes, begging for more. A loud thud vibrates under my feet, and the man Jeremy was boxing falls to his knees before tapping out. The soldier limps out of the ring. Mr. Macho holds his arms out welcoming his next opponent *if* they're up for the challenge. I stomp into the arena and shove at Jeremy's bare, sweat-drenched chest.

"Why don't you say what you want and get it over with!"

He removes his headgear and mouth guard. "You're not authorized to be in the training area. Get out."

"Not until you talk to me."

He swipes at his forehead. "I have nothing to say to you but *get out* of the training area."

I fling my hands in the air. "You are impossible!

Everything I did yesterday was for the cause! Yes, I used my cleavage and good looks to my advantage but I did it for you. For *us*. For them!" I point to the crowd watching us. "And if you are that *insecure*, then I guess we never stood a chance." I try to walk off but he grabs my elbow.

"You could have informed me of your plans. But you didn't. You kept it a secret. A relationship is nothing without trust."

"When are you going to realize I'm not *Mary*?"

"When *you* stop trying to act like her to get your way." The anger burning behind his icy eyes is for his lost wife, not for *me*. He needs to figure out which one of us he wants to fight for, because it's not fair to be forced to live in someone else's shadow.

Jeremy leaves the boxing arena, pushing people aside as he goes.

Tammy warms my side a moment later. "Let's hear it for Anna Banana!"

Our audience laughs and claps. I shake my head and brush past my supporters. "Please don't call me that, guys."

I climb the large staircase leading outside. I can't believe he thinks I'm trying to be like Mary! *Is he insane?*

By the time I reach the door, I'm out of breath. The cold wind hits me square in the chest and I shiver. I was focused on accomplishing our mission at any cost.

Isn't that what he wanted me to do?

The golden sun warms my skin while burning my pupils. I bite my lip. Maybe allowing Richard to kiss me and grab my butt was a little over the top. I shade my eyes and enter the chicken pen.

"I thought Sally didn't want you climbing the

stairs?" May asks as I join her and Billy.

"Apparently, I'm breaking all the rules today." I smile at the pair. "How is Spot doing?" May grins and tugs me to a position under the nesting box. I kneel to get a better look. "She's broody, huh? How many eggs does she have underneath her?"

"Three," Billy supplies with a puffed-out chest. "I counted them this morning."

I take a moment to really look at the young man. He's grown a lot since his mother rushed him into the compound. We were unsure if he'd survive the night, and yet here he is, thriving.

"Three eggs isn't bad." I glance around the pen. "Who does RooRoo pick on the most?" I nod towards the golden rooster strutting around his ladies."

Billy's confidence falters. "You mean other than *me*? He likes Whitey, Toffee, and Red."

"Can you collect their eggs and carefully place them under Spot? Then, in about a month, we can have some more little chicks running around here."

"You mean Spot will be a mommy?" May jumps up and down.

"If RooRoo did his part." I smirk.

"Will the chicks hatch before your baby comes?" May rests her hand on my belly.

"Maybe."

"He is taking *forever*." May snatches Billy's hand before they stalk off to collect the eggs. "Come on! I know where Whitey hides her clutch!"

I rub my abdomen. I'd be happy if my little guy stayed inside me forever. I'll miss the kicks and somersaults. I sit on the cool grass and pull at some stray weeds. With the changing of the seasons, there'll be fewer annoying pests to remove. A shadow looming over me reminds me of another nuisance. My gaze takes in his hunky form as he crosses his strong arms over his broad chest.

"Didn't Mom tell you to stay off the stairs?" When I don't take the bait, he continues. "Are you coming back inside?"

"No."

"Should I throw you over my shoulder and carry you inside?" My glare only makes his grin grow wider. "The *newspaper* arrived." I remain tight-lipped and only offer a shrug in response. "Aren't you curious if you made the front page?"

"Nope."

Something flies towards my face. I yelp and cover my eyes. When I realize it's not a bug, I peek through my lashes and stare directly at today's news. But on the front page is a picture of King Ryan and his new wife as they announce the conclusion of his selection. Below that article is a much smaller photo of me and Richard, recommending that the reader turns to the next page for the full article. I slap the paper to the ground.

"Of course, they would block my article!"

"Are you okay?"

"Why do *you* care? Five minutes ago, you weren't even speaking to me."

He lowers himself beside me. "Because I've been where you are now."

"You mean you were also forgotten by the *man* who promised to love you forever, only to trick you into sleeping with him?"

Jeremy smirks. "What can I say? I am a complicated

32

woman." He nudges my shoulder. "I had to watch Mary wed Christian. Live in the Palace. Get arrested for murder. Then I saw her dead body." He sighs. "I shouldn't have been that hard on you because of what *she* did to me. But you have to understand the reason I was mad was because I knew you were *better* than that. That those tactics were beneath you." He cups my chin. "You are smart and stubborn. Those are your superpowers. Use them to your advantage."

"Did you read the article?"

He nods and releases me. "It's good, and he was true to his word and published everything, even the pictures."

I flip through the pages. "Do you think *they* will join the video conference tonight?"

"Maybe. The paper said they weren't doing a honeymoon until the springtime."

I lean my head on his shoulder, hold my belly, and curl up my legs. "Why is Ryan ignoring us and playing King with this girl?"

Jeremy smirks. "You might want to start calling her by her name."

"How about bitc—"

"Hey." He looks around and laughs. "May is out here and she doesn't need to learn any new vocabulary from you."

"I'm sure she'd agree with me."

He strokes my hair. "I might be a jerk, but I will always be here for you."

"*Just* a jerk?"

"I was jealous, but I had every right to be. Ann, you kissed him."

"No, *he* kissed me. It didn't mean anything. Richard had a crush on me throughout school, and I played on that past affection." I look away from his tense gaze. "I'm not proud about what I did, but I'm glad it got the job done. And, next time, I promise I'll think more carefully before I act."

"I would have liked to have heard about what transpired from *you*, not one of my soldiers, in front of my mother."

"*Next time*, I'll do my best to confide in you first," I reiterate my point.

"*If* there is ever a *next time*, I will make sure *I'm* with you *and* keeping that ass's hands off you. Do you plan on using the same *tactic* on King Ryan when you travel to the Palace?"

"No. Trust me, I don't want to even *pretend* with him." I scuff my foot against the grass. "I'm furious at the situation he's put me in."

Jeremy pats my leg before pushing to his feet. "Don't let that anger consume you." He brushes the dirt off his pants and picks up the paper.

"That's easier said than done."

"That's the story of our entire lives, isn't it?" He offers me a hand up, then he lifts me into the air and I wrap my legs around him. "Ann?"

"Yes, Jeremy?"

"I love you." He brushes my hair to one side. "I want to marry you." He reaches into his pocket, pulls out a silver band, and places it in my palm. "I know we have no idea what tomorrow will bring. But I want my intentions known from here on out—not only to you but to the whole world." He rubs my belly.

I gawk at the simple silver band before searching

Jeremy's expression for any hint of a joke.

He lowers his lips to mine and whispers, "What do you say? Should we skip the whole girlfriend-boyfriend part and just get engaged instead?"

A tear warms my cheek as I hand him the ring. "I'm sorry. I cannot let you do this. There're too many *what ifs* stopping us from being together."

Jeremy tugs the ring over my knuckle. "I'd rather live *one* day by your side than forever without you."

"Are you sure? Have you had enough time to think about this?"

He removes a tarnished chain from his pocket and hands it to me. "The ring was my mom's when she married my dad, and this chain belonged to my grandmother. Put the two together and wear the ring around your neck. That way, when your fingers swell from the pregnancy, we won't have to cut it off you." He offers me a lopsided grin.

I rub the ring as it rests on my finger. "Maybe I could wear it like *this* until we do the video conference."

"Whatever you want."

We stare into each other's gaze in comfortable silence as the chickens peck at our feet.

"I love you too," I whisper, afraid that the second the words leave my mouth, he'll bolt. He presses his lips to mine and passion flares up. I pray I can make this work with him.

"How about I help you down the stairs?" He tightens his hold on me.

I giggle as he rubs his nose against mine, and my heart melts. "You better not drop me, or I'll shove this ring down your throat."

He chuckles. "You're a true romantic."

Pumpkin and Watermelon Seeds

"Are there any secrets you want to warn me about before we do this video chat with your old pals?" Jeremy teases as he tugs a comb through his hair.

"I doubt they will even show up."

"Then *why* did you suggest we do this?"

"The main reason is to get the information out to the public and let them form an educated opinion of the Black Rose's situation. Besides, allowing Richard to *see* me with my full belly will encourage him to spread the word and investigate further."

Jeremy's warm lips tickle my hand. "Hopefully he doesn't become *too* curious."

"Richard is a good man. Give him a chance."

"As long as he keeps his hands off you," he grumbles in reply.

I lean into him. "It doesn't matter who wants to place their hand on my body, it is only your touch that I desire."

Tammy pushes through with her tactical equipment. "Quit yapping and let's get a move on. We are already five minutes off schedule."

Jeremy gives me a quick peck on the cheek and collects his gear. We meet the rest of the team in the garage. I skid to a stop. It's a rare occasion when the whole gang gets together to go on a field trip. Brad and Tammy settle in the third row, Sally rides shotgun, and Jeremy sits in the middle row with me.

"Is everyone ready?" Sally questions.

"Almost. Let me get Ann situated." Jeremy leans over with the blindfold and wraps it around my head, letting his fingers tickle my neck. I shiver and swat him away.

37

He rests his hand on my belly. "He must have gone to sleep early." He kisses my bump. "Sweet dreams, little one."

My heart swells and I rest my palm on Jeremy's.

The drive is long, and by the time we arrive at our destination, my legs are cramping and I need a bathroom. Jeremy tugs the dark fabric down, and I squint at our surroundings.

"What are we doing *here*?"

"We came to the one place they won't think to look, to throw them off."

I trace a finger over my dad's tools. "Or was it to throw me off?"

"You aren't happy to be back here?"

I offer a sad smile. "It's hard to explain." I lift a hammer and turn it over. "There are countless memories here. Some good, some bad. It's overwhelming."

"I'm sorry. We assumed you'd be excited to get to spend some time at home again." Jeremy guides me inside.

"Home is where our hearts are." I squeeze his hand. "And where all my hens are too."

I watch as the rebels set up the equipment for the video conference. I side-eye my coffee machine longingly. Maybe I have time for a quick cup?

"Ann, we're ready," Tammy announces as she adjusts a few cables. "Now, remember we only have twenty minutes. Then we must be on the road before they can trace our location." She sits me on the couch and pivots the camera until she achieves the perfect angle.

Jeremy trails the room, eyeing all the photos,

knickknacks, and books. He taps on Christian's wedding picture. "You look…"

"Thinner?" I insert.

"I was going to say *breathtaking*."

I resist the urge to question him on how he thinks Mary looks as she stands next to her *new* husband. Those days are behind us now. Although our beginning was unorthodox, I'm glad we found one another in the end.

"Can we all concentrate on the mission at hand?" Tammy scowls. "Why am I the only one who's doing their assigned task? Focus, people!"

"I can multitask, can't I?" Jeremy ruffles her hair, and she slaps his arm. "If *you* were paying attention, you would have noticed that I did a sweep of the interior already."

Brad closes the front door. "There's nothing to worry about outside."

Sally examines her watch and lets out a breath. "Is everyone ready?" We all nod in response. "Okay. Here goes nothing."

Tammy types quickly into her black laptop. The camera focuses on Sally's stern face. I stick up two fingers and a pair of "bunny ears" materialize behind her head. She squints at her reflection, then side-eyes me. I burst into a fit of giggles and Jeremy, Tammy, and I share fist-bumps like we are the three musketeers.

"Can we please act our ages for the next fifteen minutes?" Sally massages her temple. "My children will never grow up."

The computer makes a noise and Tammy clicks a button. Another screen pops up. I lean closer and see a blurred face. "Elizabeth?"

The older woman squints. "Ann?"

Tammy switches the camera view to me instead of Sally. Once the fuzz settles, I wave. "Hey!" Tears well in my eyes as her blonde hair and blue eyes shine bright on the screen.

"Oh, Ann! It is wonderful to see you, dear!"

I touch the screen, wishing I could wipe her tears away. "I miss you too."

Sally clears her throat, reminding me that we are on a time crunch. "Elizabeth, let me introduce one of the leaders of the Black Rose, Sally."

The camera returns to Sally. "Good evening. I hope all is well over there."

Elizabeth's expression turns stoic. "It's nice to finally put a name to the face." There's movement in the background as the matriarch looks behind her and addresses someone in the background. "Come in. Yes, she is right here."

My best friend's beautiful face appears on camera and I all but blubber. "Karen!"

My bestie squints. "Geez, Ann! What are they feeding you? Miracle-Gro?"

I turn to the side. "Oh, you know, watermelon and pumpkin seeds."

Jeremy rubs my back before passing me a tissue.

"I can't believe how huge you are!" Karen gushes.

"Well, thanks for the boost in confidence."

"I mean it in a *good* way. You look healthy." Karen wipes at her cheeks. "Everyone here really misses you, especially Jock and Snowball."

"How's Snowball doing?"

Before they can answer, Sally taps her watch. Time is almost up. "Elizabeth, is there any way we can get together to talk face to face, in a peaceful manner?"

"I do not know if that's a good idea, Ann."

Sally moves back into view. "We have been trying tirelessly to get a response from the Palace."

Elizabeth glares. "If your group hadn't kidnapped Lady Ann, we wouldn't be in this predicament."

"There you go making assumptions!" Sally growls. "Ann came to us. We never grabbed her."

The silence is suffocating. Although Sally is right, it's not the whole truth.

"Either way, you held her against her will. She never would have chosen to live with you *murderers*."

Sally narrows her eyes at the woman on the screen. "If the Royals hadn't killed and branded us like *animals*, we wouldn't have been forced to go to such extremes!"

"What? *Your* group is responsible for murdering my husband and son!"

I ease my way into the camera again. "There's a lot of misinformation about the events that have unfolded. We'd love the opportunity to sit together and set the record straight. Please. We need to find a *peaceful* solution so there's no more bloodshed and we can all begin to heal."

"I cannot trust those monsters!"

"But, you can trust *me*, right?" I arch a brow in question, and Elizabeth nods. "Please *believe* me when I say that the Black Rose is not who you think they are. They are kind, intelligent, and compassionate." I glance at Jeremy, Tammy, and Brad. "And I will vouch for all of them."

Elizabeth rubs her face. "They won't like this."

Tammy waves her hand in a circle, giving me the five-minute warning. "I understand your hesitation. It's a lot to take in. I know… it was hard for me to believe too. But what is the alternative? More violence and discrimination?" I rub my belly. "And never being able to introduce you to my son."

"It's a little *boy*?" Elizabeth wipes her tears and Karen pops her head in, giving me a thumbs-up. "I'll persuade the King to arrange a meeting and we can discuss the facts of what has transpired. Why don't you and a small group visit the Palace on Christmas?"

"Can I have the Palace's word that no harm will come to anyone who visits?"

"As long as *they* don't bring the fight here, we won't retaliate."

"Thank you. This means a lot. I look forward to seeing everyone soon."

"And we are anxious to have you return home again, *Lady* Ann."

I don't miss the subtle undertones. Elizabeth is going to do everything in her power to keep me close. *Will she force me to move back to the Palace?*

Tammy slams the laptop closed and quickly packs up our equipment. "All right, people, let's move out!"

Promises

We pile into the SUV and Jeremy secures the blindfold, encompassing me in darkness. My mind spins with *what ifs*, while the voices in the background discuss contingency plans and tech ideas for the rebels' next venture.

I wish things could be different. That we were not at war, and everyone could show compassion and sympathy for one another. My tears fall as Karen's and Elizabeth's shocked expressions flutter in my memories. They love me so much. But what happens when they learn that I've switched sides? Will our relationships remain the same?

Jeremy's hand warms my thigh. "Do you want to talk about it?"

I shake my head, not wanting to disclose my inner turmoil with everyone in earshot. I rest my head on his shoulder and breathe in his comforting presence. *If I lose Elizabeth and Karen, then were they really my friends in the first place?* I snuggle into Jeremy's chest and relax, knowing that if things do change between me and my Palace pals, at least I'll have my rebels.

If the Royals don't slaughter them out of spite...

Before I know it, I'm being lifted out of the SUV and the blindfold is gone. I burrow into Jeremy's embrace, as he carries me into our room. He sets me on the bed and tugs off my shoes. Then he pulls the covers over my body.

I yawn and frown at his departing figure. "Are you coming back?"

He slides his hand over my cheek. "I know today stirred up a lot of emotions for you. I'd understand if you want me to find somewhere else to sleep."

"Jeremy." I rub his stubble. "So much has changed, but the one thing that *never* will is me needing my pickle jar opener close by."

His lips twitch and he kisses my palm before leaning into my touch. "Are *we* okay?"

"Yes."

"Then your pickle man will return soon."

"Can we change that to *coffee* man?" My lids fight to stay open. "I'd rather have that."

Jeremy's bulky arm is entangled around me. I grumble as I push him. He murmurs and tugs me to his bare chest. "Go back to sleep," he whispers into my hair.

"Your wild child is jumping on my bladder."

He rubs my belly. "Child, behave yourself."

"Jeremy," I warn.

He releases me and I dash to relieve my aching pelvic muscles. When I'm done, I snatch some munchies, then settle in next to Jeremy. He lays his head in my lap and I stroke his hair while the baby shuffles, getting closer to Jeremy's warmth. I crunch into my apple and take a moment to assess the small room that I've called home for the past few months.

What will happen next? Will the Royals force me to move into the Palace? Or will Ryan want the baby and abandon me?

I set my jaw. I won't let that happen. He'll never

separate me from my son.

"Who is Jock?"

I arch a brow at Jeremy's question. "I'm surprised that intel wasn't in my folder," I tease. "He's the Palace chef. Max was going to kill him but I turned myself in, to spare Jock's life."

Jeremy tenses at the mention of his former brother-in-law. "Your friend Karen said that they missed you." His thumb caresses my arm. "But I'll miss you too." I run a hand over his face, not sure what to say to that. "Why does life have to be so challenging?" His fingertips massage my back. "I'm going to miss my little buddy too." His eyes brim with tears.

My heart splinters. I've never seen Mr. Tough-Guy cry. "I'm sorry."

He wipes his cheek. "I wouldn't change the time I had with you two."

"Maybe we can video chat or something? Is Dan keeping his cover?" I ask about Jeremy's younger brother, who recently married a Palace guard.

"Yes, he's still playing contractor and happy helper to the Royals."

"Then we can always communicate through him."

"Whatever we can do, I'm willing to try." Jeremy smiles. "Besides, who knows? Maybe the Palace will release you from their claws, free the rebels, and we can all live happily ever after."

"Maybe." I stretch my legs. "Are you ready for breakfast?"

He laughs. "You are *always* hungry."

"Hey, I can't help it."

He grins and lets his lips linger over mine. "I'm always

hungry too." He nibbles my earlobe.

"You are lucky I have all these pregnancy hormones, or your butt would be bruised and on the floor." I kiss him as his hands massage my rear.

"Promises. Promises." His tongue glides over my neck.

Suddenly, alarms blare in the distance and we leap into action. I rip open our door and do a head count of the children, then turn to Sally as she watches the screen currently broadcasting the intruder as they drive up to the compound.

"Report," Jeremy snaps at Tammy.

She taps over the keyboard. "It's not an enforcer's vehicle." She uses her laptop to zoom in on the trespasser's profile. "Looks to be a middle-aged male, but until they get out of the car, I won't know for sure."

"What's that?" Jeremy points to a barcode on the windshield. "Can we get a closer look?"

Tammy bites her lip and we all lean in. "I'm not sure."

My breath hitches. I snatch Jeremy's wrist and dash for the exit before the doors can lock us inside. "Ann? What the hell?"

"Trust me!" is all I can shout as my mind reels. What the hell is *he* doing here?

"Release my hand, woman, so I can load my weapon," Jeremy grinds out. "This is the dumbest idea. But if I'm going down, I'm glad it's going to be fighting by your side."

"Please don't shoot," I huff. "Trust me."

"Yeah, you've said that already. What you haven't said is who is in the car and what they want."

Once the vehicle is in our sights, I wave around like a

46

crazy lady, hoping to get their attention. They rush out the door, dragging their weapon as they go, and aim for Jeremy. "Stop where you are!" The chambering of a round echoes against the open field.

Jeremy shoves me behind him and reaches for his weapon, but I steady his wrist. "Remember what I said."

Our eyes meet, and he purses his lips as he weighs our options. "Shit. Fine. We'll do it your way." He waves his palms around at the man. "We are approaching *peacefully*." Then he shoots me a pointed stare before returning it to the stranger. "But, if *you* attack, I'll be forced to protect the woman and child I value more than myself. You've been warned."

The other man's weapon wavers. "Let Ann come to me. Alone."

"Fuck that!" Jeremy growls.

"Jeremy," I soothe as I attempt to get around him.

"No. I draw the line at letting you walk into danger without protection," he seethes. "I trust you, but I don't know *him*."

The man in question strides to the front of his car. "Well, it looks like you've finally found someone to put you first and choose you over everything else. Does he also accept your crazy chicken fetishes?"

Jeremy's lip quirks. "I'm already working on acquiring a feathery boa and tiara for when she rules over her subjects again."

The newcomer lowers his weapon. "And do you accept this man's proposal?"

I shrug. "There weren't many other options available." Jeremy side-eyes me and I laugh. "Yes, I've accepted his proposal." I wave the engagement ring on my finger.

"Well then, I've made this long trip for nothing. Karen's

going to be disappointed." He holsters his weapon. "At least it got me off diaper duty for a while."

I give Jeremy a comforting squeeze, then I run into Vinny's arms. "You're an idiot for coming out here. But I'm glad you did. I've missed you."

Vinny rubs my back. "Ditto. My wife has been nonstop nagging me to be your Prince Charming and rescue you."

Jeremy tugs me to his chest. "Too late, *Shrek*."

"Ouch." Vinny rubs his stubble. "I know it's been a while since I shaved, but..."A muffled cry cuts him off. "Whoops." He dashes to his trunk.

I tense as the sound of kicking echoes from the car. Jeremy stands in front of me, his fingers reaching for his sidearm. "What's in the trunk?"

"A mole." Vinny releases the latch and a figure pops out.

"Dan!" I rush over with Jeremy by my side.

"What did you do!" Jeremy snarls as he clutches Vinny's shirt. "I'll rip your throat out and..."

"Easy, killer. He's unharmed. I needed a hostage, in case things went south." He slaps Jeremy's cheek. "I do have a wife and two kids at home."

"You little..."

"Jeremy, calm down." Dan rubs at the sticky spot where the duct tape was placed over his mouth. "Vinny's telling the truth. He cornered me at the house and shoved me into the trunk." He rubs his spine. "Although my back is sore and my mouth lost a layer of skin, I'm okay."

"Where's Sam?" I ask.

"She's safe and working her shift at the Palace." Vinny nods to the gravel road.

Jeremy taps his earpiece. "Stand down."

"When did you put *that* in?" I ask, gesturing to the device.

"When I was running like hell beside you." He chews his cheek. "Does this vehicle have a tracker or any undisclosed weapons?"

"Not unless you count infant car seat harnesses." Vinny crosses his arms.

A few rebels rush out to meet us. "Check the car and have Xander sweep it for trackers. Then scour the roads to make sure he wasn't followed."

"Copy that," they murmur as they get to work.

Jeremy slaps Vinny on the shoulder. "If I find out you're trying to pull *anything,* I won't hesitate to have my buddy perform a very thorough *body* cavity exam on you. Do you understand, *friend*?"

I cross my arms over my chest. "Really?"

"Oh, and I'll need your sidearm and cellular device for security purposes." The brute wiggles his fingers. *"Please."*

Vinny's jaw ticks, but he tugs the requested items out of his belt and slaps them into Jeremy's palm. "Just so you know, my wife knows where I am, and she's a force to be reckoned with when the father of her children misses dinner without calling." He smacks Jeremy's back. "Thank you for the warm welcome."

I can't help smirking as the two of them bicker. "Come on, boys, we have a lot to discuss."

Dirty Secrets

"You've got to be *joking*. You actually traveled here while you were pregnant because of a note you found in your attic?"

"When you say it like that, it sounds ridiculous." I laugh.

"Because it is! Why didn't you call me or Karen to go with you?"

"I wasn't speaking to you, remember?"

We spent the day sharing our intel with Vinny. We poured over the stolen files with Christian's signature and seal, the rebel journals, and even let him tour the facility. It's a risk, but at this point, we're running out of options. Plus, I know—deep in my heart—that Vinny is being honest. He has no reason not to be. He could have *swarmed* the facility with hundreds of guards if he wanted to attack, but instead, he came alone and mostly unarmed.

Vinny rubs a hand over his face. "That's right. Ryan was putting distance between you two."

"Distance? He was an arrogant jerk! Calling me a curse and blaming me for Christian's injury."

"Ann, please sit down and take a breath." Sally pats the chair. When I settle, she turns to Vinny. "Now that you're all caught up, it's your turn to tell us what you know."

"Are we seriously going to trust this Palace butt-kisser?" Tammy huffs. "He served under King Mark, then King Christian. And now he's Ryan's loyal pet."

"Just because I work for them, doesn't mean I follow them blindly." Vinny meets my gaze. "Christian confided in me. But he never explained the whole story, only bits and pieces, and expected me to obey when he said jump."

"Did he order you to shoot Suzie, or was that an accident?" I ask the question that's been haunting me.

"Christian instructed me to shoot first and ask questions second when they attacked you at your house." Vinny runs his hands through his hair. "But after that incident, I questioned a lot of the assignments the Royals gave me."

"Why didn't you tell *me* what had happened?" I demand.

"Christian would have killed me on the spot. You were his Kryptonite, Ann. Like Elizabeth was to King Mark. Everyone knew it."

"How did the King know Suzie was a sympathizer?" Tammy presses.

"Christian sifted through every file on the Gable family. He said his search came up clean, but when Ann visited her father in the hospital and told him about Daddy's new girlfriend, he dug deeper. He had his suspicions but no hardcore evidence… until the day we went to Jack's grave and noticed the rebels retreating towards her property."

My head swims with memories.

"How did you know Dan was our man on the inside?" Sally leans forward this time, the protective Mama Bear flexing her claws.

"It was a hunch. Ann and Dan are close friends, and even though no one had heard from her, she was still editing *his* manuscripts."

I fight the urge to facepalm. *Why didn't I think about that?*

"How did you find this location?" Jeremy narrows his eyes.

Vinny grins and taps his head. "Because I'm brilliant."

"Care to elaborate?"

"Not particularly." When Jeremy continues to glare at the lack of a response, Vinny holds up a hand. "It was a mix of a few things. Ann's last ping from her cell phone, the sighting from the bank and newspaper office, plus the report of two missing enforcers in this area."

I nibble my lip as my eyes meet Sally's pale face. That's why the enforcers have been patrolling more often.

"The vehicle is clean." Xander nods. "The cell phone is good too, but his wife is blowing it up."

"Leave it to Karen to ruin our get-together." Vinny sighs.

"What now?" Tammy throws her hands up. "We can't let him return to the Palace. He knows too much."

"But if we keep him, they're sure to send a search party." Sally shakes her head.

Vinny shrugs. "Now that I know Ann isn't here against her will and that you guys aren't the villains in this story, maybe I can help you achieve your goals. Be the man on the inside."

"Absolutely not!" Tammy screeches. "You'll rat us out the second you can!"

"Why do I get the feeling you don't like me very much?" Vinny tilts his head and looks at her.

Tammy charges, but I block her approach. "I think he has a point."

"About her not liking me?" He smirks.

"Vinny," I warn before continuing. "He can warn us

if the Royals are planning on sabotaging this meeting." I lift my gaze to meet Tammy's reddening face. "Think about this logistically. Does it make more sense to keep him here or send him back?"

Her fists clench at her sides before she turns to Jeremy. "You've been quiet over there. What do you think?"

Jeremy rests his elbows on his knees and shakes his head. "What doesn't add up is why Ryan never acknowledged Ann was missing after we sent him her belongings."

"The thing you don't understand is that with Christian's diagnosis, the country was in turmoil and in desperate need of stability, hope, and peace. All those responsibilities fell on *Ryan's* shoulders. He was drowning in paperwork and meetings. So he delegated *others* to assist him and, somehow, those items you sent never made it to him directly—likely slipped under the rug."

"What?" I push out. "By whom?"

"Think about it. Who was the one person to work for Mark, Christian, and Ryan? The same person who facilitated every document and phone call before they reached the King?"

"The secretary," Dan pipes in. "Are you telling me Tim's been hiding things this whole time?"

"Not necessarily *hiding things*, but his loyalty has always been to the current King. From what my sources told me, even though Christian was in a coma, his orders were still to be followed."

"What orders?" I question.

"That all pertinent matters concerning you... go to *him* first and Ryan last."

"That's absurd." I shake out my ruffled feathers.

"But when Christian died and Ryan became King, the information was given to him, right?" Tammy interjects. "Which means he could have done something."

"I imagine he doesn't want to stir up trouble with his new bride."

"What about the baby? Has he acknowledged his child?" Sally implores.

Vinny shakes his head. "He hasn't mentioned anything to me about the baby."

My heart clenches. The truth hurts more than the fantasies I've dreamt up in my head. The Princes never trusted me, and their so-called love for me was not even close to the real thing.

How could I have been that naive?

Jeremy squeezes my thigh. I lift my eyes to meet his gaze. "Their loss and our gain." I nod, and he turns to Vinny again. "*If* we let you leave, what can you do to assist us?"

"What do you have in mind?"

"We need the enforcers off our backs. We can't collect supplies or, hell, even cough in the wrong direction right now. And with winter on our heels, we're facing possible starvation because of it."

"I can throw them off your track and station them north for a while. What kind of supplies do you need?"

Tammy snorts. "How much time do you have, soldier?"

"Get me a list and I'll have what I can delivered to a destination of your choice by tomorrow night." We blink at his cocky grin. "Come on. It's *me*! My kids are basically family to the Royals, my wife works with the servants and collects gossip, and I stride side by side with the big man himself."

"Just like that?" Tammy arches a brow. "You're gonna jump in and help us?"

"Not you. And most definitely not him." He nods to Jeremy. "But for *her*." Vinny throws a thumb at me. "You bet your butt I will."

I wrap my arms around his neck. "Thank you for coming to my rescue."

"I'm sorry I couldn't come sooner," Vinny whispers. "If you need me to send in the calvary and take you home by force, *wink*, I'll make it happen."

I pull back and punch his arm. "Stop."

"Okay, okay." He stands and brushes the dust off his pants. "I see I'm not needed." Then he glances around the room. "It looks like you've found where you belong, Ann. Karen's going to be jealous."

"I'll see her and the kids on Christmas, at the Palace. Plus, if all goes well, you guys can retire to your farmstead when this is all over. We can be neighbors, like we planned."

Vinny shakes everyone's hands. "It was nice meeting you all. Sorry for scaring the crap out of you."

"You didn't scare us." Tammy crosses her arms over her chest. "And don't think we aren't going to tail your car on the way back."

"I wouldn't expect anything less from you." He winks and then nods to Dan. "How about you ride shotgun for the return trip?" He slaps Dan's knee. "I'll even buy you a Happy Meal for the drive."

We follow Vinny outside and wave as he and Dan drive into the night.

"I really hope you are right about him," Tammy grumbles.

I wish I could confidently say that *I am*, but after hearing what he divulged about the Palace...

"Me too," I acknowledge as I watch the taillights disappear.

Travel Buddy

True to his word, Vinny was able to acquire most of the supplies Tammy requested. The mood around the compound evolved into near contentment. It's amazing what a few staple items like toilet paper and warmer clothes can do. People are actually smiling, even sourpuss Tammy.

I sit in the dining hall drooling over my warm bread, eggs, and potatoes. "Your mom must be in a good mood. This is pretty expensive stuff." I shovel in the goods before they disappear.

"She's really impressed with the way things have been going around here. And, in a week, we'll be walking through the Palace doors, not as criminals but as invited *guests* to discuss the peace we've been working towards for decades." Jeremy sinks his teeth into a slice of toast.

"Well now, listen to *you*."

"What?"

"I'm loving all of that hope and enthusiasm." I grin.

"It's all thanks to you." He pinches my cheek.

I smack his arm. "Stop it."

"I'm excited!" May bounces over and squeezes in next to us.

"About the baby chicks coming?" I ruffle her knotted hair and feed her companion my crust.

Scarlett gobbles it up before begging Jeremy for his. He moves his tray out of reach and glares at the moocher.

"Yes, but I'm more excited about coming to the Palace with you." May pats the hen's head, discouraging it from leaping at the soldier's potatoes.

I choke on my water and cough as Jeremy pats my back. "What do you mean?"

"Sally said I could meet the King and Queen. She said you were good friends with them."

Why would Sally allow a kid to travel to the same place where blood was shed less than a year ago? I glare at Jeremy. "Did *you* know about this?"

"Well…"

"Unbelievable." I leap out of my seat, causing Scarlett to screech and flap her wings. "May is a *child*."

The girl's emotions leak down her cheeks as she stomps her foot for emphasis. "I am *not*! I am eight!"

"May, sweetie…"

She wrinkles her forehead and marches off with her pal nestled in her arms.

Jeremy rubs my elbow. "Ann…"

I ignore him, stalk off to the office, and slam the door open. I spy Tammy sitting at her desk, surrounded by wires and broken pieces of tech. She looks up with an arched brow. "I guess you found out about May." She pats a chair. "You are always being so dramatic. Sit down."

"She is too young. *Anything* could happen to her."

"But you said we could trust them, and you asked Elizabeth for a *peaceful* trip, right?"

"What's your point?"

"Do you think she'll go against her word?"

"No."

"Then there shouldn't be a problem."

"Just because she keeps *her* word doesn't mean Ryan

will obey."

"We aren't tossing her to the wolves and hightailing it out of there. May will be by our side and she will be fine. Plus, it was her idea and it's very hard to tell her *no*. You should have seen her face light up."

Tammy has a point. May is extremely stubborn when she wants something. I flick a red feather from my shoe. She reminds me of myself when I was younger. Knowing my luck, she'll stow away in the vehicle or luggage when we leave—the girl's very inventive. I guess actively keeping an eye on her would be better.

"I like the idea of having May tag along with us. It'll remind the Palace that this mandate will not only benefit the rebel adults, but the younger generation too."

"We also should protect them and not drag them into battle with us—you know, in case things don't go the way we plan."

If something happens to May, I'll never forgive myself.

"Why can't we do both?" Tammy shrugs. Brad interrupts our discussion as he strides in with a bowl. I arch a brow as he sets it in front of Tammy.

"What is this?" she snaps.

He leans back in a chair. "You never made it to breakfast, so I brought it to you."

"Do you think I need to be babied?" She shoves the dish away.

His lip twitches. "I *think* you need to take a break and eat."

"You're an idiot."

"Even *idiots*, like us, need to eat." He smirks.

She bites her lip. "I'm going to brush that comment off. But be ready to pay for it later. *Sparring* partner." Tammy grabs an orange and peels it before popping a piece in her mouth.

Brad straightens his back. "I look forward to it, *partner*." He brushes past her, then pauses in the entryway. "Ann, Jeremy is looking for you."

Once Brad turns the corner, I wink at Tammy. "That was nice."

"That *Jeremy* is searching for you?"

"No. That Brad is bringing you food." I point to the piece of fruit still clenched in her fingers.

"And did you catch the part where he nonchalantly called me an *idiot*?" She chews her food in thought. "Stop giving me that look. He's too young."

"He's *too young* to notice what you really are? A prickly old hen."

"No. To be thinking about being in a relationship."

"What do you mean? He's twenty-one."

"Too *young*." She pops the orange slice into her mouth. "I'm twenty-five."

"Is the age difference really a bad thing? I mean, he's younger… with more *stamina*."

"Not everyone sleeps around like you, Ann," Tammy teases in her sisterly way.

My jaw drops. "Ouch."

She flings a grape in my direction. "Hey, you better keep that *hole* closed."

Before I can reach over and tackle her, Jeremy interrupts us. "There you are." He turns a pointed look at Tammy. "Shouldn't you be prepping for our trip

60

and not be in here yapping?" She rolls her eyes and shoulder-checks him on her way out the door. When we are alone, Jeremy aims his glare at me. "I realize it's a risk bringing May with us, but I promise I will do everything in my power to ensure nothing happens." He places a photo in my palm.

"Where did you get this?"

"I saw it on your nightstand back at your house. It's a picture of you and Jack, right?"

I run my finger over Dad's smiling face. "What would you say to me now, Dad?" I lean my head back and gaze at the stained ceiling. "I'm such a screw-up."

Jeremy warms my arm with his palm. "Stop that. You're doing the best you can with what you have."

"Am I? I've made so many mistakes…"

"All I see is miracles and new opportunities."

"What do you think *your* dad would say to you if he were here?"

"He'd tell me to brush my teeth and to remember to change my underwear *every* day."

I laugh and glance at the photo again. "This was very considerate of you. Although, I would have preferred my coffee maker." I peek into his icy eyes. "Thank you."

"I wish I could have slipped the machine into my pocket too. Though my pants are large, they aren't *that* large." His lips graze my forehead. "I'm always here for you, Ann."

"I know." I wipe my cheek. "I'm fine. Go. I'm sure you have a lot to get done before our excursion." Jeremy stands to leave, and I stop him in his tracks. "Who's coming to the Palace with us?"

"Brad, Sally, Tammy, and May."

"What will you and Brad do with yourselves, being the only men in the group?"

"Hopefully keep you *girls* out of trouble."

"Good luck with *that*."

The door closes as Jeremy leaves me alone with my memories. And I can't help but wonder if my past and future can successfully intertwine without a cock fight.

Mighty Pen

After helping in the kitchen, I settle in near the training area while Jeremy teaches the new recruits. I flip through my newspaper with the sounds of grunts and punches echoing in the background. I scan the pages until a phrase catches my eye. I smirk as memories filter through my mind.

"You really need to stop sitting there looking so beautiful."

"Huh?"

Jeremy pats his forehead with a towel. "My guys are showing off to impress you. I almost got my butt handed to me by Jared. Almost." He flexes his bicep. I ignore his macho display and return to my reading. "What has you distracted from my good looks and smooth talking?"

I pass Jeremy the paper. "Notice anything off about the front page?"

"That the Palace is hosting a Christmas ball? That's normal."

"Look at the article's *author*."

"Richannd Olsen? Oh, it's a typo. Guess *Dick* doesn't know how to spell his own name. Why is that important?"

"It's our secret code."

"What do you mean by *code*?"

"When we were on the school paper together and had a spicy tidbit that we didn't want everyone to hear about, we would pass each other mundane notes but purposely misspell our names in the signature. Then meet up later to talk." I tap the error. "Richard needs to chat but doesn't want the Palace to know."

"Or it's a trap."

I wave off Jeremy's suspicion. "So he used *our* secret code to do it?"

He crosses his arms over his chest. "*Where* are you supposed to meet him?"

"Normally it was at the park behind the old oak tree." I rub my chin. "I wonder if it's still there." I collect my things and jog towards the office.

"Ann, where are you going?"

"I need to talk to your mom."

Jeremy watches Brad and Tammy begin their sparring match. Then he slaps his hands on his pants. "Hey, wait up."

Sally looks up from a folder as we rush into her office. "Ann. Jeremy. What can I do for you two?"

"I want to meet up with Richard Olsen again."

She stretches her arms in the air. "Why? We already got what we needed from him."

"I think he has something for us. He used an old code to get my attention in the newspaper today. A code only he and I know about." I shove the front page under her nose. "Look at his name."

"Clever. What was yours?"

"Anna."

"I guess that's where the Anna Banana nickname spawned from, huh?" Sally nibbles her lip. "What do you think, son?"

"It's risky. If something happens to Ann before our meeting with the Palace, it could ruin everything."

"I sense a *but* there," Sally prompts.

Jeremy rakes a hand through his hair. "Using the media gained us the Palace's attention and results within twenty-four hours. Something we've been trying to do for *months*." He shrugs. "I am curious to see what the reporter wants from us."

"You mean what he wants from *Ann*." Sally sighs and stands. "Let's be honest with ourselves, the man has no real interest in *our* cause. This is about his old classmate and Palace gossip."

Jeremy rubs his chin. "As much as I hate to say it… so what if he's only interested in Ann and not the Black Rose?" We stare at him with arched brows. "In the end, he's assisting *us*. And Richard knows Ann is tied down to someone else because of the baby. He can't expect too much from her."

"You guys are wrong. Richard only has one interest, his *career*. It's always been that way. As much as you think we are using him, he's using *us*," I point out.

Sally considers our words for a moment before asking, "When do you need to meet with him?"

"As soon as possible."

"We are a few hours out. Do you think he'll be waiting all this time?"

"I'm not sure."

"Brad and Jared can accompany you." Sally nods.

Jeremy steps forward. "This time, I'm going with her too."

"Son, if you are seen with the mark, this simple mission could go sideways quickly. The enforcers are still very active in those areas."

"Maybe not." I scratch my chin. "It's cold enough to wear gloves and not raise suspicion. Plus, what better cover is there than a young couple strolling through the park? And if we do show Richard the mark, he will literally drool for the photo evidence."

"Jeremy, can you control yourself if Richard gets close to Ann?"

"I will do my best. But if I did punch him out, wouldn't that be a great story to report?" He smirks.

Sally shakes her head. "We are trying to prove to the world that we are calm and compassionate people looking for *peace*. Not a bunch of brutes, who are quick to anger."

"Mom, it was a joke... mostly. I can do what needs to be done without making him bleed."

"What do you think?" Sally elbows me before tipping her head towards Jeremy. "Can he handle this mission?"

I meet Jeremy's icy eyes. "I'd bet my life on it."

"Fine, go find Jared to drive you and you can take two more soldiers to tag along. But I expect you to return immediately. There and back, nothing more." She sits behind her desk and waves us off. As Sally shuffles various binders around, I notice the dark circles and deep wrinkles on her face.

Will she ever get to retire from playing *Mommy* to hundreds of ragged rebels and focus on herself? My fingers massage my abdomen. Is this what it's like when you become a parent? You work yourself to the bone day in and day out with very little appreciation?

I wrap my arms around Sally's shoulders. "Thank you for everything you do for us. We love you."

"I don't know what I'd do without you crazy kids. But thank you. It's nice to hear that every now and then. I love you too."

Jeremy sneaks into our hug. "Not as much as I love

you both."

"Now get going before I change my mind about this mission." Sally points to the exit.

The moment we round the corner, out of sight from the office, Jeremy presses me against the wall and stares into my eyes. "Thank you for having faith in my abilities." He runs a hand down my face.

I kiss his palm. "Well, you did blindly chase after me when the alarms sounded and Vinny showed up."

His lips brush against mine. "Why do I get the feeling I'll be chasing you for the rest of our lives?"

"Because I'm high maintenance." I deepen the kiss as I lean into his body. "Wait until you meet the rest of our flock. You are going to have your hands full."

"I'm looking forward to that and so much *more*." His fingertips dance over my love handles, causing goosebumps to rise along my skin.

"Don't get any ideas. We have a mission to prepare for, soldier."

"Hey, I'm a great multitasker." He scoops me up in his arms and walks to our room. "See?"

"And you follow *my* orders well, so that's a plus." I flick my wrist, making a snapping noise to mimic a whip.

He raises a brow and I know I'll pay for that remark later. Though, to be honest, it's something I'm looking forward to.

We change into casual civilian clothes to blend in. I wear stretchy yoga pants with Jeremy's dagger resting on my thigh while a tight V-neck white sweater squeezes my chest.

I grin into the bathroom mirror. "Does it feel good

to be out of your tactical gear and in a normal outfit?" Jeremy readjusts his jeans with a grunt. "You forgot a button." My fingers work through his baby-blue shirt. "What would you do without me?" My hands still when they brush over the gun holstered to his broad chest. "Really?"

"No matter what I wear, I'll always be ready to defend the helpless." He winks. "Don't be so quick to judge, Miss High-and-Mighty." His palm grazes my thigh. "You're bringing a knife."

"It was a *gift* from a rebel jerk who failed to defeat me." I square my shoulders. "And it'd be rude not to wear it. Plus, I like to remind him that I won."

"You're right." Jeremy snatches my chin and assesses my teasing smirk. "You won me over that day and every day since for the rest of *our* lives."

I meet his heated gaze. This renegade challenges me, believes in me, and even though he knows all my faults, he accepts me for who I am. Tears well in my eyes. "I love you, Jeremy," I whisper.

He kisses my tears away. "Shit. I didn't mean to make you cry."

"I'm pregnant and my emotions are all over the place."

"Hey, kids." Sally pops her head into the room. "It's showtime—oh, Ann, are you sure you're feeling up to this?" She shoves Jeremy aside to hug me. "Do you want me to make you some herbal tea or maybe some fresh bread?"

"No, thank you. I was having a moment, but it's over now." I slip out of her mother-hen embrace. "Have you convinced May that Scarlett has to stay behind when we visit the Palace?"

Sally rolls her eyes and guides us towards the garage. "I'm still working on it. Any suggestions, from one mother to another?"

"Let her bring the bird."

"Never mind. *Look* who I asked. The same little girl who snuck a hen into her backpack on the first day of kindergarten. Your parents were beyond mad." Sally sighs. "Don't you go putting any ideas into May's head—*I mean it*."

I hold up my palms in surrender. "I won't make a peep."

Brad and Tammy nod as we approach. It's weird seeing her in jeans and a red sweater and him in khakis and a green collared top.

"Let's roll out," Jeremy barks to the crew, jumping into control-freak mode.

Jared starts the SUV and inputs the address. Jeremy blindfolds me and we are on our way. During the drive, we discuss Christmas and what we hope the day at the Palace will bring. Then we drool over the idea of all the delicious foods they'll be serving.

"Ann, do you really think King Ryan will agree to pass this vote for peace?" Tammy asks.

"I can't pretend to know what he will do," I grumble. "My guess is he feels guilty about what happened that night in the safe room. Now that he's moved on and married, I can almost guarantee Mrs. Perfect doesn't know about his little *mistake*. Which is what I can use to my advantage. I'll promise his highness that I'll disappear, if he pushes this vote through like a good little boy."

"You don't think he wants to raise the child? I mean, the baby is next in line for the throne," Brad adds.

"No, if he did, he would have tried harder to reach me."

"After everything the little dictator has done to you, will you be able to keep your mouth shut about his child?" Tammy says.

I squeeze my hands together. Ryan was pretty nasty to me before I left the Palace. Can I be the bigger person and move forward with negotiations?

"I could provoke the King by being loud about our situation to the public, but I really just want peace."

I hear Tammy shift in her seat. "You are a *better* woman than I am. I would sing like a canary."

"I'll take that as a compliment and throw it back in your face at a later date." I grin.

Before she can bark out a comeback, Jeremy removes the blindfold as we roll to a stop. Then he comes around to my side, surveying the park as he does. He opens my door and offers me his hand. "My Lady."

I place my palm in his, and he kisses my knuckles. "Thank you." I step out and rub my arms at the sudden chill.

Brad offers his arm to Tammy. She begrudgingly accepts. "Don't get *any* ideas."

We stand in a line, taking in our surroundings while keeping an eye out for Richard. Tall trees and browning vegetation trail the walking path. I can't believe winter is upon us already. Soon the ground will be frozen, and farms will focus on preparing for spring. The time of new growth and life.

I point to a man on a bench under a large oak with his back towards us. "There's Richard."

Tammy squints. "How can you tell?"

"See the ball cap he's wearing. It has our high school mascot on it."

"Everyone, stay alert." Jeremy adjusts his collar. "Let's move in."

"Dick." I greet the man before joining him on the bench.

He lowers his newspaper and uncrosses his legs. "Anna, you kept me waiting."

Children dash past us flying a bright red kite. Their giggles warm my heart.

"Why did you want to meet up?" I elbow Richard when he remains silent.

He side-glances Jeremy, Tammy, and Brad. "Did you bring the heat?"

"I think I'm *enough* heat to handle."

His eyes sparkle with mischief. "You are *more* than enough, my dear." Jeremy clears his throat, and Richard tilts his head. "Have we met?"

I motion towards the disgruntled rebel. "*This* is the real heat." I pat the spot next to me and Jeremy sits. "Dick, I thought you might want more proof of my involvement." I gently brush aside the fabric concealing Jeremy's gloved hand to reveal the angry scar.

Richard's jaw drops open. I replace the mitt before anyone else can catch on. "Does the rebel have a name?" He extends his palm to Jeremy.

Jeremy narrows his gaze and doesn't move to meet Richard's greeting.

"If you're nice, I may let you take a picture of it." I wink at my old friend. "Now tell me why I'm here before I let my new pal show you how he really feels about being singled out."

Richard leans into the metal backrest and scratches his scruff. "The public's been requesting more information about the Black Rose. They've been emailing, sending snail mail, and even stopping by the office. It's the most activity we've seen in a long time."

"That's good for business, right?"

He leans forward. "But *I* can't give them what they want. All I have is what *you* gave me. If I could get something more…"

"Like what?"

He grins. "Do you want a job?"

I roll my eyes and pivot to Jeremy. "*He* wants to know if I want a job." I rub my temples. "I'm pregnant and stuck in the middle of a war I never knew existed, while playing the mediator. I have plenty of jobs."

Richard frowns. "But you were born to be a journalist. I've always said that." Then he places his hands on mine. "Please write for me."

"Your false flattery won't change my mind. I have enough on my plate."

He groans at Jeremy. "Explain to her why this is a good idea."

Jeremy clenches his jaw. "As much as I want to disagree with the prick, we could use this opportunity to educate people and gain sympathy." He glares at the reporter. "If Ann agrees, how can we do this securely?"

"Whatever you want. Encrypted emails, messages, carrier chickens."

"What's in it for us?" I cross my arms over my chest.

"Always thinking ahead, huh? How about the community's compassionate *support* and my handsome face." Richard runs a knuckle over my jaw. "You

72

will make a difference in the world and I want to be a part of that." He fiddles with his pocket. "Here's my personal email address." He hands me the slip of paper. I grab it and he holds on to it a little longer. "Our dreams are coming true," he whispers softly before adding, "Don't be a stranger." Then he strides into the horizon without a backward glance.

"Let's go." Tammy taps her watch. "We've been out in the open long enough."

As I'm pushing to my feet to follow her lead, memories of my past creep into my mind.

Mom snatches a fistful of dirt and chucks it at her target. "Did you tell our daughter that she had to marry a farmer?"

Dad jumps and rubs his back. "What's gotten into you, woman?"

"You will not dictate who she falls in love with, cowboy." Her knuckles rest on her hips. "If she wants to marry the garbage man, she can. And you won't have a say in it. Do you understand me?"

A twig snaps under my foot as I attempt to sneak closer to their argument. I duck behind a boulder when my parents twist in my direction. I hold my breath and stroke my spy hen until the conversation continues. Once it's safe, I chance another peek.

Dad brushes the sweat as it drips towards his eyes. "Can we talk about this later? I have one hundred and one things on my honey-do list."

"Jack..."

He jabs his shovel into the earth. "You know all I want is for her to be happy."

"And marrying a farmer will accomplish that?"

"Maybe. Or she can do what you and Sal have fantasized about doing all these years." He snatches my mom's belt loop

and slams her hips into his. He tips his straw hat. "Listen here, cowgirl. We both have expectations for our child. But in the end, it'll be her choice as to how she makes her dreams come true."

"What dreams?" Jeremy tugs me out of my thoughts.

I glance out the SUV window while wondering how I've managed to escape reality and still function. "We were going to be this unstoppable media couple. Doing what we could to bring peace and prosperity to the world."

"That seems a little heavy for friends. Did you two date?"

"I couldn't open my heart to anyone after my mom died. Richard always had *his* idea of our future. It was never *our* dream. Just his." I hand Jeremy the blindfold.

He ties it in place. "Are you going to write for him?"

"I'll discuss it with Sally and get her advice. I trust that she'll know what to do."

By the time my blindfold is removed again, and we're back at the compound, I'm starving. I glance across the dining table and smile at May. She ignores me and offers Scarlett some peas.

"I guess she's still mad at me." I pick at my vegetable lasagna.

Jeremy tosses May a piece of gum. "Why are you giving Ann a hard time?"

She pouts. "Because she doesn't want me coming with her to the Palace."

"May, I *love* the idea of taking you with us, but I worry about your safety."

"But they are your *friends*, right? Why would they hurt me? I'm one of your friends too."

"You're right, May. I do trust my friends to keep their promises." I nod, and when her eyes finally meet mine, her frown melts into a smile. "I'm sure this will be a lovely trip for everyone."

"Will they make you stay there?" She unwraps her gum while keeping Scarlett from snatching her treat.

"I'm not sure, May." I outstretch a hand and pet the red devil.

"Do you *want* to stay?"

I feel the other rebels' curious stares on me. "I will stay wherever I am needed." I rub my stomach. "But this is no place for an infant. They need diapers, formula, and medical care." I wish I could elaborate further and say that the child is technically royalty and may be required to live at the Palace.

May beams. "Does that mean Jeremy will stay with you and be the baby's daddy!"

The silence is heavy as the room is hushed, but I push onward. "If he does go with me, who will bring you candy?"

"But you love each other."

I frown at my plate as I gather my thoughts. Of course, we hope to be together, but this isn't your average storybook. And it won't have that kind of fairy-tale ending either.

"Sometimes our greatest sacrifices in life benefit others more than they burden us. Rarely are there victories without great sacrifice." I ruffle the girl's hair before I clear my dish. Everyone's pitying stares follow me as I make my way to my room. When the door clicks closed, hiding me inside, I let out a breath. My lip quivers.

No. Tears will *not* resolve my predicament, only

action-oriented steps will. I unfold the paper Richard handed me, groan, and toss it on the counter. Just not *that* action. I flop on the couch with a book, but it doesn't hold my attention so I slam it shut.

Could words really be mightier than the sword?

"That little girl is very curious." Jeremy settles in at my side. He rubs my back, and I lean my head on his shoulder. "I talked to Mom. If you're feeling up to it, she would like you to test the waters and write a few articles for Richard. She also said, as an extra precaution, we can email them from a laptop offsite."

"I'll consider it."

"I know things are about to get hectic and emotional with the holiday approaching and the upcoming mission. But remember I'm here for you." Jeremy tugs on the chain around my neck and the engagement ring bounces with the movement. "We all are."

"I know."

"Good. Now get to work." He slaps a notebook and pencil into my palm.

A few hours later, I've created a decent draft. The first scribbles explain the history and unjust treatment of the Black Rose. I mention the thousands of fallen farmers and orphaned children. Then I write about their way of life and the discrimination they've faced on a daily basis. I skim the last line, then pass the document to Jeremy to double-check the facts.

"Well, it's not quite on the level of Dan's novels, but it'll do." He smirks.

"Your brother has talent in the romance department." I elbow Jeremy.

"Hey! I do too. But my talents are reserved for real life, not fantasies."

I roll my eyes. "You are unbelievably cocky."

"Can you blame me?" He flexes his arms.

"I will leave you alone with that ego of yours," I say, waving a dismissive hand before striding towards Sally with Jeremy hot on my heels.

"You are a fast writer." Sally skims the paper. "This is lovely. I'll send it out for you."

"Thank you."

She leans into her chair. "I'm proud of you, Ann, and I know your parents would be too."

"I hope so," I huff out. "I'm always second-guessing myself."

"That's adulting for you, sweetie. It'll never stop." Sally gestures to her desk. "And it only evolves with age and more responsibilities. But we do our best, which is all we can do."

I'm beginning to understand what she means. *Being an adult sucks.*

Unyoked Forgiveness

The days pass in a blur as we prepare for our trip to the Palace. I spend the time writing a few articles for Richard, and he publishes his favorite one each morning under my alias, AnnaBelle Willard.

Although I'm not ecstatic about bringing May into the danger zone, I do enjoy assisting the little girl as she prepares for her first mission. We examine maps of the layout of the Palace, discuss the servants' responsibilities, and play dress-up. She twirls in a beautiful yellow sundress and looks every bit the little princess I know she is. My heart clenches as it brings back the memories of the many exercises I performed before Christian's selection. At least May doesn't need to walk in heels while balancing books on her head.

Christmas Day arrives and it's a cold breezy morning. I don't question the lack of decorations or presents at the compound. It's sad to think they haven't had a proper celebration in all their years in isolation, and I'm eager to see how my rebel friends react to the ridiculous number of festivities the Royals have set up inside the Palace. We say our goodbyes before the sun rises as we ready ourselves for the long drive. Jeremy, Sally, Tammy, May, and I load up into the SUV and Brad settles in the driver's seat.

My leg bounces as Jeremy arranges the blindfold. "You'll be happy to know that you won't be the only one unable to look out the window. May is wearing one too."

"That's not fair," the youngest rebel whines.

"Think of it as a game of hide-and-seek," Sally tells her. "Here, let me stash your bag in the back."

"No, I'm going to use it as a pillow and nap."

"A nap sounds like a good idea." Sally buckles her

78

seat belt. "You'll need to be on your best behavior, so recharge yourself now while you have the chance."

Jeremy places his hand on my leg. "You are vibrating the whole car."

"I feel sick." I clutch my cramping stomach.

He rubs my arm. "You're just nervous. Take a few deep breaths."

What am I doing going back to that horrible place? Ryan doesn't even want me there. Before he kicked me out, he called me a curse to his family. What if they lock us all up?

I lean my head back against the seat. "Brad needs to pull over before I ruin my outfit."

Jeremy lowers my blindfold and guides me onto the side of the highway.

I heave out my breakfast into the grass. My body shakes and breaks into a sweat. "Please don't make me go back there."

"Ann, you are one of the strongest women I know. You can do this."

"No, I'm not. I put on a façade to protect myself from getting hurt, but I'm a weakling."

"As long as there're no hammers or heels involved, you'll be fine."

I smack his arm but can't help the giggle that slips out.

"Come on. Look inside yourself and remember who you are doing this for." He places a hand on my belly. "We can't do this without your help. *Saint Ann*." He teases me with my old Palace nickname.

"You guys *are* pretty pathetic," I counter.

"Says the girl throwing up on the side of the road," Tammy tosses out the window. "Can we wrap up this pity party please? The sooner we get to the Palace, the sooner we can get back home."

"Tammy," Jeremy warns before offering me a hand up. "Since *she's* the one they are expecting to be there, she can take all the time she needs."

I peek at his scar. This mission is meant to help all those who can't hold a job or buy food because of their involvement with the Black Rose. I need to convince the King to change his policies. My stomach rolls at the thought. But if I fail, all this work will be for nothing and we'll lose everything.

I groan as we buckle up again. I feel faint so I lean my head in Jeremy's lap and close my eyes. He runs his hand over my hair, and I imagine we're back at the compound in my room.

"Ann, we'll be arriving soon." Sally's voice tugs me out of my nap.

"Five more minutes," I grumble, then squint as the sun blinds me for a moment. I'm glad Jeremy forgot to replace my blindfold. The familiar cityscape greets us over the horizon and I smile as we pass Becky's Café. I turn to point it out to Jeremy. "Dan took me there to get a coffee." I watch in awe as more stores blur by. "If you follow that road, it brings you to a beautiful lake house."

Soon the iron fence surrounding the Palace comes into view. Jeremy squeezes my hand. "You can do this."

The guards at the security gate narrow their eyes at Brad. I pop my head out of the window and they nod us through. We find a parking spot up front and then we all pile out.

"Remember. Everybody is to be on their best

behavior." Sally points at each of us like a mother hen reining in her unruly chicks.

I stare at the enormous entrance, and my mind travels back to the first time I saw it. The day I met Ryan in the library.

Vinny and some of his coworkers stand guard at the entryway. I run over. He grins and opens his arms. "Ann! It's good to see you again." He smiles, but then goes stoic as my group catches up.

I clear my throat and pretend to introduce the rebels to my friend for the first time. "Vinny, this is Jeremy, Sally, Tammy, Brad, and May." The little girl smiles bright when I say her name.

"Ann told me you are one of her best friends and that you have two babies."

His mouth twitches. "She lied. I was never one of her best friends."

I elbow him. "Don't listen to him. I'm the one who brought him and his wife together. He owes me." I poke him in the chest. "Are you going to make us stand outside all day or let us in?"

Vinny straightens his shirt. "I would like to remind you all that this is a peaceful meeting. Remove any weapons from your persons, and if you fail to adhere to our guidelines or initiate a perceived aggression, the agreement is off, and we will have no choice but to apply deadly force to subdue you." May pales before she raises a hand in question. Vinny arches a brow. "Yes, little one?"

"Ann said the people at the Palace are her friends. Would they really hurt us?"

"Well, we are all, uh, friends... in a way. But we don't want anyone getting into any fights."

"Well, you should probably give them a time-out and not use deadly force," she lectures him.

I cough a laugh while Vinny rubs a hand over his face. "Instead of giggling, bestie, how about you handle this."

I make the mistake of kneeling to get eye level with the girl. "May, honey. We are all going to be nice and won't get into any trouble, okay?"

She nods and skips to Sally. Sally ruffles May's hair as she reminds the girl to be mindful of what she says. I attempt to rise but my big belly causes me to falter. Jeremy rushes to my aid. Once I'm standing, Vinny leads our entourage into the Palace.

May gasps, her head spinning around like a curious owl. "I've never seen anything this beautiful."

My fingertips graze the familiar staircase. The same one I climbed thousands of times, the same one Christian carried me up when I hurt my ankle. Now it's decorated for Christmas with garland, lights, and mistletoe. We all pause as we hear the soft rustle of fabric as an older woman descends towards us.

My eyes tear up and I run past everyone. "Elizabeth. It is wonderful to see you."

"Lady Ann, it has been far too long." The former Queen pushes me back gently. "You look breathtaking." Then she places her hands on my stomach. "Oh, my! He is a strong one! Jack would be ecstatic to meet this guy." Vinny clears his throat to get us back on track, and Elizabeth straightens her spine and pivots to my friends. "Welcome to our home. I am Elizabeth, mother of King Ryan."

May's eyes are practically bugging out of her head from overstimulation. "I love your dress! It's so shiny."

Elizabeth smooths out her gold-trimmed lavender gown. "Thank you. It was a birthday gift from my son."

"The one I'm going to meet?" May asks.

Elizabeth's lip trembles but she quickly schools her features. "Everyone is waiting. We shouldn't keep them."

I was selfish. In all the time I spent mourning Christian's death, I'd forgotten he'd left behind his mother too. I wring my hands together. And yet, here she is, leading with grace. I peek over her shoulder, hoping to catch a glimpse of her emotional support hen. But there's not even a feather to hint she's nearby. Elizabeth nods at two guards stationed at the garden doors. They bow before ushering us all outside.

"Here we go." Jeremy rubs my back. "No turning back now."

"I wonder what they have in store for us," Tammy whispers.

"Probably a public flogging." Brad snorts.

"Bite your tongue, young man." Sally covers May's ears.

The cold breeze tickles my cheek, but the warm sun seems to overshadow it. I forgot how beautiful the Palace grounds were.

"Welcome back, Lady Ann!" a crowd of onlookers calls out.

I screech and the rebels flank my sides. My hand covers my mouth, so my heart can't leap out and plop onto the ground in front of us. Jeremy steadies me. "What the hell is going on?"

But I can't speak as my eyes bounce between the welcome banner and party supplies littering the garden. There're cakes, sandwiches, carafes of tea and lemonade, cookies, pastries, and breads with chairs and tables set up where we'd normally hold press conferences.

"Is this a trick?" Tammy holds out an arm, stopping my approach.

"Only one way to know." I squeeze her wrist as she meets my gaze. She grinds her jaw but nods.

As I near the primped group, I'm bombarded with hugs and warm greetings. Many familiar faces and some new ones. Not one person speaks ill of where I've been or what I've been doing. Their love pours into my soul.

"Thank you. I'm flabbergasted by your kindness." I wipe my tears. The rebels stand by me uncomfortably. "Please allow me to introduce my new friends. This is May. She is eight years old and one of the strongest girls I know. This is Tammy. She's our intelligent strategist. Brad, our super soldier. Jeremy, head of security. And this is Sally, the leader of the group."

May steps forward and extends a hand to the strangers. "I'm very pleased to meet you all." Then she turns to me. "Can I have some of those cookies?"

She drools at the table adorned with more desserts than she could possibly name. The Palace guests laugh and shake hands with her. May captures their attention as she twirls in her dress while Tammy elbows my side and gives me her signature *I told you so* look.

Before I can give her the bird, a familiar masculine voice booms behind us. "Sorry I'm late. Yes, please, everyone enjoy the fantastic food prepared by our amazing head chef, Jock." He motions to the older gentlemen as he carries another tray to the table. "The Queen and I are thrilled you could attend our celebration." He pivots to the rebels, never meeting my gaze. "And for bringing Lady Ann." Ryan stands by the exit, dressed in a pristine tailored suit while looking every bit the part of King.

But what causes me to stumble is the woman warming his side in an elegant royal-blue gown. She's flawless and familiar. They weave through the crowd and offer greetings. I can't believe he chose *her*. After everything that's happened.

Why didn't I notice it before?

Jeremy rubs my chilled arm, reminding me of his support. For the next hour, I'm flooded by friends touching my belly, asking questions, and sharing encouraging words. Most of them assumed I returned home and have been taking time to get over Christian's loss. While others say I went off the grid to reclaim my life. Either way, I don't confirm or deny the rumors. It's enough social interactions to last me an entire lifetime. I didn't miss this. My introverted butt is overwhelmed. Jeremy senses my panic and excuses us as he guides us to a table under the shade of a tall oak tree.

"Take a few deep breaths. You've got this." He pats my leg under the table. Sally strides over with a cup and slides it to me. I accept the ice-cold lemonade while Jeremy watches the crowd. "He's good," he murmurs. "Pretending everything's fine."

"That's what the Royals do best. They put on a fake smile, while hoarding secrets and stabbing you in the back." I suck in a shaky breath. "I never expected this though."

Tammy follows Jeremy's line of sight. "What's the King's end game? Do you think he's attempting to put off the meeting?"

Ryan holds his wife's hand and laughs with a guest. I tilt my head. He looks happy. But is this another mask?

The various groups spread out as a woman with dark hair stomps through. Murder is written all over her face.

"Karen!" I grin, and her anger morphs into tears. I run to her with open arms. I pull back to take a peek at the bundles Karen's nanny is balancing a few steps away. "They have grown like weeds." I offer a pointer finger to Carter. "I have missed a lot," I whisper before placing a kiss on his cheek.

My spine tingles and I pivot as a palm warms my back. His highness has finally made his presence known. "Isn't he handsome?" Ryan strokes Carter's little fingers. "He's a quick crawler too."

I swallow, unable to respond. Jeremy narrows his eyes from where he's still positioned at our table, and I know he'll be here in less than two seconds if I need him.

"Ann, it doesn't matter how much time has passed. You are here now." Karen squeezes my hand and meets my gaze, reminding me we are surrounded by partygoers.

Ryan rubs my back, and I grit my teeth as my fists ache to punch that smug face of his. "It is good to have you home."

"I could have been here a lot sooner," I hiss in reply.

He ignores my statement and turns to the older woman holding Carter's twin sister. "Olivia, that dress is absolutely gorgeous." He brushes past me to coo at the child.

Sally offers me a cup of water—at the rate people keep offering me drinks, it's a matter of time before my bladder explodes. "You're doing great, keep it up," she whispers as she walks towards my best friend. "Karen, Ann has told us all about the friendship she cherishes with you. It is an honor to finally meet you."

My bestie grabs Sally's hand. "I wish I could say I'm happy to meet your acquaintance. But because of you, I've lost *months* with the one person I consider a sister."

"Karen, please." I frown at the hold she has on Sally's wrist.

My self-proclaimed sibling smiles sweetly as she drops the rebel's hand. "Enjoy the party, because afterwards, we have much to discuss."

Sally smirks at me as she unclenches her fingers and tips her head at Karen. "I like her."

Karen's jaw ticks as another rebel joins our conversation. "Ladies," Jeremy greets, his fingertips grazing my elbow. "Are we playing nice?"

"Please don't *ever* leave me alone again." I lean into him, begging his strength to aid my weary bones.

"Sorry. I was trying to give you breathing room." He kisses my hair. Laughter rings out from the far corner and we turn to see May. "I swear that girl will be singing a love song all the way home about those damn cookies."

Elizabeth giggles next to May as she hands the youngster another sugary treat.

"Let's hope May burns off the side effects long before then. Can you imagine her bouncing off the walls like that in the SUV?" I return my attention to my friend's frown. "What?"

Karen arches a brow and extends a hand to Mr. Muscles. "Jeremy, was it?"

"Good to know your hearing isn't as bad as Ann said it was." I smack him and he smirks. "It's nice to meet you, and I'd appreciate it if you were nicer to my mother." He nods to Sally.

"What's your position in the Black Rose?"

"Does it matter?" I jab him and he relents with a sigh. "I'm head of security."

"Is that *all*?" Karen looks between us as she drags out the last word.

Did Vinny not explain anything to his wife about the rebels? Maybe he was trying to keep her in the dark to protect her? I turn to Jeremy and his gaze tells me he's thinking the same thing.

The man in question sneaks up behind his wife. "I hear you are causing a ruckus," he whispers close to her ear. "I love it when you're being naughty." He nips her lobe.

"I'm doing nothing of the sort. I'm only gathering intel for you as usual."

"I will leave you to it then. Don't keep the babies out here too long." He hugs the rugrats. "Lady Ann, the King would like to personally introduce you to the Queen." Vinny motions towards their table.

"Oh, well…" I stutter. "I shouldn't be rude to Karen or the other guests here."

"He insists."

"I bet he does," Jeremy growls.

Karen smirks. "Don't show her any fear, Ann." She embraces me. "You can take her on and win, even pregnant." Vinny clears his throat and shoots his wife a pointed stare. "I'll return after I feed the babies." Then she turns her glare on Jeremy. "She better be *here* when I get back."

"In this exact spot? Because she'll have to pee eventually. Or would you prefer she squat in front of everyone?" He chugs his drink. "Or, hell, she can pee in my cup if that makes *you* happy."

They glare at each other until each of their mouths begins to twitch, and Karen nods. "I like him."

"He's okay." I wrap an arm around his waist.

"I'll be back soon." Karen leads the nanny inside the Palace.

"She's a real spitfire." Vinny laughs and pivots to me. "Don't make me drag you over to the King."

"Go ahead and try to pull me over there. I'd love to see you and Jeremy go at it."

The King's guard sizes the other man up. "I could take him."

"I'm always willing to take on a challenge. No matter how *small*," Jeremy counters.

"Maybe before you leave, we can make that happen." Vinny slaps Jeremy's back and leans over to whisper, "Help me drag her over there please. That way, I don't look incompetent."

"You do that all on your own. You don't need my help." I cross my arms over my chest.

Jeremy tucks his finger under my chin. "I love you and I won't let anything happen to you—remember that." I plaster on a fake smile, and he grins. "That's my feathered ninja spy." Jeremy walks beside me as we follow Vinny. "And remember to play nice with the King too, at least until we get what we want."

"Yes, *Daddy*." I roll my eyes.

"Save that talk for later."

"Stop." I shoot him a warning glare.

"I'm trying to keep that beautiful smile on your face." Jeremy pinches my cheek. Until I do as he says.

At our approach, Ryan stands and buttons up his

jacket. "Dearest, this is Lady Ann. Lady Ann, this is Queen Cherie."

With the way her eyes assess my attire before landing on my pregnant belly, it's like she's spitting in my face when she says, "Ryan, don't be silly. I've met her many times."

I want to strangle her.

"Please sit," the King commands. Then he waves a hand in the air.

Jock pulls me out of my negative thoughts as he brandishes a tray of drinks. I hug him. "What a lovely party. The food is by far the best part."

He throws a thumb behind us. "After spending some time with your little friend, I think you might be right. She adores those cookies. I'll make sure to write down the recipe before they leave." He sets the goods down. "I'm glad you're home, Lady Ann. Enjoy the rest of your celebration. I'll see you later."

I take my seat and clear my throat at Cherie's arched brow. "Jock and I go way back." I grab my water and sip past my dry throat.

Why does everyone have to stare at me?

A roar of laughter escapes Cherie. "Ryan, you were not joking about her. She definitely likes to *mingle* with the servants. Maids, cooks, guards—oh, it's too much."

Jeremy's fingers warm my thigh, reminding me that I can't choke the primped brat, while Ryan redirects the conversation. "I was just explaining to Cherie about all of the work you did on the chicken pen, Ann."

We are going to glaze over everything important and skip straight to belittling me. Great.

"It's nothing. Any *servant* of the crown could have done it."

"It was a complex project, and it's increased our numbers as you predicted it would."

"Well, pardon me, my *King*. But I wouldn't *know* if the numbers have increased or not, seeing as I've been kept out of the loop." I send a pointed glare his way and resist the urge to kick him under the table.

The Queen takes in our heated stare-off and pivots to change the topic. "I don't think we've been properly introduced." She nods to my bodyguard.

"My name's Jeremy, your highness."

"Yes, sorry. I don't mean to be rude." Ryan extends his wrist. "Thank you for visiting the Palace."

I snort. *Rude* should be that jerk's middle name. I earn myself a pair of pursed lips from the duo sitting across from me.

"The pleasure is all mine," Jeremy replies while initiating a *whose grip is more powerful* contest.

Oh boy. I watch on as the two men mimic a pair of angry cocks about to spur. When Jeremy doesn't relent, I tap my thigh against his. He releases his grip and Ryan opens and closes his bruised hand.

"Lady Ann, you look positively radiant. How far along are you?" Cherie interjects, acting as a buffer.

I know she doesn't give a hoot about me. *That makes two of us.*

"I'm in my last trimester."

"Do you know the gender of your child?"

I'd really love to remind her that it's none of her business. Instead, I respond with, "It's a boy."

"Aw, boys are the best. I love my brother dearly. We want our first child to be a boy. Don't we, dear?" She caresses the King's arm.

"Yes, boys are the *best*." I mock under my breath. "Stupid little…" Jeremy steps on my foot and gives me a pointed glare. I grab my water to keep from slapping her.

"Yes, darling." Ryan clears his throat and follows my lead, reaching out a hand and seizing his beverage.

Cherie leans forward, like she's scratching for a juicy worm. "Ann, dear, everyone is dying to know… *Who* is the father?"

I choke on my water at the same time Ryan sputters out his drink. What did *she* just ask me? Surely, I'm hearing things? We both flail to catch our breath.

The King pats his mouth with a napkin. "Cherie, that is really inappropriate to ask during a party, don't you think?"

Her Cheshire cat grin expands. "Oh, come on, Ryan. Let me indulge in some harmless gossip with your old coworker. Besides, this is between *friends*, right, Ann?"

I purse my lips. "We are certainly *not* friends, your majesty," I spit. "I agree with my ex-*boyfriend*. We're celebrating and talking politics right now. Not about my personal life." I smile. "Especially with you."

Jeremy tenses as he glances between us. Ryan pales while Cherie leans back. "I think we should attempt to be friends, don't you? It'd make these forced get-togethers… safer."

"For whom?" I bat my lashes and lean on my elbows.

A storm is raging behind her eyes. Her hackles are rising. "I am your *Queen* and I've asked you a question. I expect an answer."

The King never told his *wife* about us? How could she not know who the father is? What am *I* supposed to tell her? I don't dare sneak a peek at his highness for assistance. Ryan's useless. He's never stood up for me. Not in the past with Christian, or now as his beloved bride corners me.

Jeremy watches my internal struggle. He straightens his back, grabs my hand, and brushes his lips across my knuckles. "The baby's mine."

Water bursts from my mouth. *This was not part of the plan.* Ryan leaps from his chair as the liquid projectile sprays him. Vinny brings over extra napkins while failing to control his chuckle.

"Well, well, not only does she like to mingle with the help, but apparently share her bed with them too."

I hurl my handkerchief at Ryan's face. An unspoken threat passes between us. So help me, if he doesn't rein in his woman...

"Forgive me if I'm mistaken, but I thought you would be barred from entering the selection, since you cheated on King Ryan while you were dating?" Jeremy watches Cherie.

"Mary and her brother threatened my family," she hisses. "I had no *choice* but to spread that dreadful misinformation." Her well-practiced façade falters.

"Cherie, why don't you finish those thank you notes from the wedding?" Ryan aims to soothe her. "I'll join you in a minute."

"As you wish." She pecks him on the cheek and lifts her chin as she walks past.

Ryan sits back down and lets out a breath. "Well, that went well."

"You didn't tell her what happened in the safe room?" I grind out.

"Keep your voice down."

I'm about to smack that circle beard right off his face when Jeremy rises from his seat. "Ann, how about you show me that chicken pen the King was talking about?"

"Why are *you* covering for him?"

Jeremy takes a step back, like I slapped him. "How could you say that? I'm trying to save you from making a fool of yourself in front of all your friends. This has nothing to do with him."

"I need to go check on Cherie." Ryan scurries off without a backward glance.

"Coward," I hiss in his direction, and he pauses. For a second, pain distorts his features. But like any well-trained Royal, he continues his march, with an occasional wave to his guests as he passes.

"Ann?" Jeremy attempts to cool my mood.

I ignore him and crash into my seat by Tammy and Brad. They take notice of my demeanor and share a glance. Sally is in her element, greeting the other partygoers and making small talk, while staying close to our smallest rebel. May is having a grand old time, holding Elizabeth's wrist and tugging her to get a peek at the fishpond. The girl bounces as she points at the array of scaly creatures skimming the water's surface.

"Spill the beans, Ms. Moody," Tammy demands.

Jeremy shakes his head, a sign for her to let it go, but he should know me better than that. "Apparently, *Jeremy* is going to be a daddy soon."

Tammy's eyebrows shoot up. "Well, congratulations."

"I did what had to be done. Plus, that child is more mine than *his*." He throws back his tea and crushes the cup. "You should have heard her, Tam. The way that pompous brat was degrading Ann in front of the *spare.* The idiot just sat there and didn't do a damn thing. Spineless. Like the last King, and the one before him." Jeremy shakes his head. "Why don't they have any alcohol at this gathering? I need a stiffer drink than this." He stalks off, murder written all over his handsome face, while the guards grip their weapons in their holsters in case the rebel decides to erupt. Vinny corners Jeremy. They have a hushed argument, then go their separate ways.

"What did Vinny want?" I question as Jeremy settles in beside me. He takes in the crowd again, this time in stewed silence.

"He was commending me for taking one for the team and keeping the Queen in the dark about our situation. Apparently, Ryan hasn't told her anything and wants to keep it that way."

"Like father, like son." I nibble my bottom lip. "Thank you for what you said, but I could have handled her."

"It looked like you were doing a *great* job."

"I heard I'll be a grandmother soon." Sally side-eyes her son as she hands me a plate of munchies.

"I was only trying to help," he snaps. "Everyone needs to get off my back."

I spread my food around with my fork. "Cherie was giving me a hard time and demanding to know who the father was."

"I don't like this. It wasn't part of the plan." Sally sighs.

"The King's guard backed me up. I think I did *something* right."

"Only time will tell." Sally settles into her seat and peers over at May again. "Any word on when we're going to be talking business?" She aims the inquiry at me.

"Your guess is as good as mine," I huff out. "Nothing is as what I expected it to be."

"I agree. Something doesn't feel right." Sally pats my knee. "No matter what happens, we love you and will be here for you." May waves Sally over. The mother hen rises, but before she strides off, she hugs her son. "Thank you for standing up for them. I'm proud of you."

At the mention of the peanut, Jeremy warms my belly with his hand. "I'll always look out for you two, no matter what. Even if it starts a cock fight." My fingers intertwine with his. "Were you really going to punch the King?"

"Would you have stopped me?"

Before I can answer, Karen saunters over and claims the seat next to me. "I'm glad you're still here—oh! Is he moving?" She places her hand where we had ours. "Wow, he has some strength!"

"He takes after his father." Jeremy puffs his chest out like a proud rooster.

I deflate him with my elbow. I meet Karen's *tell me more* smirk and aim to keep the topic light and fluffy. "How are *you* doing?"

"You're asking about me when you were the one kept against your will."

"Why don't we stretch our legs." Jeremy offers me his arm. "You and Karen can show me that chicken pen." He gives me his signature *this is not the place to discuss things* look.

"That's a wonderful idea."

The three of us stroll over the cobblestone path,

away from the chatter of the party and towards my sweet flock. My heart aches. I've missed them, but guilt plagues me for abandoning them for as long as I have.

As I unlatch the gate, my feathered children rush over. "My goodness, you have all grown."

Jeremy grabs my elbows before I can bend over to greet them. "You're never going to get back up, Ann. How about you sit down here? I'll grab them one by one, then you can suffocate them with your affections."

He swipes the leaves off the iron bench and memories of Christian's gift cause me to stumble. In a way, it's as if no time has passed at all, yet everything has changed.

Christian is dead. Ryan is a jerk.

Jeremy helps me lower myself on the seat. "You're looking pale. Do I need to get you something to eat?"

"Can you grab a few finger sandwiches?"

"For you or the hens?" His brow twitches.

"Both," Karen answers for me as she warms my side.

"I'll be right back." Jeremy shoos the raptors aside, attempting to not step on any of them as he exits.

My best friend grins after him. "Yummy. I can't wait to hear that story."

I wave her off. "It's your classic enemies-to-friends tale."

"You mean *lovers*." She winks.

"Because of our past relationships, we've agreed to take things slow. We aren't lovers." I rub my belly. "Plus, I have enough to deal with in *that* area."

"You won't know if it's *enough* until you take Mr. Hunky for a whirl."

We share a laugh. I can't believe everything that's changed since I left. I recount my adventure to Karen. About how I drove to those coordinates all those months ago expecting a wonderful vacation. Then how Sally is really my mom's bestie, Sal. And Karen listens until I've exhausted every detail—leaving out the fact that her husband knows everything and has agreed to aid in our cause.

Jeremy returns in time to hear the part where I chose to stay with him after he took a bullet for me. When I finish, I break off a piece of my crust and toss it to my girls.

"You're a real hero." Karen elbows me. "You saved his sorry butt." She throws her chin in Jeremy's direction as he stands guard at the gate.

I tilt my head at her. "You knew, didn't you?"

Her hand flies to her chest. "Me?"

"And I bet I know who told you."

She peeks around before admitting, "I thought I was doing so well with my performance. He told me after he came home late for dinner one day with Dan. I just about marched to the compound to steal you myself." She sighs. "Don't be mad at Vinny. You can't blame him. He knows I'd castrate him if I found out he's keeping secrets from me."

I cringe at the thought of Sam finding out about Dan's involvement. She's a *trained* killer.

Karen grabs my hand. "Listen, I'm sorry about Ryan *and* his little witch," she growls. "None of the servants care for her holier-than-thou attitude. But the other options weren't great either. And with everyone breathing down his back to pick a Queen… well, we got stuck with *her*." She squeezes my wrist. "Try to not be too hard on Ryan. On top of all the royal duties he was forced to embrace, you represented the most challenging parts of his life. I think that's why he's taken so long to bring you home."

Ryan's words slam into my memories, and all I can picture is how he screamed at me, insisted I was a *curse* to the family. He never apologized, even when he had the chance. The trouble he's in now is just karma biting him in the tooshie.

How can she take his side?

"He didn't so much as attempt to communicate with the Black Rose *or me*, even when he found out I was with child," I whisper the last part so as to not shock the chickens.

"He's been an emotional wreck, especially after Christian died, angry and bitter to everyone. Then, like clockwork, when he turned twenty-one, he had to choose a wife."

"You're my best friend. You don't get to make excuses on his behalf. He's a grown man." I shake my head. "I never even got to bury my *fiancé* or say goodbye." Tears obscure my vision. "*His highness* took that from me."

"You mean *they* took that from you." She nods towards the rebel group. "They could have brought you home, let you move on with your life when Ryan was ignoring them and their plan was failing," she grinds out.

I swipe at my eyes. "Karen, if you saw their compound, you would understand why they were desperate to make these changes and why I couldn't turn my back on them. They can't go out in public. They can't hold a job, get married without fearing for their lives."

"You easily forgive *them* but not Ryan? You've

known him longer."

Her words slam into my chest and take my breath away. "It's two very different situations."

"Ryan was desperate to move forward and make the country stable again. Even if that meant marrying a real witch, like Cherie."

My rage boils to the surface. "Again, he made his choice and got what he deserved, after everything he did to his son and me." I still can't believe she's sticking up for that jerk. I know he's her employer and chosen uncle to her children, but I'm her best friend.

"He *loved* his son enough to keep him out of the Palace life, didn't he? And now that your *friend* has claimed the child, maybe he can still protect it from the crown."

It sounds like Ryan has opened up to Karen about more than she's willing to share. I rub my face. If the King would just talk to *me*, we could settle what happened...

But does it even matter? What's done is done, right?

"Why are you telling me all of this?"

"Because I love you and know what's going on in that head of yours. You need to try to cut him some slack. Just like you did your rebel friends." She bumps shoulders with me. "Trust me. I'm pissed at the way Ryan has dealt with this situation too. But we both know deep down he's a good guy."

I cross my arms over my chest. "He has an odd way of showing it."

"I'm sorry I didn't come after you," Karen whispers, her eyes glued to her hands. "I was so busy taking care of two little humans... I'm embarrassed to admit I didn't realize you were gone that long. I called and texted you, but I assumed you were occupied too."

Her confession breaks my heart. "You had your elbows deep in dirty diapers." I hug her. "I never once blamed you."

She wipes her cheeks. "But I'm as guilty as Ryan is. We all are. We could have—no, *should* have tried harder to locate you." She peeks over at Jeremy. "Even though I know you have been *well* taken care of."

My fingertips dance over his arm until our hands intertwine. "Yes, I have been."

"We should return to the event, or everyone will come looking for their guest of honor." She tugs us towards the group. "No more tears. It's time to *enjoy* your party and forget about everything else." She motions for the music to be turned up. "Dance with your man and have some fun. That's an order."

I try to do as she suggests, but after everything she's told me, my brain is melting from the overload.

Was Ryan really attempting to protect his son from the curse of the crown?

Invitation

When the party winds down, I scurry off, carrying my shoes and letting the grass cool my swollen feet.

I look up to see Elizabeth approaching me. "That May is spunky."

"You have no idea." I smirk. "She seems to have latched on to you."

"She's certainly warmed my heart with her antics and innocence." The former Queen nods at the little girl now chatting animatedly with Karen.

The silence is awkward between us. There're many things that've been left unsaid.

"Where are Dan and Sam?" I ask her, hoping to generate conversation.

"They are still on their honeymoon."

"Oh, I didn't realize." It's not a lie. I knew they tied the knot, but I assumed they were going to wait to travel until all of this mess with the Palace was cleared up. "I hope they will be happy."

"They seem to complement each other well."

"What about Ryan and Cherie?"

"Just like all newlyweds, they are still working out the kinks." Elizabeth's gaze travels skyward as a bird flutters to a tree branch. "It looks like the clouds are building. How about we go inside?" The former Queen then turns to address the dwindling crowd. "Thank you for joining us. This concludes the evening. I hope you have safe travels back to wherever you call home."

We offer our final goodbyes to the guests, the guards hold the entrance open, and Elizabeth waves our rebel group inside.

"Follow me, please." When we make it to the third floor, she nods to the conference room. "I know you didn't come here to party. We have business to discuss. Thank you for being patient. Please have a seat."

Jeremy assesses the space, making sure nothing's amiss. He pulls out my chair. I fall in it, glad to be off my feet. Once he warms my side, I shove my toes in his lap. He works his witchcraft on my sore muscles, massaging all the way up to my calves. I groan and melt. His touch is magic. I yelp as he tweaks a knot.

"Sorry." He smooths the lump until it's gone.

May fidgets with her backpack but even the young girl looks exhausted from all the fresh air and vigorous festivities.

"Do you want me to rub *your* feet?" Brad nudges Tammy.

"Touch my feet and die."

He leans towards her. "Why? Are you ticklish?"

"Yes," Jeremy interjects. "And her sides are too."

Tammy glares back at him. "Why are you spilling all my secrets?"

"Call it payback from being mean to Ann when she arrived."

"Oh, really?" she hisses, then turns to me. "Jeremy's nipples are super sensitive."

"All right, you two. We are in the *Palace*. Try to act intellectual," Sally demands. "The next thing to spew out of either of your mouths better be something clever."

When Sally looks away, Tammy flips Jeremy off and moves a safe distance away from Brad before he gets any ideas. Thank goodness May is entranced by her bag and doesn't seem to notice the squabbling.

The door swings open and his highness graces us with his presence. "Thank you all for your patience. I hope you enjoyed the social gathering." Ryan joins us at the head of the table. "I have received many inquiries from concerned citizens about the Black Rose and my family's history. Enough to make me question what's happened between us and consider how this situation should be handled in the future." He meets our gazes. "Even though we have had a bloody past, meeting peacefully like this can ensure a more optimistic future." He sits, concluding his introduction.

My jaw ticks. This is a well-*rehearsed* speech with no explanation of what action is going to be taken to accomplish the goal. We lean back and let Sally sweeten the mood with her honey-laced words.

"Thank you, King Ryan. We appreciate your generosity as you welcome us into your home. We know our pasts are complicated, with casualties on each side, and hope this visit can start the healing process for both of our families."

"What are you looking to accomplish *specifically* with this trip?"

"We would like you to pardon those with the Black Rose mark." She flashes her scar. "And enact a law permitting us to have the rights that all citizens of this great country hold, privileges like employment, marriage, and owning property. No more discrimination."

"And call off the enforcers," Tammy adds. "Make them stop branding us like livestock."

"And in turn, what is it we get?" Ryan counters, like the pompous jerk he is.

I almost leap across the table. How can he sit there

and demand something in return when the rebels obviously have *nothing* to give him?

"While living with us, Ann and the baby have been well taken care of. This proves we are not the animals you have treated us like all these years. Also, we have kept your secret hidden from the press, allowing you the right to claim the child if you please."

"Except your *stooge* told my wife that the baby is his." Ryan throws a thumb at Jeremy.

The rebel twitches and I wait for him to jump. But he grinds his teeth and shakes his head. *Pity.* I would have liked to see that.

When Jeremy doesn't take the bait, Ryan drags on. "If we pardon the group, do I have your word that no more attacks will occur?"

"As long as we are not attacked first."

"After the more recent events, the citizens have been banging down our door demanding justice for your cause."

My heart skips a beat. My articles have been reaching them.

"Will we vote on the pardon?" Sally whispers.

Ryan plows forward. "They've already voted to construct a contract in your favor. There'll be some *terms* and signatures that will be necessary to make this proposal official but consider yourselves pardoned. We've been asked to make the announcement at the Christmas Ball tonight. Which you are all requested to attend."

I squeeze Sally's hands and tears well in her eyes. Everything is happening so quickly. Could this really be the end of their discrimination?

"We have arranged guest rooms for you on the

first floor and waiting inside will be a maid or butler to assist you in whatever you may need during your stay." Elizabeth's eyes flit to our clothes. "You have access to our wardrobe of dresses and suits, and I am confident you will find the *proper* attire for this evening's festivities."

May squeals in excitement. She claps her hands in delight and I can't help but laugh at her enthusiasm.

"That's most generous of you. Do we still have your guarantee of protection during our stay?" Sally inquires.

"Our Palace guards and servants have been instructed to treat you like guests. You may stay the night and return to your home tomorrow after our press conference," Elizabeth answers.

"That's wonderful. Of course, we'll be more than happy to stay and celebrate," Sally concludes.

Ryan stands and buttons his suit. "Vinny, can you please have someone show *our guests* to their rooms so that they may relax and get ready for the ball?"

"Right this way." Vinny nods towards the open door, gesturing to where a group of servants is waiting to show us to our rooms.

Ryan grabs my wrist. "I need a word with you."

Jeremy crosses his arms over his chest. "It's my job to protect Ann, at all costs. Whatever you have to say to her, you can say with me present." He leans forward, almost touching Ryan's nose. "You assume you have us all fooled, but we've been dealing with your bloodline long enough to know something reeks of deception."

"Ann trusts us. I'm sure she will be comfortable with the head of the Palace guard watching over her." Ryan nods to Vinny. "She doesn't require *your protection*."

The air is suffocating, as I watch two roosters ready to spur. I rub Jeremy's arm until he tears his gaze from Mr. High-and-Mighty.

"You should make sure the others are settled into their rooms. I'll see you soon." I rise to the tip of my toes and press my lips to his, to further my point. He is *my* choice. There are no other cocks. His tongue caresses my seam, begging for an intimate taste. When I let him in, he devours every inch of my mouth, like this might be the last time we embrace.

Maybe he's afraid I'll slip away like Mary did...

When Jeremy pulls back, I'm breathless. Nothing remains in the room, except us. I cup his cheeks. "I love you."

His grin is magical, satisfying every insecurity I possess. "I love you *more*."

My lip twitches at the challenge. "Only time will tell."

"I look forward to proving it, every day for the rest of our lives." Jeremy shoulder-checks Ryan as he leaves the room.

"Charming." The King rubs his sore arm.

I lean on the edge of the table watching him. The wrinkles are deeper in his face than when we last spoke this intimately. I squint and notice grey strands poking out of his scalp. Or maybe it's just the lighting? Surely you can't get silver streaks at twenty-one. I run my hand through my own hair. If anyone should have them, it's me.

Elizabeth slides over her notes from the meeting to her son. She squeezes his wrist and gives him a look. The same look I've seen her give Christian many times in the past. She doesn't want him to lose his composure.

"I should check on Snowball."

"How is she doing?" I inquire about the snow-white beauty.

"She's been a little under the weather, but I'm sure with you here, she'll perk right up." Elizabeth embraces me. "I ensured you were given the best guest room in the Palace. You'll be staying next to me, on the third floor. I will see you both soon."

Once the door closes, Ryan hands me his mom's notes. "Please have *AnnaBelle* write an article, explaining that negotiations are underway to make our country united again."

Has he *caught* my hand in the cookie jar?

"She is a very busy woman. I don't know if she'll be available."

Wait a minute. Is *this* why they agreed so quickly? Not to offer equality to the rebels but to appease the nosey citizens and get them off their backs?

"Anything I can do to persuade *her*?" He chuckles.

Yup. He knows. Chicken's out of the bag. No use in denying it. His laughter elicits my own, and our longstanding barriers tumble over. For a moment, it feels as if no time has passed, and Christian should be strutting past the threshold to scowl at us. I peek in that direction and sigh.

"What happened to you?" I whisper to the man I used to love.

And that barrier slams back into place. "You must be exhausted from today's events. Maybe you should nap before the ball."

"Ryan, please."

"It's been an emotional day for me too." His gaze

wanders to my belly. "I thought I could talk about it, but I can't right now." He rushes out the door and I'm left in the silence of my thoughts.

"Jeremy and I agreed to wrestle after the dance." Vinny leans against the wall. "That should turn that frown upside down."

"I would love to see that." I grin and he offers me his arm. "You guys will be shirtless, right?"

"Whatever you want."

Vinny guides me to my room. As usual, the space is furnished with an obnoxiously big queen-size bed, a dresser, a walk-in closet filled with clothes, a bathroom with a shower and a jacuzzi tub, a couch, a coffee table, a desk, and an enchanting balcony. Despite the niceties, I miss my tiny accommodations at the compound.

My hand glides over the comforter before meeting a red dress with an open back. Of course, Elizabeth would be micromanaging everything again. Making sure I was every bit the woman she expects me to be.

"Is this what I'm supposed to wear?"

"You are going to be breaking hearts all night." Vinny smirks, ignoring my question. "I'll get Karen to assist you with your hair and makeup. Then you two can have some girl time."

I wave him out of the room, then ease myself onto the bed. Memories skim the surface, threatening to choke me. I rub my hand on my belly, wishing Jeremy was here. Everything is much quieter when he's gone.

It isn't long before Karen is striding in with a smile. "How does it feel to be among the civilized again?"

"Even though we didn't have fluffy decorative pillows, it was *civilized*."

She maneuvers me to the vanity and runs her hands

through my hair. "I cannot imagine how hard this situation must have been for you." She tugs a knot loose. "What happens now?"

"I don't know. Ryan chickened out of talking to me privately, so your guess is as good as mine."

Karen primps and pulls with expert focus. She steps back to take in her handiwork. "You are an absolute masterpiece." She kisses my cheek and whispers, "Remember, these walls have ears." Then she fidgets with my diamond earrings. "No matter what happens, I'll always be here for you."

I groan at my shoes. "Can you grab me flats? I'm done with these." I kick the heels aside. "My balance was bad enough when I wasn't pregnant, and lately, I've been spoiled with boots."

"Same Ann, different day." Karen shoves a pair of ballerina flats my way. "Here you go."

I slip them on. "Wish me luck. I'm going to get my Prince Charming."

"I'll walk you down. That way, I can check on the kids." She tugs me to the staircase. "I can't wait to show you what Olivia can do! She does this cutest thing where she pretends to cry to get Vinny to read her an extra bedtime story."

"She has Daddy wrapped around her little finger, doesn't she?" I carefully descend the steps until I make it to the first floor. "Any idea what room Jeremy's in?" I ask while eyeing the hallway of doors.

She lifts her chin at the first one. "They wanted to keep a close eye on Mr. Bulky-Biceps."

"Thanks."

When Karen skips off, I knock, and Jeremy yanks the entrance open. "I told you I can dress myself!" His eyes travel over my gown. "Well, look at you. You're like a juicy apple." He tugs me inside before he presses me against the wall, his blue eyes sparkling with mischief. "Has anyone told you how incredibly beautiful you are?" He cups my chin.

"Keep talking."

He nibbles my earlobe. I groan and arch my back, exposing my neck. He trails delicious kisses over my skin, pausing to admire my overflowing cleavage. "How much time do we have before the ball?"

"You haven't changed into your suit and your hair is a disaster. We don't have time for anything *extra*." I push him away from my heated frame.

"It's been years since I've had to dress in anything fancy." He points to the suit still sitting on the bed.

"Where's your butler?"

"I told him to leave me alone."

"But he was here to help you."

Jeremy tugs my hips to his. "But I prefer *your* help."

"You are hopeless."

"Hopelessly in *love*." He lowers his lips to mine again and my body flares up. I wrap my arms around his neck as he intensifies the kiss.

I lean back to meet his gaze. "Vinny told me you were going to battle it out later."

"I'm going to make him cry in front of all of the other Palace guards."

"Do not break him." I laugh at his frown. "He's our *friend*."

"I'm making no promises." Jeremy flexes his arms. "Once I release these puppies, it's hard to leash them back up again."

I shake my head. "If you hurt him, you'll not only have to answer to me and the King but also to Vinny's wife." I help Jeremy dress and knot his tie. "Now brush your hair and put these on." I hand him his cuff links.

"Why? I can just roll up the sleeves."

"There will be cameras everywhere tonight and we need to show that we can be civilized."

Wow. I sound like Elizabeth. Have I come full circle, from farm girl to Palace representative? I need to get out of this pampered place before it's too late and I start craving pointy heels and ruby-lined underwear.

"You are really amazing, you know that?"

I shift his collar. "You aren't so bad yourself."

Jeremy kneels. "How is my baby boy doing?" He rubs my stomach. "Are you behaving?"

"He is his father's son." I ruffle the rebel's hair. "A troublemaker, through and through."

"Hey!" Jeremy jumps up before gliding the comb through his mess again. "I'm not a troublemaker. You are."

"That's a really mature comeback." I lean my forehead against his. "Whatever happens, know that my heart is yours."

"And you have mine." He glances at his watch. "Well, it's showtime, my lady."

"I sure hope you don't embarrass me on the dance floor."

"Hey, I can do more than the *Chicken* Dance."

Christmas Ball

Soft plucks of classical music echo in the hall as we near the event. I squeeze Jeremy's hand, my nerves prickling my skin with every step we take. Christmas colors wrap around the ballroom with tiny glittering snowflakes made of crystal, fresh mistletoe, and twinkling lights guiding our way. The Palace staff have created their own winter wonderland. A string quartet is nestled in the corner. Waiters scurry from guest to guest with sparkling beverages and glistening pastries. Jeremy and I continue to weave through the crowd until we locate the other rebels looking uncomfortable at a table in the corner.

"You guys clean up nicely," I say as Jeremy pulls back my chair.

"These outfits are absurd." Tammy adjusts her cleavage. "Whoever designed this should be hung."

I think Brad would disagree. He's having a hard time keeping his eyes off Tammy's emerald gown.

"I think everyone looks pretty," May announces as she fans out her pink dress.

"I'm with Tammy on this one." Sally tugs at her dark-blue fabric. "How long do these things last?"

"Any amount of time is too long," Tammy grumbles.

"At least the grub is top-notch." Brad snatches a macaroon from a passing tray.

"Welcome, everyone." Elizabeth materializes at my side. "Thank you for joining us."

"Not like we had a choice," Tammy mutters into her water glass.

Ever the polite Royal, Elizabeth ignores the retort. "Lady Ann, King Ryan would like you to sit at our table please." The former Queen offers her hand. "I can show you the way."

"Of course." I peck Jeremy on the cheek, follow her to the front, and offer a nod of acknowledgment to Cherie and Ryan before I take my seat.

The King buttons his jacket and stands. "Welcome to our annual Christmas Ball. I am very pleased to see you all here tonight. Especially since we're celebrating alongside Lady Ann." He motions for me to rise.

Does he not realize how hard it is for me to lift my fat butt? But I do as he commands and wave to my peers. The guests clap and I hear a few shouts from the back, then I return to my seat.

"Lady Ann has accomplished a great feat. After decades of failed peace negotiations between the Palace and the Black Rose, she has successfully united us. Tonight, we celebrate in her honor." He lifts his wine glass. "To new beginnings and a brighter future."

"To Lady Ann," the flock tweets in response.

Thank goodness the waiters present our meal, and everyone turns their attention to the roast, mashed potatoes, glazed carrots, brussels sprouts, and fresh rolls. It's been a long time since I've devoured an all-you-can-eat buffet. My gaze flicks to the rebels and it seems they are happy about the dinner too.

Sitting here with the Royals is awkward. I wish I could trust them, but after everything that's happened...

Maybe Karen has a point. I forgave the Black Rose easily. *Why can't I do the same with the crown?*

Soon our dirty plates are picked up, and Cherie stands and clinks her glass. "Again, thank you all for spending Christmas with us. We will now open the floor for dancing. As is tradition, the guest of honor and the King will start us off." She nods to her husband and me.

Never mind. I still hate them.

The King offers me his arm. Can I tell him to flock off and get away with it? He gives me a pointed stare. Guess not. I concede, and Ryan leads us to the middle of the room, where he wraps a warm arm around my waist. The string quartet plays a slow melody as Ryan glides around.

"I am glad I decided to wear flats," I blurt out.

"You and your distaste of heels."

"At least I don't have *tacky* facial hair."

I yelp as he swings me out, then tugs me back in. "Why do I feel the need to apologize?"

"To whom? Me or the rest of the world?"

He ignores my jab. "Listen, I did not mean to put you on the spot like this. Mom thought of this *first dance* nonsense last minute."

"Your wife isn't too happy about it either." I nod to the Queen.

"She'll be fine."

Why did he say *fine* that way?

"Are you happy, Ryan?"

His jaw ticks. "You mean after my brother *died* and I was forced to take his position? Yes, I'm thrilled."

His sarcasm cuts deep, but before I can question him further, the song ends and we separate. Ryan darts into the crowd, eager to put distance between us—which is fine by me—and I turn to make my way back to my seat, only to be stopped in my tracks.

"Lady Ann, can I have this dance?"

"Richard, I'm surprised to see you here." I allow him to take the King's place, and we sway to the beat.

"The people demanded full coverage of this event and who better to cover it? And I'm glad I came because I get a front-row seat to tomorrow's press conference too." His tone causes my brows to rise, and he continues. "I mean, I get to witness your return to the Palace, first dance with the King…"

"Richard, what are you asking me?"

"Is your ex-boyfriend going to confess to being the baby's *father*?"

I stumble and step on his foot. "Why would he do that?"

"Why wouldn't he?" Richard counters.

"That's none of your or anyone else's business." I pull away but he tugs me to his chest.

"Or does it belong to the rebel… *Max*?"

"I'm only going to ask you nicely *one* more time. Stop."

"I'm going to find out eventually."

He freezes as a shadow looms behind him. Jeremy squeezes the reporter's shoulder until Richard releases his hold on my frame. "I believe you've had enough dancing, Dick," the rebel snarls in a hushed tone, applying more pressure when he adds, "If I see you harassing Ann again, I'll make sure you won't have the ability to write for months."

"I apologize if I've made you uncomfortable, Anna. I'll see you tomorrow." Richard shakes Jeremy off and dashes to his table to hide.

"You didn't have to do that," I scold Jeremy once

Richard is out of earshot.

"A simple thank you is all I need to hear." His fingertips weave to my lower back. "Prince Charming is ready for his dance with Cinderella." He twirls me in a circle.

I crush his toes when I regain my balance. "Where did you learn to do that?"

Jeremy swallows a lump in his throat. "I trained with Mary in ballroom dancing."

I cringe. I forgot about that. "Oh," is all I can push out. Of course, he would know how to glide effortlessly across the floor.

"Do you want to stop?" he questions.

"No, I enjoy learning and experiencing your many talents." I meet his gaze. "You can even touch my butt if you feel the urge. No pressure though."

Jeremy's hands drop to the spot in question. "I thought you'd never ask."

It's as if we've known each other our entire lives. Two best friends hanging out at a stuffy, forced function and taking comfort in each other's presence. I'm safe in Jeremy's embrace and the world is blocked out around us. When I'm out of breath, we migrate to the rebels' table and chatter with the group.

A sudden chill is my only warning before we are interrupted again.

"How is everyone doing? Did you enjoy the roast?" We all pivot to see the Queen gracing us with her presence.

"It was delicious," Sally answers. "Thank you."

Cherie dips her chin, then turns to my man. "Jeremy, I was very impressed with your waltz. Would you do me the honor and dance with me?"

He side-glances me and I shrug. Then he clears his throat and rises to the occasion. "I guess I can't say no to our Queen, now, can I?"

Ryan's voice startles me. "Don't I know it." He steals Jeremy's chair.

I arch a brow at the smell of his breath. "How many drinks have you had?"

"I'm not sure."

"You never drank like this before. Do you do this often?"

"Ever since I lost Christian." He throws back the rest of the amber liquid. "My big *brother*. How I miss him telling me what to do." He laughs and grabs another glass from a passing tray. "Do *you* miss him?"

His question catches me off guard. Does he think I'm that cold-hearted? "Of course, I do," I whisper more to myself.

"Jeremy looks like him, kind of."

"It's the blue eyes." I smile. "And the bossy attitude."

"Christian really loved you." Ryan traces circles on the tablecloth. "When you left, the guilt was unbelievably hard to bear, especially after he died. I couldn't even look at *pictures* of you." The King runs his hands through his tussled locks. "I assumed the rebels wouldn't harm you and you would be happier there."

"They sent you my blood and hair. How could you think I was safe?"

"I guess ignorance is bliss."

Before I can tell him he's an idiot, his wife saves him.

"I've brought him back to you in one piece," Cherie

announces. "Now, my King, I believe you owe me a few dances before we retire for the night."

"As you wish." Ryan entwines his fingers with hers and guides the Queen to the center of the room.

"How bad was she?" I elbow Jeremy.

"She stepped on my feet twice." He munches on a pastry.

"Are you lying to me to make me feel better about my dancing abilities?"

He smirks and I shake my head. I watch as the royal couple sways to the soft melody. Cherie rests her head on Ryan's shoulder, and he kisses her hair. I wonder if he's found someone to fill the hole in his heart after losing his brother. Then my eyes flick from corner to corner.

"Where's May and Elizabeth?"

"May wanted to go to bed early." Sally nods to the hallway. "Elizabeth offered to read her a bedtime story." She holds up a hand to Jeremy. "Don't worry. I sent Tammy to trail them to make sure nothing happens."

"All of this excitement is too much for me. I'm going to get some air." I squeeze Jeremy's arm. "I'll be back."

"Do you want me to come with you?"

"No, I'm just stepping into the hallway for a minute." I brush past the crowds and take a deep breath. The halls are noiseless at night. It used to be comforting, but now it's eerie.

"You can't do that to her!"

I pivot towards the ruckus of high-pitched squeals. Oh no. I can't believe this. Two guards are manhandling *Scarlett* by the tail while May jumps up and down to try to save her friend.

How did she get here?

I stomp over, steam escaping my ears. "What are you doing?" The guards freeze as they take in my *I'm gonna rip your feathers out* demeanor, and I hiss in their direction. "Put. Her. Down."

"The only hen allowed inside the Palace is Snowball." The tall guard tucks the rebel chicken under his arm. Once her beak is close enough, she bites his finger as if it's the juiciest mealworm. He roars and I take the opportunity to snatch the agitator from his hold. "Hey, you can't do that!"

"*Hay* is for horses." I lift my chin. "Not for chickens." Then I hand Scarlett to May, who promptly adds her pal to her backpack and zips it.

"We have our orders."

"Well, you have been *overruled*," a strong, feminine voice replies, and I don't need to turn around to know Elizabeth is asserting her dominance over the pair of lackeys. "This hen is a guest and will be treated as such. Is that understood, gentlemen?"

"We apologize." They bow and scurry off.

The Royal kneels to meet May's tear-stained face. "Did they hurt you, dear?" Her eyes scan the little girl's trembling body.

"They…" She chokes on her hiccups. "Pulled her tail." She waves at a pile of red plumage.

Elizabeth wraps her arms around the child. "There, there. They won't hurt her again. I promise."

The two share a heartwarming moment as they comfort each other. One likely remembering the lost child she'll never see again and the other missing the parents who will never again remind her how important she is. The backpack vibrates and May unzips it an inch to let the bird get some fresh air.

"I think your friend would be more happy walking around, don't you?" Elizabeth questions.

I tense. I'm not sure Scarlett can behave herself inside the Palace. I snort. She reminds me a lot of myself when I first arrived and got lost, found the gorgeous library, and set my heart on a mission to know the wrong prince.

"Can she get a tour of your home, Elizabeth?" May gives the former Queen her best puppy-dog eyes.

"I thought I heard you screaming." Sally stumbles to our group. "May, you told me you were going to bed."

The older women stare each other down. Tension builds, and I swallow, afraid that Elizabeth might know that Sally's son was the one who shot Christian. May picks up on the internal feud, but gracefully tugs on both of the ladies' wrists. "We were going to tour the Palace. It's pretty with all of the twinkling lights. I begged Elizabeth to show us and she was about to say yes."

May is good. She glazed over the fact that she's supposed to be asleep in her room right now.

Elizabeth clears her throat. "Yes, of course, I can give you a tour."

"And can Sally join us?"

The former Queen's jaw ticks. "Only if *she* wants to."

"I appreciate the offer, but I should check in with the others."

"Ann can do that, right?" May smirks at me.

This little *diplomat*. "Yes, I can check on the others and let them know you are exploring the home."

"Great!" May shoves the backpack in my hands. "Scarlett is hungry."

"You brought the *chicken*?" Sally screeches as her face turns red. "I specifically asked you to leave her outside with the other hens before we left." The rebel rubs the bridge of her nose. "I'm sorry about this."

"It's not a problem. Any friend of May is welcome here." Elizabeth pivots to the small girl. "Now, how about we get some freshly baked cookies from the kitchen before we walk around?"

"Yes!" May claps in response.

The trio strolls down the Palace halls. Elizabeth points to the many paintings decorating the walls and explains who created them. I shake my head. Everyone underestimated May. I can't wait to see how her future unfolds. A nip on my hand brings me to the feathered renegade.

"You are a troublemaker," I scold her. "You could have gotten us kicked out." She chirps in reply, reminding me she's hungry. "Let's go." I take the hen to my room, set a dish of water on the floor, and let her roam. Then I tiptoe to Elizabeth's room to borrow some squirmy treats and tasty feed. "Snowball!" I rub my face over her back. "I missed you." I remember when she was a tiny cotton ball. Now she is fully grown. "You are beautiful." She leans into my touch before stealing a goodie.

"There you are," Jeremy grumbles as he's flanked by two guards.

"Are you guys on your way to having a threesome?" I poke a worm at them. "Because I'd love to watch a video of that."

"Very funny. These *peons* wouldn't let me up to this floor. Apparently, it's off-limits to us commoners."

I flip my hair over my shoulder. "And rightly so. You'll track mud and *self-doubt* on the carpet."

His lips tug at the sides. "I take it you found our hitchhiker?"

"You knew Scarlett was with May?"

"I'm head of security. I know all."

"Then why didn't you do anything about it!"

"I wanted to see if the guards were doing their jobs correctly and would search us before we entered." He throws a thumb over his shoulder. "They've proven themselves incompetent, *again*." The soldiers bristle but don't take the bait.

Light catches my eye and I groan. In my rush to get here, I didn't notice that I left my door open. I dash past the men and search my room. "Scarlett?" I call out, but she's nowhere to be found. "Jeremy, have you seen..."

A flash of red runs head-on into a blur of white. *Oh, no!* I smack the closest guard. "Elizabeth's chicken is getting her butt beat." Their eyes go wide before they leap to save her fluffy highness. If I could bend over to separate the hens, I would. Seeing as that's not an option, I turn to Jeremy. "Shouldn't you help them?"

Jeremy coils an arm around my waist. "Give me a few more minutes. I'm analyzing their movements, seeing if I can learn a thing or two before our next scuffle." I jab my elbow into his stomach. "Fine."

He tugs tail feathers until Scarlett rests in his arms. She's puffy and heaving but looks unharmed. The guard collects Snowball and dabs her bleeding wobble. Then glares at the red devil.

I hold up a hand stopping him. "Snowball is perfectly fine. This is normal behavior. They are fighting to be head of the coop."

Jeremy chuckles. "It looks like Scarlett gets to be the queen now."

I jam my heel into his foot to shut him up. "We'll bring Scarlett to my room and keep her there."

Snowball squeaks and attempts to wiggle out of reach. I stroke her neck. "I'm sorry about this, Snowball. Scarlett is a little rough around the edges but she's a sweetie once you break through her tough exterior." The feathered highness narrows her eyes at her new enemy, likely doubting my words. "She'll stay out of your way. I promise." Before the guards can argue, I guide Jeremy to my room and shut the door.

Jeremy flops onto my bed. "Nice save."

I settle Scarlett on the desk with her discarded snacks. Then I run a hand over her body to make sure she's unharmed. "Do you think the two of them will ever get along?"

"The chickens, or the Royals and the rebels?"

"All of the above."

"I sure hope so. Or all of this will be for nothing, and we might as well tie our nooses now." He collects me in his arms. "Why did they give you the nicer room?"

"Because I'm obviously better than you." I smirk.

He tickles my sides until tears kiss my cheeks. "You are just as feisty as the rest of the flock."

"I take that as a compliment."

"I knew you would."

The Curse

A knock on my door pulls me from Jeremy's icy gaze. "Come in." Tim pops his head around the corner, and I glare in his direction. "What do *you* want?"

He blinks. "Are you upset about something?"

"Drop the act. I know you kept things hidden from Ryan until Christian passed away." I poke a finger in his chest. "And it makes me wonder what else you're hiding."

"I was doing my job."

"I thought we were friends."

"We are."

"No. Friends help each other."

He rustles around in his pocket and tosses me a piece of paper. "My family's safety comes first. Always."

I examine the photo. "Who is this?"

"King Christian helped me and my partner adopt a child. She's our whole world. I owe that man so much. And following his last order was more important to me than hunting down a cheating woman who did nothing but cause him pain and suffering." He sucks in a breath and straightens his tie. "I came here to let you know that King Ryan has some forms for you to sign, at your convenience."

I run a finger over the photo. I remember when Tim told me about the possibility of adopting a child, but I didn't realize all the hoops he may have had to jump through to accomplish that. But Christian did, and of course, he helped his assistant follow his dreams of completing his family. If it meant ensuring the man maintained his loyalty to the crown...

I return the photo. "Congratulations."

The words flutter around us and Tim nods before leaving.

"Why does he want you to come to the office so late?" Jeremy yawns from where he's positioned on my bed.

"He's probably drunk and drowning himself in work." I grind my jaw. "But the quicker I deal with him, the sooner we can go to bed."

"Do you want a bodyguard?" Jeremy tosses a pillow at my butt.

"Speaking of, have you seen Vinny?"

"No. He was supposed to meet up with us at the dance."

"Maybe he took the night off to be with Karen and the kids," I suggest.

"Do you want to go to Karen's room and see what's up?"

"No, let me deal with his highness and then we'll check on them in the morning."

Jeremy kisses my nose. "Hurry back."

"Don't get into any trouble while I'm gone." I crack the door and scan the hallway.

"No promises," he fires back. Scarlett attempts to squeeze out behind me but Jeremy catches her. "Oh, no. You've caused enough mayhem for one day." Then he closes the door.

"You wanted to see me?" I lean on the King's office doorframe a few minutes later.

"Please sit." Ryan closes me inside his domain before settling behind the desk. The same one Christian once occupied.

How many times have I sat in this chair? I focus all my attention on the container of pens in front of me and not the spot where Ryan once beat the fluff out of Max.

"You must be very *proud* of yourself."

"Excuse me?" I itch my ear, wondering what's clogging it.

Ryan leans back and feigns regalness. "Come on. Don't play the village idiot. It's beneath you."

"Are you drunk?" I lean forward to sniff his breath.

"I've never been more sober or seen more clearly."

"I'm not taking the bait. If there's nothing else you want to discuss, I'm leaving." I clutch the doorknob.

"How could you do it?" he snarls. "Choose them over us."

"You think I chose?" I snip. "My hand was forced, remember? When *you* kicked me out and didn't make any attempts to rescue me."

"You're sleeping with the enemy!" he barks.

"What happened to all that crap you spewed earlier about forgiveness and moving on? I knew it was all for show. You've learned *nothing* from your family's mistakes."

"You acknowledge you *are* bedding that rebel." He shakes his head. "Anything with two legs, huh?"

Red flashes behind my eyes before a resounding slap echoes around us. "How dare you. For your information, I haven't had sex with anyone but the piece of shit in front of me."

Ryan rubs his cheek. "Good, I wouldn't want you to get too attached, considering…"

My heart stops. "Considering *what?*"

"Remember those terms and conditions I warned you about earlier?"

The door flings open and Cherie bursts in. She slams her palms on his desk. "What did you do?" She side-eyes me. "What's going on in here? Why is *she* alone with you?"

"I was explaining to Ann that someone needs to be held accountable for the King's death."

My pulse quickens. Ryan is no longer the man I once loved, but a replica of his father.

"Don't do this," I whisper. "We came here for *peace*, but if you do this…"

He thumps his hands on the table as he stands to meet my threat. "You'll do what exactly? Attempt another attack? Send more articles to the press?"

"Honey," Cherie urges. "This is not what we discussed."

"I'm done *discussing* everything while waiting for justice! I'm the King and what I say is law!" he shouts. "My brother's murderer will hang!"

Cherie's plump lips hang open like she's trying to catch flies. "Don't raise your voice at me. We are partners, ruling this country side by side."

"Go check on Mom, Cherie." He waves her off as if she's a nuisance.

"This discussion is not over." She stomps out.

"Ann!" May's screech vibrates from down the hall.

I tumble my chair as I run to her voice. "I'm coming, May."

It's my worst nightmare. A group of guards push back the crowd as two soldiers wrestle with a man on the floor.

"Stop!" Sally shoves Tammy and Brad aside. "Don't provoke them. We can still fix this." She holds May to her chest.

"You said you wanted peace!" Tammy snarls as Brad clutches her waist. "You're all liars!" She kicks and screams. "I warned you that they weren't going to listen to us! This is all *your* fault." She turns her rage on me.

My knees grow weak. I crumble to the ground as Jeremy meets my gaze. Not wanting to cause any more distress, he throws his arms up in surrender. The guards cuff him.

"You can't do this!" I grab the closest uniform. "I order you to release him!"

"Look at me," Jeremy demands. "Take a deep breath. It'll be okay," he soothes. "Stay with Mom."

"No, please don't," I whimper, watching in horror as the love of my life is dragged to the same place his wife died. I've sentenced him to the same fate. I told him it was safe to come here, that we could trust Elizabeth to keep her word...

I clutch my hair.

Tammy breaks through Brad's hold, and like a wild rooster, she spurs the guards holding Jeremy. Brad is close behind her, throwing his own fists. But they're no match for the dozens of enforcers rushing to their comrades' aid. Blood is spilled before they, too, are detained. The one thing we were trying to avoid at all costs. May wiggles out of Sally's grasp and runs after the group.

"May? Wait!" Sally trails her.

I glare at Ryan as he stands there watching. Not doing a thing to stop the brutality he once said he didn't want.

"You said *I* was the curse!" I shout as tears stream past my chin. "But the crown is the curse, and if you continue down this path, you're going to be next." A sharp pain jabs my abdomen and has me doubling over.

Even my body is against me.

"What is going on out here?" Elizabeth tightens her robe. "Oh my! Ann, are you hurt?" She crouches beside me. "Ryan! Come quickly! Ann needs the doctor."

"Not him," I push out. "Anyone but him."

"Don't just stand there, young man!" Elizabeth hollers.

Ryan collects me in his arms, without saying a word, and rushes down the hall. Everything is falling apart and there's nothing I can do about it.

How is my world crumbling so quickly?

The King sets me on a bed. His voice sounds far off as he explains my plight to the doctor.

"When was the last time you saw your obstetrician?"

My hearing fades back to reality as the blood pressure cuff squeezes my arm. "I've *never* seen one before."

"You have never seen one?"

"My father was a farmer, and we didn't have health care. I only went to my primary care doctor in emergency situations."

"We will need to perform a full exam, bloodwork, and an ultrasound." Before I can protest, the doctor pivots to the King. "I will be right back."

Once the door closes, the air between me and his highness is electrified. We both want nothing to do with each other, but this child is tethered between us, forcing us to act civil.

"Why haven't you seen a doctor?" Ryan demands.

I cross my arms over my chest and stare at the wall.

"Ann, answer me."

"Why? You don't care about me, or anything I've been telling you for the last few hours. Go back to your wife and leave me alone."

A nurse breezes into the room, waving around a gown. "Lady Ann, I'm going to assist you into something more comfortable." Ryan at least has the decency to face the wall as I'm stripped of my ballgown. "Are you in any pain right now, dear?"

"Yes."

"Where?"

I nod to the jerk in the corner. "He's a giant pain in my rear."

She laughs, before quickly turning it into a cough. "What about in your abdomen?"

"I had sharp jabs of pain earlier, but not right now."

"Well, the doctor will give you a thorough examination to make sure everything is good." The nurse ties the flimsy fabric, then nods at her handiwork. "There. Much better than that restrictive dress. She's decent, your highness," she calls over her shoulder. She rubs my arm with an alcohol wipe. "I'm going to draw some blood. It won't hurt but you'll feel a tiny prick."

"I got a *prick* right here already," I mumble to the shadow tapping away on his phone.

The nurse's lip twitches as crimson fills the tubes in her hands. "I'm going to drop these off. Sit tight." She exits with the vials in hand.

"That was more than a prick." I rub my bandage.

"I am sure popping the child out will be a little more intense."

"If it has your massive head, it will be."

Ryan rolls his eyes. "It's not that big. Unless you mean my other head."

My neck snaps in his direction. "We both know *that* body part is not as big as you wish it to be. Why are you still here anyway? I told you to leave. I want nothing to do with you."

His practiced façade splinters and he growls, "I'm here because I was *instructed* to be here, and unlike you, I can't run off whenever I want."

We stare each other down. Two headstrong individuals, each never giving an inch to the other. I should spit in his pompous, know-it-all face and leave. I clench my fists. But I need to set the rebels free first. I won't leave them to fend for themselves. I'll play nice for now, then when his back is turned, I'm going to claw his heart out.

He doesn't use that organ anyway.

"Am I interrupting?" The doctor's eyes bounce between me and the King.

Ryan clears his throat. "No, of course not."

"Lady Ann, are you ready for your physical?" The older man snaps his gloves on and pulls a curtain in place, so it separates me from my enemy. "It should be painless and quick."

"That's exactly how I got into this mess, doctor," I respond loud enough for Ryan to hear me.

The doctor takes a second to process my humor and chuckles before moving to my feet. I can't explain how awkward it is to have your feet high up in the air while a complete stranger mumbles from between your legs. Whoever named these crazy contraptions *stirrups* must have been clinically insane. "Well, everything looks good."

How the heck am I supposed to answer *that*? Seeing as gratitude is far from what I'm feeling right now.

"That wasn't too bad, was it?" He removes the divider, then pulls the ultrasound machine to the head of the bed. "Now, let's take a closer look."

I don't know... You were pretty close before. I bite back my retort.

He turns the lights down and lifts my gown to reveal my baby bump. Then he squeezes on a dollop of cold liquid and runs a wand over it. The screen is fuzzy, then a giant blob comes into focus.

The warmth on my arm causes me to side-eye Ryan as he leans in. For once, he seems genuinely interested. His eyes grow wide as his gaze bounces from my belly to the screen. "That's the baby?"

The doctor nods. "Yes, my King. This is his head... hands, abdomen, and feet." He taps the screen. At Ryan's shocked expression, the older man smiles. "I will give you a moment." Then he steps out of the room.

The King's fingertips graze the screen. "What have I done?" he whispers, a hand flinging to his head and raking through his hair. "I abandoned my child. I am a failure." He drops into his chair and hides his face as his frame shakes.

I rub my eyes. Is he... *crying*? I imagined him breaking, the celebrating I would do afterwards, but now that it's here...

He rushes out of the room, slamming the door behind him, while a pair of tiny feet jabs my side. I rub my belly, my mind wandering to a future full of unknowns.

Can this tiny human melt the King's frigid heart and bring harmony to our great nation?

New Deal

Before I leave the hospital wing, the doctor informs me that I have a urinary tract infection and gives me a bottle of antibiotics. He also said that my iron's low, and I need to ramp up my intake, or I'll need pills to remedy that too.

Not too bad, considering my lack of proper medical care.

After the whole ordeal with Ryan, I can't remain inside the Palace any longer. Were those tears in his eyes a sign of his *regret*? Is he going to change his mind and claim my son?

I need space to clear my head. Then I'll track down Sally so we can build our contingency plan. I rub my arms as the chilly breeze caresses my cheeks. That's what Tammy and Jeremy would do if they were in my shoes. Keep a positive mind while plotting their next move. The moon shines brightly as I stare at where my feet directed me. Of course, my subconscious would bring me *here*. My fingertips trail the engraved name. The granite headstone is cold and unmoving, like the bones it's concealing. Memories slice through my next breath and I sob into my hands.

"Christian," I whimper, begging his soul to answer all my questions of *why* he did what he did.

What I would give to return to simpler times before my life mingled with the Royals. I swipe at my eyes.

No. I don't regret all of it. There were tender moments between us. I know, in his own way, Christian loved me. It just wasn't how I wanted him to.

My solitude is broken by the sound of crunching grass. "What a weird way to spend your time, Lady Ann."

I clench my fists, not bothering to look at the beast stalking me. "I could say the same thing about *you*."

"I followed you out here because I was worried about your well-being."

Her voice grates on my last nerve. "Liar."

"You'd dare call your Queen a liar?"

I pivot and glare. "Leave me alone. You have other matters that need to be dealt with, considering the way your husband dismissed you earlier." Her jaw ticks. "He isn't who you thought he was, is he?" I purr. "I know all too well what's going through your pretty little head."

"You have no idea what I'm thinking." Despite her words, her composure falters. "Everything was wonderful until *you* came back into his life. Now he's consuming too much alcohol and making dreadful choices as he seeks vengeance."

Her observation washes over me. She doesn't like the way Ryan is handling things. *Interesting.*

"And you turned the King's guard into a spy," she spits. "The one man my husband trusted more than anyone else."

My chest tightens. "What do you mean?"

This snaps her mask back in place. "Don't deny it! I know more than you think."

"What did he do with the guard?"

"He's packing his bags now. We're sending him and his family away with a warning to never return if they know what is good for them."

Poor Vinny and Karen. That's why he didn't meet us. "Where are you sending them?"

She snorts. "They're returning to their farm in the

country. Waste of talent, really."

I release my breath. At least they are safe and back home.

She eyes my stomach. "I know Ryan's the child's father."

I swallow my terror. "You're mistaken. Jeremy is the father." My hand reaches for my baby bump on its own accord.

"You *believe* you are intelligent." She *tsks* her tongue. "Didn't your fiancé ever warn you that the Palace has ears?"

She's right. Christian said as much. So did Karen for that matter. But how did Cherie know about Ryan and me?

"Don't give me that look. It's beneath you," she snarls. "When I came to pay my respects to Christian before his passing, I kept to the shadows in the hallway just long enough to overhear your pitiful confession at his bedside. The one where you admitted to *sleeping* with his brother. I've been a part of this family's inner circle since I was three years old. They were *brothers* to me. Then you waltzed in here and destroyed everything."

I don't dare to point out that if she does consider the Princes her brothers, she's now committing incest. But the pain etched in her gaze splinters my silence. "You can't put all that blame on *my* shoulders. They had a hand in everything that happened too." I straighten my back. "And now your beloved is choosing to continue the reign of terror started by his father and sentence my fiancé to death. When will it end?"

"It ends with me." Cherie lifts her chin. "I will do everything in my power to convince my husband to end this madness and fight for the peace he swore to uphold."

For the first time since I met her, I actually *see* the woman standing in front of me. She doesn't want to be Queen any more than I did. She just happened to fall in love with the man whose fate led him to uphold the crown. What I wouldn't give to hear her story and know how she became who she is. But that's a tale for another day.

That being said, I'm not dumb enough to take her word at face value or doubt that she has ulterior motives. "What is it you want in return?"

She jabs a finger at my belly. "That *thing* will never be part of our family. I want no part in its life."

I cover my unborn baby's ears the best I can. "He's only a child…"

"Stop!" she screeches. "What he is… is a *mistake*! Ryan never would have done anything with you if he weren't so traumatized by the events that played out." She smooths her gown. "You will go on record and state that the rebel is its father, then we will free him and work on the peace you covet."

"No."

"No?" she seethes. "You do realize this is not open for discussion, right?"

"Oh, but it is." I rub my bargaining chip. "Because according to the laws, this *mistake* is our next King."

She falters. "You wouldn't dare…"

"I'll move *mountains* to ensure Jeremy's freedom. I'd even break up a royal marriage. So, let me tell you how this is going to go. Once you get his highness to release Jeremy *and* sign the petition, I'll go to the press with the name of the father and not a moment sooner. And I want you to convince Ryan that Vinny's family deserves the right to resume their employment at the Palace *if* they want, because they are loyal to their friends and never meant to hurt him."

Cherie chews her bottom lip as she sizes me up. "You've learned a thing or two from Christian. I see a lot of him in your proposition."

I glance at the headstone. "He taught me a lot, and for that, I'm grateful. No matter the cost of those lessons," I whisper to the wind, hoping it'll carry my words to the man himself.

"You really love the rebel, don't you?"

"With every breath that I have."

"Then I guess we have some work to do." She holds out a hand.

I accept the challenge. "You know, Cherie, you aren't as evil as I thought you were."

"It's *Queen* Cherie to you." There's a twinkle in her gaze, and I question if one day our rivalry can melt into camaraderie.

"Let's hope your reign ends better than Mary's." I elbow her as I walk towards the garden. I pluck free a stem with blue flowers and rest it on top of Christian's headstone.

"Why that one?"

"I guess you don't know the boys as well as you claim." I rub my arms to stave off the sudden chill. "The forget-me-not was Christian's favorite blossom in the garden."

"I didn't know that," Cherie whispers more to herself than to me.

"Well, maybe I can teach you a few things."

"Doubtful." She pivots on her heel and strides to the

door.

The Palace is quiet. Even Sally and May's room is dark when I poke my head in. I give them each a peck on the cheek, then continue to my own room. My hand stills on my engagement ring dangling from my neck and I detour to the one place I swore I'd never visit again. I knock on the heavy wooden door. The last time I was here still haunts my nightmares. Images flash through my mind of Max's violence and Joey's bloody corpse.

"Yes?" The Palace guard arches a brow.

I lift my chin. "I would like to see the prisoner."

He steps aside to let me pass. "Five minutes."

I swallow down the suffocating memories and stare straight ahead.

Jeremy is sitting on a cot in one of the cells. When I walk in, he rushes to the bars. "Ann, are you all right? Is the baby okay?"

I warm his hand with mine. "Yes, we're fine." My lip quivers as I take in his black eye. "Are you ready to say I told you so?"

He runs his fingers over my face. "Never."

I lean in and whisper, "They know about Vinny." He tenses. "He's safe with Karen and the kids at the farmhouse."

"Is everyone else okay?"

I know he's thinking about Dan and Sam. "As far as I know, yes, they are."

"Where are you getting your intel from?" Tammy pipes in from the other cage.

"The Queen."

"Great. Another person we shouldn't put our trust in," Tammy hisses.

"She's our only ally right now and she's literally sleeping with our enemy. Trust me, I don't like it, but I've struck a deal with her."

"What?" Tammy growls. "Haven't you learned your lesson?"

Jeremy ignores her and squeezes my wrist. "What was the deal?"

"I can't say." I eye the guard in the corner. "Just know that it's worth it and it'll grant you your freedom."

"What about Brad and me?" Tammy is quick to question.

I roll my eyes. "I'm sure she meant you all as a package deal."

"Well, you might want to find out before you start celebrating."

"I only really want Jeremy." I wink at her.

"Time's up," the guard hollers.

"I love you." I kiss Jeremy's knuckles. "Try to get some rest."

"I love you too. Thank you for fighting for me." Tammy snorts and he adds in, "I mean fighting for *us*."

"Don't make me tell you again," the guard warns me.

I can hear his approaching footsteps, so I head to the door but pause to look over my shoulder. Jeremy watches me and gives a nod, encouraging me to fight for another day.

Birds of a Feather

The wind whistles through my hair. I clutch my bundle to my chest. No one will harm him. Wispy blue and black feathers stroke my hands, beckoning me to relax. Then they combine, forming a stunning set of wings. They flutter beneath the blanket and ease the weight from my arms. They don't stray from my side, and I know in my heart that they will aid me in my travels.

My eyes flutter open and I groan at the morning light. It feels like I just fell asleep. I toss the covers aside and yelp when two beady eyes glare back at me.

"When did you get in here?" I stroke Snowball's feathers. "I'm glad Scarlett didn't leave a scar." I poke her wobble and the hen puffs her chest in outrage. "I promise she'll behave herself." She narrows her gaze, as if doubting my words. "I'll watch her more closely next time," I correct.

After the royal hen has given me a proper scolding, she scratches my door so I slip on my fuzzy slippers. As I turn the knob, it moves on its own and the door opens. Snowball struts out and I'm left staring into a pair of dark eyes.

"These are yours." Ryan shoves a box into my arms. "They're items I thought you might want, but if you do not, then please return them to me."

I assess Ryan's dress pants and light-blue button-up shirt. Is he *serious*? After all the crap he's put me through, he thinks a box will change my mood.

"They belonged to Christian," he clarifies.

I set the container on the table, remove the lid, and gasp when my eyes land on the contents. I stare at the wall for a moment as memories flood my mind. I never expected this.

Is Ryan trying to come at me with mental warfare now?

I run my hands over the picture frame showcasing Christian and me posing for our engagement photo. I miss that handsome, strong, blue-eyed man. Next, I pull out the jeans I bought him for Christmas. I shake my head as I remember how ridiculous everyone thought the outfit made him look. But he knew how much it meant to me so he wore them anyway.

"You got it back?" I smile at the chicken-themed engagement ring Christian customized for me. I pawned it to help the rebels buy food and clothes. I never thought I would see it again. A laugh escapes me as I bring my *Mother Clucker* shirt to my lips. Oh, how he hated this top. I thought it was safe at my house, but he must have snuck it away again so I couldn't wear it. When I look up again, I'm surprised to see Ryan watching me. I clear my throat. "Thank you for these." Since he's acting somewhat rationally, I test my luck and try to convince him to release the rebels. I walk to my dresser and hand him a strip of fabric. "Are you going to fix the mistakes of our past kings or perpetuate them?"

Ryan stretches the material between his hands. It's the blindfold that's kept me in the dark during my many outings with the rebels. "Do you think it's really that *easy*?"

"No. If it were, your family would have already done it." I lift my chin. "They revel in the *easy* ways. It's the hard choices that they ignore for too long until it literally kills them."

Ryan scrunches the cloth in his fist. "Don't pretend to know everything about us."

"I won't. But don't you pretend to know everything about the rebels either."

"Get changed and join us for breakfast." He throws the command over his shoulder as he exits. I fight the urge to smack him in the back of the head while I nestle everything back inside the box and close it, locking away the past.

"Good morning, everyone." I hug Sally and May before sitting next to them. "I went to check on you last night but you were both asleep."

"We said goodnight to the others, then passed out pretty fast." Sally strokes May's hair but I can see her clenched jaw. She doesn't want to break bread with the Royals any more than I do.

May lifts her apple juice. "Miss Elizabeth let me pick whatever drink I wanted with my breakfast! She even let Scarlett sit next to me too."

I stroke the red hen as she pecks a ceramic bowl of grapes. "That was very thoughtful of her."

"She also told me I could stay at the Palace a little longer." May grins at Sally. "Can I?"

I know May misses her friends at the compound, but the thought of having everything she's ever dreamed of seems to be stronger at the moment.

"I don't know, May. It seems not everyone around here likes to keep their word, so I don't think I can entrust them with your care."

"Now, wait one minute," Elizabeth interjects.

"Enough," the King demands. "We will have a civil

breakfast."

Cherie meets my gaze before looking away. *When is she going to follow through on her part?*

I lift my chin and work to soothe May's tears. "May, I'm sure you can come and visit the Palace another time." I nod towards the rebel matriarch. "Sally loves you a lot. She and your brothers would miss you dearly if you were away for too long."

"How many children live at the compound?" Elizabeth questions.

"If they survive the streets and the branding process, normally at least two or three a year seek sanctuary with us. Right now, we have about ten children under the age of eighteen."

"Where are their parents?" Mr. I-Want-False-Peace has the audacity to ask.

"The adults are usually the *first* to be tortured and murdered. Most of the time, they are killed trying to *make* their way to our compound."

"Could you get me exact numbers of men, women, and children?" Cherie pipes in.

Sally nods. "Of course."

This meal is going smoother than I thought it would. Maybe hearing the facts will remind the Royals what we're fighting for.

My eyes light up as the familiar nutty aroma beckons my senses. My mouth waters. After months of waiting, I can't believe it's finally happening. The waiter pours the liquid gold into my mug. I finger the intoxicating steam.

"Do you two need a room?" The King's rude comment brings me back to reality.

"I have dreamt of this moment for *months*," I reply before sipping the heavenly coffee.

"Caffeine isn't good for the baby," Ryan counters.

"There are a lot of things around here that jeopardize the safety of my child. Things far worse than a caffeinated beverage," I spit. "Like me trusting you to keep your word."

"I was just saying..."

"The only thing I want to hear out of your mouth right now is an apology!"

"Please don't fight. Here, have some of my juice." May pushes her coveted glass to me and turns to Ryan. "*Juice* is okay for babies, right?"

"Juice is very healthy for a growing child," Elizabeth answers for her son. "And I agree. We all must find a common ground to stand on and stop this bickering." She throws a pointed stare at the King, while May sips her beverage and claps as the waiters pour into the room with our breakfast of steak and eggs.

I hate the tension-filled atmosphere and the fact that Jeremy and the others are probably dining on moldy bread and water in their dank cells.

"How is your steak?" Ryan asks.

Like you care.

I force a smile. "It's good. I'll have to make sure to compliment your *chef*."

"I remember the doctor mentioning that your iron was low, so I requested that the staff include foods to accommodate your new dietary needs."

Oh, how I wish I could vomit. I want nothing from his highness—nothing except freedom.

Sally's gaze snaps to mine. "When did Ann see a

doctor?"

"Last night, after the King's true intentions were on full display." I pat my lips. "Right, Ryan?"

"Is everything okay?" Sally squeezes my wrist. "Are you and the baby healthy?"

"Yes, the *rebels* took very good care of us. Even though they are still being punished." I lift my chin to Cherie, who gracefully ignores me. I throw my napkin on the table and rise. "I'm going to check on the hens."

"Can you bring Scarlett with you?" Elizabeth nods at the chicken as the troublemaker in question scratches her food, sending the bowl crashing to the floor. "I'm sure she wants to spread her wings a bit."

"That's a great idea." May hands the feathered rebel to me. "She'll probably need a nap or she'll get cranky."

"No problem."

"Thanks, Ann." May pops a piece of fruit into her mouth.

I turn my back on the table and stride out to the gardens. "You can search for bugs out here, girl." I set the hen in the grass.

She stretches her wings and the morning sun reflects off her crimson plumage. She looks around, unsure what to do next.

"I'm going to check on my flock. Do you want to come?" She tilts her head but makes no move to follow me. "Suit yourself. But they have food, water, and a wonderful dust bath." I open the gate to the pen and a blur of red dashes past me and to the pile of grit in the corner.

I smirk as Scarlett rolls in it, throwing sand all over the place like it's a luxurious bubble bath. The other girls side-eye her before attempting to join in on her fun, but the hen demands her privacy.

I settle on the bench and massage my cold arms. *Stupid winter*. I always forget to grab my coat. To keep my mind off the chill, I pull out my cell phone and dial my bestie.

"I was wondering when you were going to call," Vinny answers.

I double-check the number I dialed. "Where's Karen?"

"The kids are still adjusting to being here, so she was up late with them."

"I'm sorry..." I offer, because I don't know what else to say.

"Me too."

"I'm working on getting you guys back here. Cherie—"

"I don't want to talk about the Royals right now," Vinny cuts me off. There's an edge to his voice that tells me he must think our conversation isn't private, and he's probably right.

"I miss you guys. I finally get you back in my life and it only lasts a few hours. I just need one of your hugs right now." I don't stop the tears as they fall off my chin.

"I know this is overwhelming but remember who you are, Ann."

"That's the thing. I don't know who I am anymore."

"Yes, you do. You are strong, compassionate, and full of love."

Scarlett plops down in my lap, stealing the baby's warmth. I stroke her and she purrs. "Those are not strengths. Those are weaknesses."

"You are wrong. They are your greatest weapons right now."

"They have my friends in custody and are talking about punishing Jeremy for Christian's death."

"What would *he* want you to do? Sit there and cry over it or get off your butt and demand justice."

"Can't I do both?"

"Nope." Speaking of crying, I can hear a twin in the background. "Olivia is awake. I need to grab her before she…" Vinny's cut off by the sound of more wailing. "I should help Karen with the twins. Try to call her later to catch up. I'm sure she'd love to hear your voice right now. She's bummed to be out of a job *and* a high-class nanny."

"I will. Good luck, Vinny." I have to shout over the noise, causing Scarlett to screech and leave my lap.

"Good luck to you too."

I guess he's right. It's time to pull up my big girl panties and deal with the Royals head-on. "How about we skip our nap and go straight to whooping butt?" I ask the rebel hen before collecting her in my arms. She narrows her eyes at me. "Fine. I'll drop you off in the room." When we enter the Palace, I shift her weight. "You really need to learn to walk on a lead like Snowball."

Scarlett wiggles and flops on the tiled floor. She ruffles her feathers and struts forward, reminding me that she's as good as the white fluffball in question. I roll my eyes but maintain my pace towards the staircase.

"Ann!" May waves.

Scarlett slides to a stop. The little girl has *Snowball* in her arms. "Scarlett, we need to behave, remember?" I remind her before she gets jealous.

The red devil screeches and runs to her beloved owner. May clutches the feathered queen to her chest, unsure what to do. Snowball senses her uncertainty and leaps to the girl's aid. She puffs her chest out and leaps in front of May. The two hens circle each other with their hackles raised.

Elizabeth claps her hands, gaining their attention. "Enough!" She shakes a bag. "Good girls are rewarded with mealworms." The chickens eye each other, then waddle to the goodies, begging for a taste. They peck the ground, side by side without incident. When the crumbs are cleared from the floor, they blink at the bag. Elizabeth strokes them. "Now, if we can all get along, we'll get treats like this, okay?" She sprinkles a few more.

"I should try this tactic with your unruly son. I'll dust some mealworms on his lunch and see what happens."

May wrinkles her nose. "Please keep them off my food."

"As long as you behave, I will." I grin at her.

May tucks a hen under each arm. "Let's play dress up!" The girl skips off, red and white feathers fluttering behind her.

"She looks happy," I whisper to myself.

"She is an extraordinary young lady." Elizabeth nibbles on her lip. "I want to meet the other children."

"That'll be hard, considering your son is trying to kill one of their caregivers."

She lifts her chin. "I'm traveling to the compound when they return."

"What does Ryan have to say about that?"

"I've lived my entire life for the *crown*. I've dealt with a lying, cheating husband and disgraceful politics, all while maintaining my composure. It makes me sick to know the aftermath of my silence." She swipes the memories from her cheek. "But it's time I do something for myself."

I squeeze her hand. "I'm lucky to have you fight in my corner. We all are."

Elizabeth meets my eyes. "I wish I had the courage to step up to them before all of this. Before May lost her parents..."

"There are many more families like hers who are in danger still and could use your help." I pull the former Queen in for a hug. "Thank you."

She returns my embrace. "This doesn't mean I excuse *Jeremy* after what he did to Christian. But I do agree that executing him will only continue to lead us down a destructive path. May doesn't deserve that. No child does."

"Elizabeth, Scarlett is too fat for the pink dress," May hollers from her open door. Snowball takes off, attempting to escape the runway show.

"I'll alert my seamstress immediately." Elizabeth strides to the little girl. "I'll have her take measurements and bring you fabric samples." She bends to clutch her highness, but the hen slips past with a squeak and heads to the open kitchen door.

"I'll grab her." I wave to the duo.

It's nice having Elizabeth on the same team, but a small piece of me wonders if I can trust her. Could she be deceiving us? Do we really have a choice? We need as many people backing us as possible.

I turn the corner and skid to a halt. Jock and Sally are

talking in hushed tones.

"Ann, I know you were raised better than this." Sally sips her steaming mug. "Quit snooping on us."

Jock rushes to pull out a barstool. "Yes, please join us. We were swapping war stories." He slides over a cup.

I elbow my adoptive mother. "She is definitely something special."

Sally finishes her drink and stands. "Thank you, Jock, for your time and your reassurances that my son is being taken care of."

"Anytime. And don't you worry, I'm personally making sure your friends are getting fed." He dries his hands on a towel.

Hope rises in my heart. Are Sally and Jock working together to free the prisoners?

"*You're* bringing food to the jail?"

"Yes. There's no way I was going to let them eat moldy scraps. I've been sending snacks every three hours on the dot."

"That's very kind of you." Sally squeezes his wrist, and he nods. Then she pivots and snatches Snowball. "I'll return her to May while you two catch up," she whispers as she hugs me. "Don't worry, I'm working my magic."

When she pulls away, I change the subject to avoid suspicion. "Did you know Elizabeth plans on returning to the compound?"

"Yes. We had a heart-to-heart last night after everything that transpired. We are very blessed to have friends here. I can see why you found it hard to leave them behind." Sally offers me a reassuring nod and strides off with a squealing hen.

"You two looked cozy." I wiggle my brows at Jock once the rebel is out of earshot.

He chuckles as he pours cream into my coffee. "Yes, I owe her more than I realized."

"What do you mean? You knew who she was before she came here?"

"No, of course not. But when she told me her story..." He lets out a huff. "There's no easy way to say this, but Tammy is my *grandchild*."

I'm at a loss for words. I scan my memory for any mention of the chef having children, but *nothing* comes to mind. Then it clicks. Before the raid, he gave me advice on loss that touched me to the core. Did he lose his family to the Black Rose?

"What do you mean she's your granddaughter? When did you talk to her?"

"I don't have to talk to her to know she's my kin. That spunky attitude and crimson hair is all I need for confirmation." He drags his hand through his locks of wisdom. "My daughter got mixed up with a bad batch of kids in college. She fell in love with one of them. He was a medical student, and she was an artist. Once they graduated, they eloped and disappeared from our lives. Clara was our only child, and my wife was distraught when our girl never returned home. Then my wife had a massive heart attack, and I lost her." He swipes at his face. "I drowned my grief in my work at the Palace. It was all I had left to live for. My entire family was gone."

"Oh no." I place my hand on his arm. "You don't have to continue if it's too much." I've never seen Jock this sad. He's usually upbeat.

"No, I want you to know." He takes a steadying breath. "One day, I overheard King Mark celebrating his having captured a massive group of rebels. When I glanced over his shoulder, his dinner tray slipped from my grasp. Because clutched in his hand was a picture of my baby girl, but she wasn't alone. She was holding the wrist of a young child while her free palm was tightened around her husband's." He sniffles. "I knew there was no hope for them."

I wait for him to continue but he doesn't. I can't imagine the emotions he must be experiencing right now. "Jock, you couldn't have known the rebels were actually *good* people. At that time, everyone thought that the members of the Black Rose were the bad guys. Don't blame yourself." I squeeze his elbow. "And don't let that stop you from approaching her. You can still be in her life. Tammy is a wonderful woman, and she would be lucky to have a grandfather like you."

"No, I'm a coward. I should have spoken up for my child. I should have sent her help. My wife would be disappointed in me. I'm *nothing* to the girl and will remain nothing to her."

"Please, Jock, for me, talk to her and tell her your story. She has lost a lot and should at least have the opportunity to know all there is to know about her mother, father, and *grandfather*. And if you need a buffer, I'm your girl. I'll help you reconnect."

"Sally said the same thing. I'll think it over, but please don't mention anything to Tammy unless I say otherwise." He uses his fatherly tone, and I can't help the tender smile that crosses my face when I nod.

"Do you have any fresh biscuits?"

"Yes, and some blueberry preserves." He busies himself in the pantry while I lean back and rub my belly. It's a small world and it seems to be getting smaller by the minute. Now it looks like I've added another goal to my list. I need to get those two reunited on top of rescuing the rebels. "Here we are, fresh blueberry preserves." Jock twists off the lid. "One of my daughter's favorites."

"I'd love to hear more about her."

The twinkle in his eye returns as he unravels the tale of his family, and I soak up every last detail.

"Sorry for the intrusion, but King Ryan requires your presence in the office, Lady Ann." Jock and I both pivot to see a guard holding the door open for me. "Now," the man adds when I don't immediately jump to do his bidding.

I sink my teeth into my third biscuit. "He'll have to wait. I'm eating. *Yum.* Good to the last delicious morsel." The guard narrows his eyes, drawing my attention to his rigid features. I blink at the rank pinned to his jacket. "You took Vinny's spot?" When he doesn't answer, I continue to peruse his frame. There's something strikingly familiar about him, but I can't put my thumb on it. "Have I seen you here before?"

"My orders are to bring you to the King. Either shove the crumb down your throat or leave it here."

"Damien, that's no way to speak to a lady," Jock bristles.

"It's okay." I pop the piece into my mouth and brush off my hands. "I was done anyway." I push past the jerk. "Now look who's falling behind, soldier."

"I would rather have a quiet trip," he grumbles from beside me.

That voice. I peek at him as a shiver racks my spine. "You're Derek's son, aren't you?"

"My lineage is none of your business."

Memories of his father's hands on me cause me to stutter. Then I remember that Derek is dead. "It's your crooked nose and husky tone that gives you away. Let's hope his morals didn't rub off on you too." I slide to the left, putting distance between us, just in case.

"Our *parents* do not define who we become."

"You're right. Our *actions* do." I nibble on my cheek. "And the only way Christian would have let you stay in the Palace after what your father did is if you proved yourself worthy of the title."

"I don't have to justify my actions to you."

"No, you don't but I'm warning you: if you treat me like your father did, I won't hesitate to correct Christian's mistake."

His lip twitches. "*You?*"

"Maybe not me, but I have friends who are more than capable if it's warranted."

He pauses before we enter the office. "I may have his physical features, but I have no intentions of following in my dad's footsteps."

"That's good to know, but remember *actions* speak far louder than words."

Flock Together

My fake smile automatically activates as Derek's son escorts me to the conference room with the others. I nod at Elizabeth, Sally, and Cherie before I take my assigned seat next to Ryan.

The King nods at the guard. "Thank you, Damien."

The man in question hovers by the exit with his arms crossed. I would rather have Vinny here. No matter what the guard claimed, his outward appearance screams *Derek.*

"What were you thinking?" The King slams a newspaper on the table. "This is not what I asked you to do."

It takes me a second to realize he's shouting at me. "Do what exactly?"

"Don't play stupid!" He rips the newspaper in half and continues to shred it. "You lied to the press. You told them I was signing the petition and that all the rebels were going to be pardoned. Then you continued to state how I extended my forgiveness to *Jeremy.*"

I wish he didn't ruin the evidence, because I'm at a loss. I have no idea what he's talking about. *When would I have had time to write that?*

"Darling, what's done is done." Cherie squeezes his wrist before giving me a pointed stare. Then the pieces click in place. *She* penned the article under my name.

Well, well, how the mighty have fallen.

"And you've managed to turn Mom against me too," Ryan continues.

"I'm a grown woman and you'll be wise to remember that, young man. I make my own choices," Elizabeth bristles.

Cherie guides the conversation back to the matter at hand. "The reporters will be here soon, dear. What are we going to do?"

All eyes are on the King as we hold our collective breaths.

He appears to consider his options, then straightens his blue tie. "We will announce our pardon on the rebels." Hope rises in my throat. "Anyone caught mistreating the former members of the Black Rose, which will disband immediately, from this day forward will be detained." He nods as if convincing himself to continue. "Also, as suggested in the article, the Palace will reimburse land and funds to those who can prove hardship or that their property was taken from their family in the process."

"I think that is a wonderful way to move ahead." Cherie kisses his cheek, attempting to smooth his ruffled feathers.

Sally clears her throat. "That is a *start* but what about a government reform? That way, this incident doesn't happen again?"

"One step at a time." Ryan waves her off.

"But this is how the rebels came to be. Without real representation, we had everything taken from us. We need the people to have the ability to voice their opinions so they can be represented properly."

"Don't you think we've done enough already?" Ryan booms.

"How about a compromise?" Cherie adds. "We'll give this pardon a few months to settle, then come back together to discuss the next step."

I look to Sally for a response. "Fine, but may I request that we mention this at the press conference so the people know more change is coming."

"I have no problem with that." Cherie glances at her pouting husband, who just shrugs.

"And what will happen with Lady Ann? Is she free to choose where she wants to go next?" Sally nods to me.

The room is quiet. I nibble my bottom lip. Now that his highness can't punish Jeremy, will he keep me as his prisoner instead?

"I'm sure she will want to return to her farmhouse with her fiancé. There's no reason for her to remain here." Cherie laughs. "She'd just be in the way at the Palace."

"What about my chickens?" I won't let him get his claws on them to hurt me.

"The Palace has plenty of meat birds and layers already, so unless you want to donate them to one of those categories, you may bring them home with you." She smirks, knowing darn well I won't let her touch my ladies.

I wish Ryan would grow a pair already and speak to me directly. Dealing with his wife is grating on my last nerve. "And Vinny and Karen?" I prompt.

"The King proposed employment *similar* to their former positions, but they declined his generous offer."

I bet his *generous offer* consisted of lower rank and pay. But that was their call to deny or accept. Having my best friends live next door to me is better than them staying here with *her*.

"Ryan, you are Olivia and Carter's uncle." I place my hand on his until he meets my gaze. "I know you love them as much as they adore you. Please don't punish them for their parents' mistakes."

"He is not a blood relative of the *servants'* children,"

Cherie huffs out. "They are lucky he didn't imprison them for their deceit to the crown."

Ryan turns to Damien. "Escort everybody to the dining room for some refreshments before the press conference." The group begins to shuffle out, but the King grabs my wrist. "Not you."

Cherie looks between us. "I should stay too."

"No. You should entertain our guests. We won't be long."

She presses her lips together but does what she's told. She pauses in the doorway to give me a pointed glare as a warning. I wave her out with a smirk.

Once we're alone, Ryan rubs his face. "Why do you antagonize everyone?"

"Where is the recorder?

"I have no idea what you are talking about."

I lean back, crossing my arms. "You are as bad as Christian but at least he fibbed better. Don't play dumb with me, Mr. Royal-Pain-in-My Butt."

Ryan reaches under the table and retrieves a black machine. He presses a button, then turns to me. "It's procedure. You know that." The silence around us is heavy. "I heard Jeremy is going to claim the child as his."

I swirl my pointer finger on the table's surface. "No matter whose blood is coursing through my son's veins, Jeremy will *always* be his father because he chooses me every day. He's my rock and strength. This baby will thrive under his attentive eye and adoring heart."

"What about his position in the Black Rose?"

"With this new peace, he won't be needed at the compound."

Ryan shakes his head. "I knew you didn't want this life and I made it easier for you to escape it."

I grind my molars. *Now he wants to play the hero.*

"All I wanted back then was *you*, Ryan. To be loved and cared for. To be a part of your life, not shunned like some *curse*. You did this to us. To me."

"I knew they weren't going to hurt you, that you'd be happier without the Royals breathing down your back."

"That wasn't your call to make. It's my life, remember? I choose."

"No, Ann, our lives are chosen for us."

"Maybe for you." I lift my chin. "But not for this farmgirl."

"Are you really that naive?" His harsh laugh bounces off the walls. "The Black Rose snuck your application to the top of the list in the contest for Christian. They wanted you here for a reason. You want to blame me for everything, fine. Make me the beast of your tale. But I'd take a deep dive into why they wanted you in the selection."

"Sally's husband was a bad man. He made that call and he's dead now."

"Why didn't anyone warn you about what was going to happen?"

"Because it would have been too dangerous to get me officially involved."

"Excuses." The King slams his palm down on the table. "I protect you, and I get shunned. They do it, and they are the heroes. I'm never going to win, am I?"

"This isn't a game, Ryan."

"No, of course not. It's all one-sided, with them the victors."

I wish I could say he's completely wrong, but he's not. In the last few hours, Ryan's done a lot for us. Plus, he isn't forcing me to claim the child as his. He's not attempting to lock me up in the Palace. He's allowing me to have my freedom and his firstborn son without asking for anything in return.

I release a puff of air, with a pinch of my fight. "I'm sorry."

He itches his ear. "Can you repeat that?"

"No." I smirk as his lip twitches. "Listen, I may not understand why you did what you did, but I'm glad you are not letting history repeat itself."

He tugs out the blindfold I gave him. "Thank you for reminding me to not let my anger get the best of me."

"I guess I need to take my own advice. I've been mad at you for everything." I run the fabric through my fingers. "But if I'm being honest with myself, I miss our goofy friendship."

"Goofy?"

"You know, the one where you are terrified of ducklings and bring me pizza and chocolate when my cycle is out of whack."

"I wasn't *afraid* of the duck," he clarifies. "And at least I'm not a klutz, stumbling over myself and letting hammers fall on my head."

"Let's hope this kid is more graceful and less fearful." I rub my belly.

"I hope so too," Ryan whispers. "I know I have no right to ask you for this, but do you think the child can have Christian as his middle name?"

I blink, taken aback by his sudden request. "Why would you want him to have your brother's name?"

162

Ryan meets my eyes. "Because Christian asked me to do it."

What did he say? When? Does that mean...

"How did he find out about the baby?"

"He didn't know for sure that you were pregnant." Ryan sighs. "All he knew was that we had unprotected sex in the safe room and demanded if you became with child, that his name would be on the birth certificate."

"But he never told me he knew."

"And why would he? You could do no wrong in his eyes." Hurt drips off every word. "Me, on the other hand..."

"Ryan, I'm sorry. I didn't know."

"I know you didn't, because that's the way the King wanted it," he sneers. "Even on his deathbed, he still ruled over me."

I rub his arm. "I'll uphold your promise to your brother. The child will have Christian as his middle name."

Ryan swipes at the corner of his eye. "Thank you."

"And I'm willing to put our troubled past behind us and continue our friendship... *if* you promise to remain in the baby's life."

"As what exactly?"

"What would you like to be? The Big Bad Beast?"

"How about a self-proclaimed uncle?"

"I'd like that."

Ryan stands and opens his arms. "To new beginnings."

I embrace him. "Make sure you don't neglect your

duties with Karen's kids either."

"I know. I owe them an apology."

"I'm sure if you send them their nanny back, they'll forgive you. They could use the extra hands."

"Can't we all?" Ryan strides to the exit. "Let's go visit your rebel friends and allow them to enjoy their newfound freedoms."

"Release them."

Two words and my heart soars. The jailer unlocks Brad and Tammy first, then Jeremy, who rushes forward and smashes me to his chest. "I'm sorry I couldn't be there for you."

"It's okay."

He stalks past me and slams the King against the wall. "If you hurt a single hair on her head…"

Guns are drawn and aimed.

"Jeremy! Let him go!" I tug at his elbow.

"Did he hurt you?" he demands. "Try to manipulate you in any way?"

I squeeze between the two men. "No. He's giving you your freedom and pardoning the rebels. He's even offering them land and financial reimbursement."

Jeremy arches a brow, then steps back before dusting off Ryan's suit. "And here I thought I'd be hung by my neck before he'd do *something* right for this country."

"You and me both." Tammy crosses her arms over her chest. "What's the catch?"

"I offered the King the title of uncle to *our* son." I grab Jeremy's hand and place it on my belly. "In exchange, he would be honored if the child takes Christian as his middle name."

Tammy visibly cringes while Brad steps closer to aid his commander if things go south.

"And does his highness grant us permission to go wherever we want?" Jeremy's jaw ticks. "Or are we to be leashed like dogs?"

"You all are free to roam the country as you please," Ryan answers.

Jeremy nods to me before addressing the King again. "Are you good with her terms and conditions?"

"Yes."

"Then it's fine with me."

"Great. Now, who's hungry? We'll eat some finger foods, then attend the press conference."

Everyone files out, but Jeremy presses me against the wall and devours my mouth until I'm breathless. "I was so worried," he admits. "A hundred scenarios were running through my mind and driving me insane."

I press my fingers against his lips. "We're getting our happily ever after."

Jeremy kneels, wrapping his arms around my abdomen. "I missed you both." He kisses my belly button, then meets my gaze. "Is he okay?"

"He's healthy. Me, on the other hand…"

Jeremy leaps to his feet and looks me over. "What's wrong?"

"My iron is a little low and I have a tiny infection. But don't worry, I'm eating more red meat and they have me on antibiotics."

He tucks his arm around my waist, and we follow the group towards the dining room. "I'll give you some of my meat."

"You've been out for a whole five minutes, and you've already started up with the inappropriate jokes."

"Would you have it any other way?"

As we enter the dining hall, Sally runs over while blubbering. "Jeremy!"

He releases me to hug his mom. "I'm fine."

"Scarlett got a new dress, Uncle Jeremy." May shoves the red hen in his face. "It matches mine."

He chuckles and ruffles the girl's hair. "You both look beautiful."

"Elizabeth is going to go to the compound with us too."

His neck snaps to me. "What?"

"Let's sit down and catch you up on what you've missed." Sally guides him to a chair and does just that.

The waiter sets down water, pastries, and a variety of cheese and meats with crackers. As I pop a blueberry scone in my mouth, I glance at our reunited team. It seems Tammy and Brad are closer. I wonder what happened in that jail cell. Jeremy's hand hasn't left my thigh as he listens to his mom.

"The reporters are in the garden," Damien announces.

Ryan finishes his beverage and stands. "We'll be right there."

Then we all make our way outside where the press is waiting.

"There's a nice crowd." Jeremy tightens his hold on my hand.

"Don't worry, the Palace only allows certain individuals access to these events." I wave to Richard.

"They need to screen them better," Jeremy grinds out.

"This way." Elizabeth guides us to the chairs behind the podium.

"Thank you all for coming today as we make history and look forward to a more peaceful future." Ryan recounts the ill-treatment of the Black Rose, then explains that the pardon will be effective immediately and will allow the rebels to hold jobs, buy homes, and regain their lives.

"Is it true that the rebels took Lady Ann as a hostage?" a woman in a tan suit asks.

"No, that's inaccurate," Ryan clarifies.

"Ann!" A man in a blue suit waves. "Who is the father?"

Well, I guess I should hold up my end of the bargain with Cherie. I open my mouth to speak, but Ryan answers for me, "We are not here to discuss Lady Ann's private life. Just know she is healthy and eager to return to her home. Are there any questions regarding the *pardon*?" They spend an hour going over what is to be expected over the coming months. Then the King concludes with the promise of another get-together to discuss more changes, possibly with our government as a whole. "You are welcome to stay for some refreshments." He waves to the finger foods. "Thank you for coming."

We're corralled into different areas for pictures.

"You owe me what you promised," Cherie says between her teeth as she smiles for a photo.

"Your husband cut me off. I was going to announce it."

"Ladies, this is not the time," Ryan orders in a hushed whisper.

"That's the last one." Elizabeth ushers us towards the warmth of the Palace.

"Sally, how about we meet again next month?" Ryan asks as we stride through the hallway.

"That would be amazing."

"And to ensure my mom is comfortable during her trip to the compound, I'm sending a chef, maid, and doctor."

"We can definitely use their expertise at our facility."

"Good, it is settled. You can head out later today once Mom has packed her things. Now if you'll excuse us, we have a video conference to attend." Ryan and Cherie stride hand in hand up the staircase.

"I should supervise the maids as they pack." Elizabeth rubs May's back. "And you have some things to collect as well."

"I have to grab all of Scarlett's new dresses!" She tugs Sally's wrist. "Can she ride in my lap on the way home?"

"As long as she keeps her diaper on and doesn't poop everywhere."

May slides to a stop. "Is Snowball coming with us too?"

"I'm not sure," Sally answers.

I turn to Jeremy. "Do you want to return with them and grab your things?"

He tugs me to his chest. "I have all I need right here." He kisses my forehead.

"You don't want to escort them back, just in case?"

"I trust Brad and Tammy to do their jobs."

"What's going to happen to the rebels now that they are free?"

"It'll take time for everyone to adjust to the new laws, and I expect some resistance at first, but then it'll be a new normal. How did the baby look on the ultrasound?"

"Bigger, less like an alien, and more like a possible baby."

He laughs. "I'm sure he will be *perfect*."

"He's a man. He won't be anywhere near perfect."

"That's a very sexist comment, *Lady* Ann."

"What can I say? Girls are better than boys."

"I'm not arguing with you right now." He kisses my knuckles. "So, we have the baby's middle name. Do you know what his first name will be?"

"Jack." My eyes mist over. "After my dad."

Jeremy glides his fingers through my hair. "I think your dad would be honored that you made that decision."

"Are you sure you're ready to take me on 24/7?"

He chuckles. "There's only one way to find out. But before we leave, I need to do one more thing."

"What's that?"

"You'll see." The glint of mischief in his eyes warns

me that I'm not going to like whatever it is he's about to do.

Cock Fight

"This isn't a good idea."

"Why? Are you afraid Jeremy will get pummeled?" Ryan taunts.

"I agree with Lady Ann," Cherie jumps in. "This is unprofessional."

I wrinkle my nose. I don't want her on my side. "Jeremy's going to win anyway."

"Want to make a bet?" The King holds out his palm. "The loser is getting a drum set for their child's first birthday."

"This is ridiculous. Enjoy your immature playdate. I'm returning to the office to complete the paperwork for the negotiations we discussed." Cherie stalks off.

Ryan tugs her into an embrace and kisses her deeply. "I look forward to *our* playdate later." He cups her rear.

The Queen turns crimson. "Ryan. Release me at once." She pretends to be appalled, but the desire in her gaze gives her true feelings away.

He watches her hips sway as she leaves. Then he focuses on the task looming in front of us.

"Aren't you guys going to use gloves for protection?" I ask the men as they approach.

The duo makes their way to the mats. They wave off my comment and begin dancing around each other. Soft patters are the only sounds echoing around us in the training room.

"I can't believe you are letting your guard fight your battle for you," I scoff.

"He volunteered and your fiancé had no problem agreeing to it," Ryan declares. "Jeremy said something about *clearing the air* for past transgressions."

I roll my eyes at the thought. Damien's dad, *Derek,* was the one who broke up Jeremy's parents' marriage, stabbed Vinny, and hurt me—not the man the rebel is presently eyeing with disdain.

"I hope you don't value your fiancé's face." Damien grins. "Because I'm about to rearrange it." His wide swing misses Jeremy's cheek.

"Focus, Damien!" Ryan shouts.

"Aw, are you worried about your soldier's well-being?" I coo.

"No." But like his wife, the King's features speak for themselves.

A few more swings miss their target, and I immediately know Jeremy is toying with his prey. I've watched him spar enough to know the way he fights. And right now, he's teasing his opponent.

"We don't have all day," I remind him.

His right fist slices through the air, grazing Damien's chin. Then before the guard can recover, Jeremy's left hand slams into the man's stomach. Damien bends over, attempting to catch his breath, and holds up a palm, signaling a pause.

"I'm thinking we should up the stakes, your highness." Jeremy shimmies out of his shirt and throws it in my direction. "How about a drum set and microphone for toddler karaoke?"

"Okay, tough guy, you've proven your point. Let's call the match before someone draws blood in the first hour of our peace contract," I snip.

"Have you had enough?" Jeremy provokes Damien.

"I'm just getting warmed up." The guard pulls off his

top and tosses it at my face. "Be careful or I might finish what my father attempted with your fiancée."

I dodge the projectile. "Guys…" I warn.

The sculpted men ignore me and battle it out. Grunting and moaning as they grapple each other on the mat.

"Ryan, are you going to stop this?"

"You heard them. They want to continue."

Tammy rubs her hands together. "I like being on *this* side of the mat." She slaps Brad's back. "Are you going to challenge the winner?"

"No."

"Not as tough as you pretend to be, huh?" She elbows him, then cheers Jeremy on.

Soon, the fighters' bodies are glistening with sweat and spotted with blood as they both lie on the mat, catching their breath.

"Can we call this match a draw?" I ask again.

"I've got a better idea." Damien sits up. "How about we settle this at the range?"

Jeremy rolls to his feet. "You're on."

I hesitate. "I'd rather settle this *without* bullets."

"Are you afraid my guard will win?" Ryan taunts as we trudge to the weapons arena.

"No." But I chew my lip. Fists are easier to control and predict. Firearms, not so much.

This time, all of us get to have fun. The targets are set up before the 9mms are distributed. We each fire six rounds at our assigned silhouettes, then tug them forward and compare our marksmanship.

I laugh at the results. "Well, gentlemen, it looks like Tammy and I are the real winners." I high-five her as we gloat over our perfect head shots.

"That's not fair. I want a rematch," Brad demands.

Tammy drapes an arm over his neck. "Don't be a sore loser."

His fingers glide over her waist. "I may have lost this battle, but trust me, I will win when it counts."

"Dream on," Tammy snarls, shoving him aside.

Brad grins at her departing figure. "I'm going to marry her someday," he says with a wistful sigh.

"Good luck!" I shout as he jogs after his reluctant bride-to-be. Then I pivot as Jeremy and Damien begin to argue over who was more accurate.

"Jeremy is a pretty good guy." Ryan nudges me. "He seems to really care about you."

"And Cherie is… interesting. *She* wears the pants in your relationship." Before he can whine, I add, "But she loves you."

"I need to grab my bag, then we can meet the others." Jeremy's lips brush mine.

"You need to shower too. You aren't going to stink the car up with your body odor."

He tugs me under his armpit. "I thought you loved everything about me?"

As we walk towards the staircase, music thumps down the hall and lulls us forward.

"Was there a party planned for today?" Damien asks the King.

"No."

We continue to follow the noise until we peek

inside the servants' break room. Maids and guards are enjoying their time off as they shake their hips to the cheerful tempo.

"It's funny how something as small as a pardon can make a huge difference and lift everyone's spirits." Jeremy nods to the group.

"That's what they are celebrating?" I scan the crowd and spot several rebels amongst them.

"Is it hard to believe that all of our hard work has affected them too?" He smacks my butt. "Freedom and equality are always worth celebrating."

Sally twirls May in the center of the room. Brad and Tammy bump and grind in the corner. And Jeremy tugs me towards the growing crowd.

"Let's give it a try. We've earned it."

It's great not having to worry about how to move or where to place my hands. There's no judgment either. This is how dancing is meant to be, not a stiff display of proper etiquette but just having fun and enjoying the music. Jeremy slithers behind me. He nips my ear as he squeezes my hips to his.

"Are you having fun?" he asks as if he can read my mind.

"It beats kicking your butt at the gun range."

"That was all luck. I wasn't at my best because I spent an hour wrestling with the King's guard."

"They are loading the vehicles now for our return trip," Sally announces, drawing our attention to her.

"So much for showering," Jeremy answers.

"You have time to clean up really fast," I point out.

"I'm not staying in the Palace any longer than I have to."

We follow the rebels outside and help the servants load Elizabeth's bags into the back. May giggles as Scarlett flaps her wings in Tammy's face.

Sally hugs us tight. "Be safe and keep in contact." She rubs my belly. "I will see you soon, little Jack."

"Are you sure you don't want to come back to the house with us?" I bite my lip, not wanting to say goodbye to my surrogate mother.

"Not yet. I need to get a few things situated at the compound before then. But don't worry. I'll come and visit you two soon."

"You better. We have a wedding to plan." Jeremy returns her embrace.

"We should pop out the baby first." I elbow him.

"Speaking of wedding bells." Elizabeth drapes a garment bag over my arm. "This belongs to you."

I unzip it and gasp. "My feathered gown." I clutch it to my chest. "You kept it?"

She shrugs. "I knew you'd need it eventually. And don't worry about the fit. My seamstress is at your disposal with any alterations you may require in the future."

Tears blur my vision. For as long as I can remember, I've been upset about losing my biological mom, not having her here for all the major moments in my life, but I've been blessed with so many others who have eased that burden. Suzie, Elizabeth, and now Sally. Even Jock has provided me guidance during my time of need, just like my dad would have. I'm lucky to have these people in my life.

"Thank you."

"And don't forget to invite me to the big day." Elizabeth wipes my tears.

"Of course."

"I always knew you were meant for greatness." Memories swirl in her eyes. "From the first day I met you, I knew you were special."

May warms my side. "I'm going to miss you and Uncle Jeremy."

"You'll have your hands full with Scarlett and Snowball." I stroke the girl's hair. "And you can visit us anytime."

She pulls Elizabeth to the SUV. "I can't wait for you to meet my friends Billy and Spot."

Jeremy ushers me to our own vehicle. "How does it feel to travel without a blindfold?"

I settle into the leather seat. "Like I was once blind, but now I'm seeing clearer than ever before."

The scenery blurs by, transitioning from city to country. The farther we travel from the Palace, the easier it is to breathe. Like a weight is being lifted off my shoulders.

I jump as the cell phone Sally slipped into my bag *clucks*.

"Look who's finally free as a bird," Karen says on the other end.

"Hey! It's good to hear your voice. How are you?"

"Much better now that the nanny is here helping with the kids' routine. Thank you for having Ryan call and make up with us."

"I'm glad he gave you some extra hands."

We talk about babies, pregnancy, and even discuss a little about me and Jeremy.

"Any idea on what you're going to do at your farm?"

I squeeze my fiancé's wrist and his icy eyes meet mine. "We haven't decided yet."

"Well, if you're interested, I have a proposition for you." Karen goes on to explain that she fell in love with the local diner, but the owner needs some investors to keep it from going belly up. I smirk, knowing the exact place she's talking about.

"Let's do it."

"Really?" Her voice rises with her excitement.

"Absolutely. It'll be a fun project that will also help the community."

"It'll be tough between the kids and husbands," she warns.

"When have we ever had it easy, Karen?"

"You have a point. Oh, and I insist that we sell your photographs in that cute artist shop next to the café."

"I don't know…"

"We can even turn it into a little gallery!" There's a crash in the background. "Whoops, got to go." Karen ends the call and I drop the phone back into my bag.

"What's with the grin?" Jeremy pokes my cheek. "Why are you so happy?"

"I'm finally doing something for *me*." I pat his thigh. "And for our future."

"Let me know how I can help."

"I was hoping you'd say that, because I'm going to require your muscles."

He flexes. "I always aim to please my girl."

The driver parks the car in front of the small farmhouse. "I'll unload your bags, Lady Ann."

178

"Can we hire him? I could really get used to that." Jeremy throws a thumb behind us.

"No way." I shake my head. "He drove so slow. I swear a finch was flying faster than our car was moving on the highway."

"Not everyone can have a lead foot like you."

"How would you know?"

"It was in your folder." Jeremy opens my door. "Welcome home, Ann."

For the second time today, tears well in my eyes. "It's wonderful to be back."

"What's the first thing you are going to do when we step inside?"

"Make a hot cup of coffee, sink into my recliner, and read a book." I breathe in the crisp country air. "I can't wait for our flock to settle in."

"I'll get the heated waters set up for them too. Elizabeth said they should arrive in the next day or two."

After being confined in the stuffy car for hours, I have a better idea. I glide my fingertips through Jeremy's hair. "It's a perfect night for a stroll around the property, but I'm exhausted. Can you carry me outside for a little bit?"

He lifts me in his arms. "I thought you'd never ask."

The garden is blanketed in darkness. Only the stars and crescent moon illuminate our path. Coyotes howl in the distance, creating a melody of peace. Jeremy lowers us onto a bench, and I close my eyes as memories of my childhood wet my cheeks. Playing in the flower beds. Camping in tents, with a roaring bonfire ready for s'mores. The weight of my parents' hands tickle my shoulder and I know their hearts are

179

bursting with pride.

Feathered Kingdom

I stretch and moan into my fluffy pillow. I forgot how amazing my room was. I slept like a rock. But now my bladder is screaming at me. When I return from the bathroom, I'm surprised to see the other side of the bed is empty. I make my way to my glorious coffee machine but pause at the guest room. Jeremy slept in there last night. *Why?* Sizzling from the kitchen catches my interest and I pursue the wonderful smell wafting from that direction.

"Good morning. How did you sleep?" Jeremy scrapes a spatula on the frying pan.

"Good," I draw out. "How'd you sleep?"

The nutty steam fills the area as the mocha-colored liquid drips into my chicken-shaped mug.

"Why are you saying it like that?" He splits the scrambled eggs between two plates.

"Because you didn't want to spend the night with your fiancée."

I trail behind him as he places the food on the table. "Ann, you need your space. That way, you can rest comfortably."

"You were sleeping by my side at the compound." I stab my breakfast.

"But now we are at your house and there's plenty of other places to sleep."

"Jeremy, what's really going on?" I demand as he sits in front of me.

"You fell asleep before we could discuss how this is supposed to work." He eats a mouthful of fluffy eggs. "I don't know if you want me to sleep in another bed until we are married, or if I'm allowed to share the same room with you now."

I squeeze his wrist. "I never want you to leave my side."

"What about when you have the baby?"

"If you want to be in there for that too, I'm okay with it."

"You're fine with me moving my things into your room?"

"It's now *our* room and our house."

"I don't have much. You know how little we had at the compound."

"Then feel free to use whatever you need, and we'll go shopping for the rest when things settle." When he remains silent, I elbow him. "What's wrong?"

"It's overwhelming." His fork scratches the plate as his eyes flick up to meet mine. "I never realized how much catching up I'd have to do. Did you know I need to take a driver's test before I can get back on the road?"

"That's normal."

"Not for rebels who've never been allowed to get one."

"We'll take things one day at a time."

"You're right." He nods and collects our empty utensils. "I got a call from the Palace informing us that your chickens will be arriving within the hour."

"I totally *forgot*." I scurry down the hallway.

"I thought you'd be happier," he calls out before following me.

"I'm ecstatic, but I need to go buy supplies." I fish through my dresser for warmer clothes. "Nothing is going to fit me."

Jeremy tugs something out of the dresser. "What's

this?"

"Hey! Get out of my underwear drawer."

"These are not underwear." He dangles the lacy material in front of me. "Who were you planning on wearing these for?"

"Don't make fun of my clothing choices." I snatch my underwear back.

"Oh, I'm not making fun. I'm trying to figure out when I get to see those on you." His lips graze mine. "I bet they'd look amazing." He cups my rear. "In all the right places."

There's something very intimate about being alone with Jeremy in this big house. I swallow my desire. No one's here to supervise us.

"Do you want me to model them for you?"

His gaze smolders and almost catches me on fire. "I'd love that."

I stretch the material. "At this point in my pregnancy, I doubt I'll be able to pull these over my thick thighs though."

Jeremy's chuckle warms my heart. He runs his hands through my hair. "We need to take you shopping, and when we do, I'll find the perfect lacy accessory."

"Can I pick out something for you?"

He arches a brow. "Like what?"

"Grey sweatpants that hang low on your hips and shape other things."

"Ann Gable, what a dirty mind you have."

"At least I didn't suggest special underwear to go with them." I collect the largest clothes I can find and change.

We settle into the car Christian bought me. I can't believe it's only been a little over a year since then. Many things have changed. As we drive to the feed store, I point out all the local establishments.

"I volunteered at that library and read to the kids. It was an exciting adventure."

"I have no experience with handling children," Jeremy blurts out.

"What? All the kids at the compound love you."

"But I'm the fun uncle, who gives them candy, not a father figure."

"I have complete confidence in your abilities. I know we'll make a great team."

We stride into the store and are greeted by the workers. They help us purchase feed, bedding, hay, oyster shell, and more treats. While we check out, the cashier bats her eyelashes at Jeremy. "Ann, who is your handsome friend?" Megan asks.

"My fiancé, Jeremy."

She shakes his hand. "What an absolute pleasure to meet the man who stole Ann's heart."

"Thank you."

She quickly passes me the receipt. "Thanks for coming, Ann. We hope to see more of you. Are you returning home for good now?"

"Yes, we are." I rub my protruding belly.

"Oh. When are y'all going to have the wedding?"

"It'll probably be after the baby comes." I wrap an arm around Jeremy and guide him to the exit. "Bye, Megan."

She waves as we walk out into the early-morning

sun.

"She's nosey."

"That's small-town living for you." I grin.

"We should start ordering everything *online*. That way, we can avoid people," Jeremy grumbles before loading our supplies into the car.

We make it home as a trailer with the Palace's emblem on it pulls into the driveway. We assist the crew and settle the hens in their pen.

"Welcome home, girls," I call out as they peck at the yard. "No more back-and-forth traveling." I wrap an arm around Jeremy. "I think we need more chicks. What do you think?"

"I think we should wait until after the baby is a little older."

"But fluffy chicks are adorable." I bat my lashes. "Please."

"Anyone home?" a male voice calls from inside the house. "The front door was unlocked."

"Saved by the stranger." Jeremy pecks my cheek. "Let me go see who it is, in case I need to redirect a nosey neighbor."

I follow my protector inside the house. "Those neighbors are our friends. Karen and Vinny are on one side and your brother is on the other."

Jeremy's hand rests on his sidearm as we turn the corner.

"Hey, you two," Dan greets from the doorway.

I hug him tight. "What are you doing here? Elizabeth said you were on your honeymoon."

"We are. We went to the beach for a week and now

we are settling into the house. After rearranging the entire place, Sam is out getting some groceries. So I thought I would come back and see why there was a truck parked in the driveway."

"Those were Ann's feathered subjects, returning to their kingdom." Jeremy punches Dan's arm. "How's married life treating you?"

Dan rubs his neck. "Good, for now. But I'll have to explain everything to Sam soon and I'm afraid I may not be a husband for long."

"I'm sure she'll understand." I offer him a glass of water. "We can talk to her too if you want."

"Thanks." He sips his beverage. "Because of our little getaway, I'm out of the loop. I thought you guys were still at the Palace with Mom?"

Jeremy and I side-eye each other. How much should we tell Dan right now? Especially when he's due back to see his wife.

I shrug and Jeremy gives his brother a quick summary. "We received the pardon, and we'll reconvey next month to discuss a government changeover."

"That's great." Dan's words don't match his tone. I know he's nervous about the future of his relationship.

"Mom called this morning and is already planning to visit us as soon as she can get away." Jeremy's quick to change topics.

"We'll plan a barbecue or something," I add.

"In the middle of winter?" Dan's brow raises and I can tell he's starting to feel better.

"Why not? Just because it's chilly, it doesn't mean we can't smoke a brisket."

"It won't be easy." Jeremy shakes his head.

"It'll be a nice challenge for you men." I cross my arms over my chest. "We can even have a *whose hotdog is tastier* tournament."

We laugh and Dan relaxes. "Just add in some s'mores and that sounds like the perfect weekend adventure."

Jeremy brags about how he defeated Damien in a sparring match. I slip in and remind my over-inflated rooster that I beat them both at the gun range.

"Well, that's only because I wasn't there." Dan smirks.

"You know darn well you wouldn't have lasted two seconds in the ring," Jeremy counters as he pinches the other man's bicep.

"Wanna bet?" Dan lifts his fists and jabs at the air.

Jeremy wraps an arm around his sibling's neck, tugs him to his chest, and grinds his knuckles on his scalp until Dan surrenders. "I'm glad we live so close now — gives me a chance to constantly remind you how much I *love* you."

Dan dusts his shirt off. "Right back at you, bro." Before I can blink, he grins and tackles Jeremy to the ground.

I leap out of the way as they fling insults at one another. I step forward to stop them but quickly realize what my fiancé is doing. He's letting his little brother release some of his pent-up frustrations the only way they know how. I make a mental note to assist my man in finding healthier alternatives.

Eggstra Cafe

"I thought we were investing in the café?" I whine at Karen.

She affixes the flaps of Olivia's diaper as she focuses on the task at hand. "But the owner wants to spend more time with his daughter and not waste it managing the restaurant." She places the child on the carpet. "I understand where he's coming from. You know?"

I lean back in her recliner as Carter smacks blocks in my lap. "Frankie lost his wife early in their marriage. But he told us he wanted to keep the café in his name so that he could keep his partner's dreams alive."

Olivia squeals and takes off towards the stuffed chicken I bought her. She squeezes its face before tossing it at Carter. The little boy hollers and throws his wooden toy in retaliation. Karen dives in its path before it can blind her daughter. After she lectures the twins on sharing and playing nice, she returns her attention to me.

"That was *before* Aurora started school. Now he feels like he has no time with her. Do you want to back out of the new deal?"

We've put many hours into reorganizing the café. If we let him sell it to someone else, we'd lose all that time and they'll profit from our labor.

"Let's do it."

"Yes!" Karen hugs me. "You won't regret this!"

"Under one condition." I smirk. "We name it Eggstra Café."

She wrinkles her nose. "That sounds like a breakfast place, and we serve all country fixings."

"But wouldn't it be funny?" I elbow Carter. "You like

it, don't you?" He nods. "See?"

We turn as a tearing sound gains our attention. Olivia waves her diaper over her head like a victory flag. When her mother gives her a look, the toddler takes off laughing.

"Get back here, young lady!" Karen leaps but misses.

"Does this belong to you?" Jeremy snatches the wild child and she giggles in his arms.

"You're right on time." I kiss Carter's head, then stand. "Karen was asking me to buy the café."

"Buy?" Jeremy reiterates as he passes the naked toddler to her mom.

"I'll explain on the way home." I kiss him softly. We hug our goodbyes before walking outside. "You didn't need to drive here, Jeremy. We could have walked home."

"I need to drop by the feed store."

"Why?"

He chuckles. "How about *you* tell me why? Because, technically, that bag of treats should have lasted months, not *weeks*."

I shrug. "I'm allowed to spoil my flock. They need the extra fluff for winter anyway."

"If they gain any more weight, they'll crack their own eggs."

An hour later, having stocked up on more goodies, Jeremy and I step over the threshold of our home.

"*Surprise!*"

Thank goodness Jeremy's behind me, or I would have fallen on my butt. "What's going on?" My gaze bounces to Karen, Vinny, Sally, Elizabeth, Tammy, Brad, and May.

"We wanted to throw you a surprise baby shower." Sally drapes a sash over my neck, that reads 'mother-*hen*-to-be', but it appears someone penciled in the '*hen*' part and glued on hundreds of fluffy feathers. Then she places a feathered tiara on my head. "You look stunning."

I'm on the verge of blubbering. They decorated the living room with streamers and balloons, while gifts are stacked up on every available surface. They did all this for me. I rub my belly. For *us*.

"Thanks, guys."

"Now, *Queen*, sit on your throne and relax those sore feet." Karen leads me to my favorite recliner. "And your King will make you coffee." She pushes Jeremy towards the kitchen. "I even got you a little bell." She jingles it before setting it beside me.

"Oh, this will come in handy." I ring the instrument. "Sugar and cream please," I shout to my newly appointed manservant.

I share a giggle with Karen. Then May places Snowball on my chest. "I painted her nails for your party."

"That's very sweet of you." I grin as Scarlett struts past, glad the focus is off her for a change. "There's a bag of freeze-dried mealworms in the garage, if you want to give them a treat."

190

My man sets my coffee on the table and the party begins. We play games, eat cake, and laugh so much my cheeks burn.

A few hours later, Vinny starts picking up the assortment of wrapping paper scattering the floor. "Did Ryan talk to you about forming a tactical force?" He elbows Jeremy as he tosses some ribbon into a bag.

I lean forward, hanging on to their words. This is news to me.

"He asked me to take a look at the guards he has available and assemble a mixture of rebels and uniformed personnel for the project."

"Does that list include the best?" Vinny puffs out his chest, and Jeremy quickly deflates the former guard with a jab of his finger.

"I added Sam."

"Why would he need a tactical force?" I ask.

They share a glance, then Jeremy pats my hand. "Don't worry, it's just a precaution. We expect some resistance to these changes and we want be prepared. Plus, it pays well."

"I have plenty of money. You don't need to work if you don't want to."

"And let you save the world all by yourself? No way." He kisses my forehead. "We are a team, and I need to pull my own weight."

"Will you have to travel all the time?" I can already feel the tears welling in my eyes and I try to fight them off. I know the hormones are making me extra emotional.

"No, I'll be home every night. Ryan is organizing multiple task forces in every city to help patrol."

"That sounds serious."

Jeremy shrugs. "It's better to be prepared. You know that. He's basically redirecting the enforcers and employing some rebels to join their team."

"Babe, we need to get back to the kiddos." Karen dries her hands on a dish towel, before turning to me. "The kitchen is back in order."

"You didn't have to do that." I hug my sister from another mister.

"Well, you're always doing the dirty dishes at our house. I'm just returning the favor."

"But I do them because you have double the trouble. *Triple* if you include the biggest child." I throw a thumb at Vinny.

"Hey. Stop talking crap about me." He tugs his wife to his chest and kisses her until she's breathless. "Now, let's go home so I can continue this punishment."

"Yes, sir." She salutes before he guides her out.

I stroke Snowball as she snores by my side, tired from the day's events.

"When are you guys heading out?" I pivot to Sally as she yawns on the couch.

"After everyone uses the bathroom." She pats May on the back, urging the girl towards the hallway.

"You guys can stay the night."

Sally brushes my hair off my cheek. "Maybe another time."

"Make sure you stop at the graves and say hi to Mom and Dad before you leave."

"Good idea." Sally hugs Jeremy goodbye, then twists to Elizabeth. "I'll meet you guys in the car."

I smile at the two women. I never thought they would become friends. But I'm glad they did.

Once everyone is on the road, Jeremy locks the door. "I missed the peace and quiet." He sinks into the sofa and collects me in his lap. His gaze drifts as he appears to ponder our new life. "I never thought this day would come for my family."

I burrow into his neck. "I'm lucky to be a part of your journey."

He warms my belly with his palm. "I can't believe I'm going to be a father soon."

"Are you still scared?"

"Yes."

"You'll be amazing, Jeremy."

An interrupting knock causes him to groan. "I'll be right back."

I wrap a fleece blanket around my shoulders and snuggle up with a paperback.

"I forgot my phone when I stopped in to help Mom decorate." Dan strides in. "You look comfy." He pats my knee as he goes to the kitchen.

"Yes, and she'll remain that way for the rest of the night," Jeremy warns his brother. "Don't bother her."

"I just came for this." Dan waves his lost device in the air.

"Why didn't you guys come to the baby shower?" I comment.

An uneasy silence thickens the air with tension. Jeremy leans on the counter. "Dan, you know I'm assembling a tactical team, right? Well, guess who Ryan put on the list to join me?"

Dan's smile fades. "Samantha."

"You'll need to break the news to her before she finds out who your *family* is."

I cringe. *Why hasn't Dan told Sam yet? What is he waiting for?*

Many different emotions simmer behind his eyes. I know he loves her, but will she accept him after she finds out he used her to break into the Palace?

Jeremy slaps his brother's back, pulling him out of his despair. "Let me show you all the baby shower gifts Ann received. There's this weird contraption called a breast pump."

"Wait. A *pump* that draws out milk?" Dan wrinkles his nose. "Like they do for *cows*?"

"Exactly."

The boys sift through the newborn outfits, bottles, and equipment. They pretend to extract milk from their chests and their childish laughter brightens the home. My little man kicks, and I wonder what it'll be like to have multiple children. I grew up as an only child, but watching Dan and Jeremy interact creates an ache in my heart that I never had before.

Fluffy Members

Jeremy assists the Palace with locating a facility to set up the new task force. Somewhere they can train and discuss what's going on in the area. It's not a big space, but it does its job and is located near the café Karen and I are rearranging, in hopes of bringing in new patrons. She's amazing. Her attention to detail is exactly what the restaurant requires. And since I worked in the office at the Palace, I'm handling the business side of things.

In the future, I hope to incorporate our farm products. I can expand the chicken pen so that we can utilize the eggs, plow the garden wider to cultivate more vegetables, and fertilize the fruit trees for more sweet treats. These dreams fuel my desire for knowledge and I shut myself in my room with my agriculture novels. It's easier on my back and feet if I lean on the headboard while I study.

Maybe I can add beehives to manufacture fresh honey too?

I tap my pen to my lips. We can add homecare products like soap, essential oils, and baked goods to the café and clients can purchase them on the way out. It can expand our inventory and variety to the shop.

The front door closes, and I shimmy past my mess to greet Jeremy.

"Hey, beautiful." He stands in front of me in his tactical outfit.

I hug him. "You're home early."

"Because I missed you." He rubs my cheek. "Why is there marker on your face?"

"It's pen ink." I swat his hand.

His eyebrow lifts but he doesn't question me. He sets his bag by the front door and shrugs out of his jacket, then pauses. "Did you check on the chickens?"

I frown at my watch. Is it really that late? "I'll check on them now."

"I'll help you."

With winter in full swing, I'll need to make sure no hidden nests go unnoticed, or the eggs will freeze and be no good. I shiver as the cold air smacks me in the face. I grab the goodies the girls laid in the nesting boxes. But when I notice some on the pen floor, I attempt to grab them and quickly realize my belly gets in the way. When I straighten, I find Jeremy grinning at me.

"Stop laughing at me."

He throws his hands up. "I wouldn't dare."

"Well, are you going to pick up those eggs?" I envy how easily he bends at the waist to collect the goods.

"Maybe you should leave this chore to me for a while."

I pout. "I love grabbing their butt nuggets." I sprinkle treats at the hens' feet.

"But you already have such a full plate. Let me help so I can lighten your load."

Once we return to the kitchen, I make a cup of coffee while Jeremy grabs his bag from the front door and holds it behind him.

"Let's make a deal. If I can get you to smile or laugh within the next two minutes, you have to take a break and relax."

"I find studying very relaxing."

"I mean, you should watch a movie or read a book for pleasure, not education."

"And if I don't, you'll let me return to planning my world domination, without judgment."

"Absolutely."

I glance at his dad's old watch on my wrist. "Your time starts now." He keeps me on my toes. I never know what will happen next with him.

He offers me a plain box. I grab it and arch a brow. "Just open it." I jiggle the contents, hoping the sound will give something away. "Don't shake it!" he chastises.

My eyes widen at his tone. I lift the lid and smile from ear to ear. "Jeremy!" I pull out a fluffy baby chick. "Aw." I kiss its tiny neck as it tweets its greeting. I tilt my head and stare. Its neck has a little bowtie on it. I giggle as I notice that all five feathered children have one. "How did you do this?"

"I dropped by the feed store to pick up some more food and there they were. Megan told me you had everything you needed for them except chick pellets, so I picked those up too."

"It seems like small-town living *is* starting to rub off on you."

"If you don't want them, I can bring them back."

"Don't you dare," I warn. Then I situate the cuties in a pen in the sunroom. I remove the bowties and hand them to Jeremy.

"Thank you for my gift. It was very thoughtful." I kiss him softly. He turns up the heat as his tongue slips inside my mouth. I groan and mold my body into his. He lifts me up. "Jeremy, put me down."

"Oh, I plan to." He walks into my room and pauses. "Well, someone's been busy."

I smirk at the mess of books. "I was doing more research."

"Any room for a partner in crime?"

"Other than Karen? You are definitely high priority for a partnership." I clean up the notebooks. "Can you put these on the bookshelf in the living room?"

Jeremy wraps his arms around my waist, ignoring the pile. He places warm kisses down my neck until I can't stand. His rapid heartbeat thunders from under my palm. "If I'm moving too fast, tell me."

Before I can respond, my cell phone *clucks*. I quickly answer it. "Ann, it's Elizabeth."

I flop on the bed with a groan. I didn't want to be thinking about her right now. I lean against my pillows. "What's going on? Is everything okay at the compound?" Jeremy kisses my belly, then moves his way up. I swat his hand and giggle.

"Ann?"

Did she say something?

"Yes, I'm here. Sorry."

"I was wondering if you had a chance to locate a physician?"

Does she think I can't handle my health? I bite my lip. Well, I did forget to make a follow-up appointment like the Palace doctor recommended.

"Remember we discussed it at the baby shower? I'm going to have a *home* birth, so I'm using a midwife."

"I recall that conversation. That's why I had the doctor write up a list of recommendations for you. I'm sending you their information now."

"Thank you."

"Not a problem. I know you've been busy with Karen so I figured I'd offer some suggestions." Voices echo in the background. "I need to help May clean the chicken pen, but I'll talk to you soon."

I almost laugh out loud when she says this. The image of the former Queen shoveling poop is absurd.

I fall into the pillows and toss my phone to Jeremy. "Is the Palace family ever going to let me relax?"

"Are you ready to meet the midwives?"

"Don't *you* start too."

He shoves my lit-up screen in my face. "According to these confirmation texts, Elizabeth set up interviews with three midwives for *today*."

"What?" I shoot up and scroll through my messages.

"She had it all set up before you even made up your mind."

I leave the bed and run a brush through my hair before our guests arrive.

"Can you move those to the guest room?" I point to the items I brought home from the Palace. "So the house doesn't look too disastrous for the midwives."

"When did we decide on a home birth?" he grunts as he grabs the stack.

"I don't like doctors, or hospitals." I swallow my fear. "The smell… the sounds… I've always been that way, especially after my mother died."

"I'll be here for you no matter what you choose." The box on top of his pile tumbles to the floor, spilling the contents at my feet. "Sorry." He collects the pieces, then pauses as he pops open the velvet case concealing Christian's engagement ring.

"You *kept* this?"

"You aren't seriously jealous of him?"

"I know Christian isn't around. But the thought of you being with another man, it stirs up a lot of

199

emotions."

I rub my belly. "Then *this* must be killing you."

Jeremy snorts. "I can handle Ryan if he oversteps the boundaries you set for him. But there's not much I can do about someone who haunts us from beyond the grave." Then he snaps the container shut, locking away the past before handing it back to me.

I shake my head. "Put it with the rest of the stuff and we'll store it in the attic later."

His face brightens. "With pleasure."

The doorbell rings and I groan. "The first midwife is early."

"We could always go to the hospital instead. Then you won't have to meet any of them."

I swing the door open with a groan before plastering on a fake smile. "Hello, Mrs. Shelby. I'm Ann and this is Jeremy."

She shakes our hands, and the fun begins.

After she leaves, the other two arrive right on top of each other. Once they are gone too, we dig into the spaghetti Jeremy cooked while I was chatting. He's not the best chef. My pasta is still crunchy. But I love that he made the effort.

"Which one do you like?" he inquires over dinner.

"Mrs. Shelby was really sweet, and she seemed to approach our *unique* situation without judgement."

He laughs. "The *other* midwife looked like she was about to faint when we told her we weren't married and she saw my scarred hand. I think she was about to sacrifice an animal to atone for our sins."

"I'll call Shelby and give her the job. That should get Elizabeth off our backs for a little bit," I say, and Jeremy gives me a pointed stare. "What?"

"You should consider setting *boundaries* with Elizabeth."

"She's trying to help."

He shrugs. "It's just my opinion."

"What time are you planning on leaving tomorrow?" I bring the dishes to the sink.

"I have training and meetings lined up, so pretty early. Why?" He follows with more plates.

I bite my lip. It's been nice having Jeremy home, but I need to remember he wants to work. I was eager to go shopping for maternity clothes, but maybe I'll ask Karen to tag along instead.

"I was hoping to wake up with you, so we could have coffee together before I start on the housework." I soap the sponge.

He puts a hand on my arm. "Not *too* much heavy-lifting, okay? Make sure you are taking it easy."

I sprinkle water at him. "Stop worrying so much."

"Or what?" His phone rings. "Sorry, I have to take this." He pivots out of the kitchen. His hushed whispers are fierce, and his face distorts with rage. He jabs his screen to end the call. "I need to head out for a few hours." He kisses my forehead.

"Where? Why?"

Jeremy's gaze searches mine. I hold my breath. Will he trust me with the truth, or lie to pretend to save me?

"There was a riot in Cambridge, not too far from here, and they asked me and some Palace guards to check it out."

Bile rises in my throat. He should have lied. "Why

can't they send someone else?"

He glances at his feet, then at me again. "They sent Brad and some guards this morning, but no one has checked in."

"Then you'll be walking into a *trap*."

Jeremy cups my face. "I'll go in as I always have. Very carefully and with guns drawn." His fingertips caress my cheeks. "Plus, I will have Palace guards to back me up." I lift my chin, ready to offer my services. "You know I want nothing more than to have you fighting at my side. But you are *pregnant* and we can't put Jack in danger. I'd never forgive myself if he lost his life because of me." He puts his hand on my belly. "Stay here so you can protect *him*."

"I don't need to be on the battlefield to be an asset. I can watch from the getaway car."

"Trust me, I know you can. But not with *this* mission. Please." His icy gaze darkens. "I will call you as soon as I can." My stomach twists in knots as Jeremy tugs on his tactical gear. "I'll be back before you know it." He warms my wrists. "Dan's going to stay with you. He needs your comfort more than you need his." He grins.

"Sam is going with you?"

"Yes."

"Why can't Ryan send in the calvary?"

His frown deepens. "*You* don't think I can deal with this?"

"I think you could use some extra assistance."

"The King is monitoring the situation, but he wants to see what our task force can do. It's a great opportunity to show him we can handle this."

"If this is a stick measuring contest..." I warn.

"A what?"

"You know, to see who has the bigger *stick*."

"That was never a question because *my* stick will always be bigger." He kisses my nose. "And you are stalling this *rod* from departing."

"Is it working?"

Tears slip out and run down my cheeks as he loads his duffel bag into the SUV. Out of the corner of my eye, I watch as Sam settles in the passenger seat.

Jeremy rubs my arms. "Go back inside once we leave and light the fireplace."

I snatch a fistful of Jeremy's shirt and slam my lips on his, reminding him how much he means to me. "Don't you dare break my heart."

"The sooner I leave, the quicker I can return." He starts the engine, then salutes his brother. "Good luck with her."

"Take care of my wife or I'll take yours," Dan shouts as the car pulls onto the main road. He wraps his arm around my shoulders. "I'll make soup." His smile is as fake as mine is. "You like soup, right?"

"As long as it tastes better than your brother's crunchy noodles."

Dan guides me into the brightly lit house, which feels more like a prison every minute Jeremy's life's in danger and I'm stuck on the sidelines.

Until the Bitter End

Dan is a much better cook than his older brother. After I clear our dishes, I excuse myself to spend time with my hens. As they frolic at my side, I mentally exhaust myself with planning the dimensions of next season's garden.

What would the restaurant need more, tomatoes or lettuce?

I venture to the rear of our estate to determine the location of the beehives. I don't want them too close to the main house, especially with Karen's children exploring the yard connecting our properties. It should be a safe place for them to venture. I crane my neck at the old treehouse my dad erected. Many years have passed since he nailed the lumber together. It needs tender love and care before I'd allow the kids to pretend to be pirates aboard its foundation.

Dan pops his head out to check on my progress. I smirk at the hat he's wearing. "I can't believe you still have that."

He adjusts his 'Dan the Man' cap I gave him last year. "Why wouldn't I?"

It's a reminder of the deception that's blanketed our friendship since the first day at the Palace. Even though I know he was protecting me, it still hurts.

"What does your wife think of it?"

He understands my double meaning. "She's mad." He stares at his feet. "We're sleeping in separate beds and only speaking when we have to."

What can I say to that? Christian lied to me for years, and if he were still alive, I'm not sure I'd be able to look past all of his deceit. Hopefully Sam is a better woman than I am.

"It's getting dark. Let me help you put the chickens

up for the night."

Once the girls are settled, I sink into the sofa with a beekeeping paperback while Dan types out his next novel. But after I read the same paragraph five times without comprehending any of it, I slam the book on the table.

"Do you want me to grab you a cup of coffee?"

"No." I scroll through my phone. "Why haven't we received an update yet?"

"We have to be patient," he tells me. I glare at him in response and his confidence falters. "I'm worried too—what are you doing?" He watches me push from my seat.

"I'm going to hunt them down."

"No, you aren't."

He's chosen the worst time to grow a backbone.

"Your *wife* is out there. Man up and help, or I'll tie you to a chair and leave."

"At least let me call Vinny first. He has more experience with this."

I imagine Karen without a husband, her kids fatherless. I shake my head. "We'll check out the situation, and *if* we need his assistance, I'll contact him.

"Jeremy asked us to *wait* here. If they haven't returned by tomorrow morning, then we'll reach out to the King and my mom." Dan squeezes my hands, reminding me why his brother was always a better match for me than he ever was.

"*You* may not be willing to fight for the person you love but I am!" I shoulder-check him as I pass. "I'll let you know when I reach them."

"You don't even know where they went," he shouts

at my back.

"Cambridge," I respond simply. "Do you think the newspaper has any reporters on this?" I ask myself.

"Maybe?"

My plan of action builds as I gather essentials. "I shouldn't be long."

Dan puffs out his chest. "I'm going with you."

I pause for a moment, considering if he'll be more of a liability than an aid. "Fine. Grab a backpack with medical supplies, water, and protein bars."

I jog to my room, where I shove my feet through black leggings and a pair of boots while nibbling my lip. If this place is dangerous enough that Jeremy needs reinforcements, I'm going to need more than I originally thought. I sift through my dad's old clothing until I find a concealed carry tactical shirt with two gun holsters sewn in the sides. I slide it over my baby bump. It's snug. Thank goodness my father was tall and had a dad bod. I then locate some ammo clips and a handgun, removing them from his safe, and arm myself with a few hunting knives.

"I'm loading the car!" I shout as I make my way to the garage.

"I'm right behind you." My partner in crime falls in line with his backpack in tow.

Within five minutes, we are speeding down the highway towards Cambridge. My mind is racing as I grip the steering wheel. I throw Dan my phone. "Call this number for me." He dials and I speak as soon as the call connects. "Richard, this is Ann."

"It's been a while," the reporter answers. "The last time we spoke, you told me to leave you alone."

"That's not exactly what I said," I grind out. "Can

you quit yapping and listen to me?"

"Why are you up so late?"

I ignore him and continue. "Do you know where the riot was today?"

"Maybe," he draws out.

"I'm in a hurry, so either tell me *now* or I'll be at your house with a loaded gun and a really bad attitude."

He chuckles. "Look at you, throwing around orders, *Lady* Ann."

"Oh, look, it's Peach Street. See you in five," I counter.

"Please turn around. You're *pregnant*."

"I'm pregnant, not incapacitated. You have three seconds before I make the turn into your neighborhood."

"I'll give you the address of where we last heard anything, *but* I want something in return."

"What?"

"Tell me who the baby's father is."

"Give me the address, and if it checks out, I'll tell you."

"I'll hold you to it." He rattles off the location. "Be alert. These men were laid-off enforcers and are not happy with the recent changes made with the Black Rose."

"I'm going in quietly. Don't tell the King what I'm up to or the deal is off."

"I don't like this, Ann."

"I didn't ask your opinion. Sleep well." I nod to Dan, gesturing for him to hang up.

"Do you think he's telling the truth?"

"He has no reason to lie to me."

"Are you really going to tell him who the father is?"

"God is the father of us all." I grin.

"He's not going to like your answer."

"If things pan out, I'll tell him what he wants to know. But on my terms, not his."

I reduce my speed and turn off the headlights as we near the building. I park in an alleyway a few blocks down. "Grab the backpack and stay close."

"Shouldn't I be the one to lead you?"

"I can outshoot Jeremy and Vinny." I hand Dan a knife. "Follow me."

We exit the vehicle and make our way onto the street. There isn't anyone standing guard. A chill runs up my spine but I force my feet forward. We locate a rusty side entrance and I glance to Dan, wondering if we should test out our luck. He dips his chin and I tug on the knob. The squeaky door creaks open and we slip inside. When it clicks closed behind us again, we're encased by complete darkness.

I listen for voices, creeping forward with Dan at my heels. My fingertips graze the wall, until it bends around another hallway. I pause. There's a tapping echoing around us. I knock on the closest surface in response. Then there's a louder, more urgent rap. I still can't see a thing, so I use my phone's backlight to illuminate a path.

There's an entrance at the end of the corridor. I run towards it as quietly as I can and place my ear to the drywall. Then I thump my knuckle and wait. It's repeated back to me. Dan grabs my hand and shakes his head no. A silent warning that this could be a trap.

He pushes me aside and opens the door himself. I aim the gun and pivot with my phone's light until my eyes are able to take in the scene in front of us. On the dirty tile floor is a group of Palace guards and rebels, all tied and gagged.

Dan and I use our knives to free them while I question, "Where's Jeremy, Brad, and Sam?"

Dan looks around. "They must be in another room."

I pivot to the haggard-looking group. "Listen. Follow the hallway and take your first left. It'll lead you to a back door."

"We're going to stay to help you find the others," a guard interrupts. "We won't let you have all the fun, Lady Ann."

"How will you defend yourselves? It'll be more helpful if you stay out of our way."

"These are all the weapons I need." The man lifts his fists. "And I know where to go." We trail the guard until he suddenly stops. There're two armed men blocking a room. "We need a distraction, or we'll have to fight our way in."

"Dan, hand me a water bottle," I whisper.

He passes me the item in question. "Be careful, please," he hisses in reply.

I wait until the men turn their heads, then I toss the bottle. It bangs in the opposite direction.

"Who's there?" They jog into the darkness in search of the sound's origin.

I tug open the door and gasp. Sam's on the ground with blood pooling around her. Dan kneels at her side. "No, no. Please be okay." He grabs the first aid kit and rifles through the contents. "Sam, stay with us," he begs her.

Her swollen eye twitches. "Dan?" she croaks. "Ann?" She coughs as we help her sit. "They knew we were coming and surrounded us."

"She needs an ambulance," Dan demands. "We have to call for assistance."

Things are getting out of control. "I agree."

"Brad's over here." Someone shouts in the distance as I hear grunts. "He's in better shape than she is, but he'll need help escaping."

"Where is Jeremy?" My nerves are on edge.

If Brad and Sam look like this, will my fiancé be worse?

"There's another interrogation room," Brad squeezes out between hissed breaths. "Continue down the hallway and take a right."

Dan grabs my arm. "Wait. I don't know about this."

I know he's conflicted. He wants me to tell him who to prioritize, his brother or his wife. "You stay with Sam and Brad until help arrives. I'll be right back with Jeremy."

Dan snatches up some bandages for Sam, then hands me the backpack. I slide it over my shoulders and turn the corner with a small group following my lead.

The sounds of knuckles meeting flesh echo behind the closed door. I peek inside. Jeremy is tied up in the corner while a guy screams at him. I tiptoe into the darkness while the others either keep watch at the exit or trail at my heels. I point my gun at the enemy as he brings back his fist to land another blow.

Then I chamber a round. "Give me a reason *not* to fire."

The man raises his bruised knuckles in surrender. "You have some balls…"

Before he can spew any more nonsense, I slam the butt of the gun across his temple. He crumbles at my feet. "Jeremy?" I pat his cheek. "Wake up."

His lips are oozing blood. He lifts his chin. "What are you doing here?"

"Rescuing you, old man." I use my knife to cut the ropes binding him to the chair.

He groans as his hands fall to his sides. I push water past his mouth. He sips it eagerly. "I don't think I can stand."

"Well, you sure as hell can't stay here." I pivot to the others. "Can you carry him out?"

"I'm not a child." Jeremy spits crimson. "Help me to my feet."

The group rushes to his side and he curses as he rises but quickly shuffles towards the exit.

"Hands up," a voice demands once we make it past the frame. Three men glare at us with their guns drawn.

"Listen, we're here for a peaceful rescue. We don't want to hurt anyone."

"Well, boys, look who we have here? It's Lady Ann," one taunts.

"Why are you doing this?" I push out.

"Because that's what *they* trained us to do. Hunt, torture, and destroy the rebels." He points to Jeremy's scarred hand. "They were once *murderers* and thieves, and now suddenly they aren't?"

"And *you* aren't?"

The man steps forward so that he's inches from my face. "*They* started this war."

"So that makes it right? That's a very childish way of

thinking."

His face contorts with rage before he grabs a chunk of my hair and pulls me off the ground. My scalp is on fire, but I swing my fist into his nose. His scream cuts through the air as his grip loosens. I fall to the floor and my group subdues the enemy.

Heavy footsteps are approaching in the distance. We aim our weapons at the dark hallway, my trigger finger itching to fire as sweat drips over my chin.

"Woah! We're on the same team."

I sigh with relief as Richard dashes over. "You couldn't let me have all the fun," I groan.

His palm rubs over my sweaty face. "Never." He looks around. "That hallway's clear. This way."

I squeeze Jeremy's hand, making sure he's still with us. When he returns the pressure, I allow Richard to pull me to my feet before turning back to my fiancé. "You never called."

"You defied my orders."

"I guess we're even then." I gulp in the frigid air and lean against the closest wall.

"It was incredibly stupid to place our child in harm's way." Jeremy closes his eyes. "But thank you."

Once the ambulance arrives, we're taken to the hospital, where they examine our injuries. Sam needs stitches, has one broken rib and a cracked tooth. While Jeremy has bruises littering his body and a busted lip. I'm fine, suffering from a few mild Braxton-Hicks contractions.

When we return to the house, I know I'm about to get a king-sized earful. His highness storms over with a huff. "What the hell was that?"

"Ryan, it's been a long night. Can we talk about this in the morning?" I plead.

"No! We will talk about it now," he insists. "This pardon was supposed to decrease the bloodshed, not draw more."

"It's going to take some time," Jeremy pushes out between clenched teeth.

Ryan points a finger at him. "Why didn't you call for backup?"

"I told you we had it covered."

"Obviously not. You're fired," he blares. "For putting your crew in unnecessary danger." Jeremy cringes, but the King isn't finished. "Dan, you and Sam are excused and can return home."

I'm in shock. Ryan is actually being bossy.

Dan helps Jeremy to the couch. "Let me know if you need anything, Ann." He hugs me and whispers, "Good luck." Then he leaves.

I sit next to my fiancé while resting my feet on the coffee table. I explain to the King what happened and how we saved the team. "I knew you would try to do something stupid," he accuses.

"Stupid? I was saving lives," I'm quick to remind him. His scowl boils my blood. "You want an apology? Fine, I'm sorry there's so much ignorance in the world." I throw my hands in the air. "We need more resources to counter the riots. And firing the one person tasked with ensuring peace and defending both sides is not a smart move."

Ryan appears to chew on my words. "I assumed everyone wanted peace. But now I see that the hatred towards the rebels runs deeper than I imagined." He sits on the couch. "We should consider bringing you back to the Palace until this situation simmers down. Otherwise, you're a target, Ann."

"I won't let these idiots ruin my life. Besides, I've proven I'm a worthy adversary."

"We need to keep you safe."

"What we *need* is to prevent the brutality, not hide behind stone walls."

Jeremy's voice cuts through the tension. "These men are angry that they've lost their jobs. They feel like all their training and years of dedication were for nothing. Most of them spent their entire lives bringing the rebels 'to justice' and now they have nothing to show for it."

"I offered them jobs on the task forces, but some refused to work with the *bad* guys," Ryan says.

"Maybe we can reeducate and find new purposes for them, like in the Palace under the watchful eyes of the guards," Jeremy suggests.

"How can we know if they're safe to return to duty?" I ask.

"Lie detector?" Ryan questions.

I snort. "They aren't accurate. Don't you remember? Mary was able to pass one without batting an eyelash, yet she was lying through the skin of her teeth."

"If you have the proper training, know how to control your blood pressure and so on, then it's possible to lie," Jeremy interjects. "But even then, it's not an easy task."

"Then we'll give it a shot, starting with the goons we picked up tonight." Ryan straightens his suit.

"Does this mean I have my job back?" Jeremy questions.

"Only if your report is accurate. Leave nothing out.

No more of this lone ranger crap."

Jeremy salutes the King. "Aye, aye, Captain."

Ryan rolls his eyes before he meets my gaze. He appears to consider his words carefully. "I wish you nothing but happiness. You know that, right?"

"I'm beginning to see that."

"And you're sure Jeremy is the one you want to spend the rest of your life with?" He hooks a thumb in the direction of the man in question.

"I'm injured, *not* deaf," Jeremy snarls.

I touch my ring and smile. "I raided a warehouse to rescue his sorry butt." I laugh. "As much as I tried not to, I love him with all my heart."

The King nods to Jeremy. "Well, now it's *your* job to keep her in line. But be warned. Many have tried and failed."

"Excuse me?" I growl.

"I look forward to that *challenge*." Jeremy grins.

"I should head home. Cherie must be worried. I'll be in touch soon." Ryan saunters to the door. I rise from the sofa, but he holds up a hand. "I can see myself out." He pauses in the entryway. "Can I stop by later and visit Jack's grave? I'd like to pay my respects."

My heart clenches at the sorrow-laced words. "You can fly by any time."

"But, seriously, *call* first!" Jeremy adds with a shout.

We are *finally* fighting for the same side. It's not perfect, but it's a step in the right direction.

First Date

Early the next morning, I slither off the sofa and glide my fingers through Jeremy's hair. He looks peaceful. With a desperate need for a shower, I stride to my room. As I drop the concealed carry shirt in the hamper, I freeze. I almost didn't get out of the warehouse unscathed. I hold my belly as tears wet my lashes. But I would do it all over again. Jeremy is worth the risk.

After I finish in the bathroom, I head towards the back door to let the hens out. I slip on my jacket but fight the zipper.

"I think you need new clothes."

I clutch my pounding heart. "Jeremy, you are supposed to be resting."

He leans against the wall. "Why did you come for me last night?"

"You would have done the same for me."

"That's twice that you've saved my butt and I don't know how I feel about that."

I smirk. "Well, it *is* a great butt."

He chuckles and grasps his side. "Stop. I can't laugh right now."

"Go and rest. I am going to let the chickens out of their pen *alone*."

"While you do that, I'll make breakfast."

Pots and pans bang around, and I block out the noise as I greet my feathered pals. "Willy, you need to chill out with Whitey. Poor girl is getting bald spots from all your mounting." I stroke the pale hen's back where the male's spur scratched her.

The rooster struts off, unfazed by my reprimand. I

216

make a mental note to search for chicken saddles before infection spreads. Once my contingents are taken care of, I deposit my boots and coat inside the warm home. I brush past Jeremy as he flips an omelet and half of the goop drips onto the stove and sizzles.

"I made a pot of coffee for you."

"Thank you."

As I pour the liquid gold, he declares, "I'm taking you out of the house today."

"Why? We can stay here and enjoy the fireplace."

"After being rescued by my woman, I want to pamper her. Is that okay?"

"I'm fine with watching a movie on the couch in my chicken pajamas."

He grabs my hip and brings me to him. "You need maternity clothes—plus, we can buy any supplies you didn't get from the baby shower."

"You need clothes too." I wrinkle my nose at his tactical outfit. "Maybe jeans and a few button-up shirts."

He nips my earlobe. "And grey sweatpants."

The visual does magical things to my girly bits. "Fine, you twisted my arm."

"Great. Let's eat, then we can head out." While we munch on breakfast, we discuss the events of last night. "I'm thinking about leaving the task force once Jack is born."

My fork freezes an inch from my mouth. "Why? I thought you liked this job?"

"While I was in that warehouse last night, all I could think about was *you*. If something happened to me, how would that affect your life." He sighs. "I was forced into this field by my father. It's all I've ever known and I'm curious what else I can do with my talents." I stir my eggs. "Ann, what are you thinking about over there?"

"That it'd be nice to have you home at regular hours and not shot at all day, but I don't want you to feel like you have to sacrifice what you love for me or Jack."

"We can build an empire together."

"You're actually going to take up farming?"

"Why not? It can't be worse than being a mercenary. And if staying home doesn't work out, I can always start my own security company."

"Whatever you want to do, I'll support it." I squeeze his palm. "We're a team."

"Should I invite Karen or Vinny?" I ask as we clean the dishes.

Jeremy tugs on a jacket. "Why? Are you afraid to go out alone with your fiancé?"

"No, I was thinking we could go on a double date."

"Maybe next time. Today I want you all to myself." He kisses the top of my head.

I snuggle into him. "Sounds good."

Jeremy jingles the keys. "Are you driving or should I?"

"No, you sit and relax."

"You're lucky I love you," he grumbles as he opens

my door.

"I know you like to be the one behind the wheel, but you're also healing from last night's battle."

A few minutes later, we park near a huge mall. Jeremy grabs my hand and squeezes. It's nice doing something normal. The sun beats on us as the wind blows. I shiver and bring my jacket closer to my chest. It'll be nice to have a coat that zips up.

The venue is bustling with crowds. We weave through the small groups while laughing and talking about items we're planning to purchase.

"First stop." Jeremy tugs my arm. "We're getting you something comfortable to wear."

The maternity store is larger than I expected. We gather clothes, jackets, and other essentials. Then I drag him to a men's apparel retailer and purchase him a few new outfits. After that, Jeremy stops inside a computer store and we acquire a new laptop for my business.

"I'm starving," I grumble. "And my feet hurt."

"Do you want me to carry you?"

"No."

The smell of fajitas wafting in the air makes my stomach growl. I spot a Mexican restaurant and dash towards the entrance. Thank goodness it isn't too busy and we are seated immediately. As I drool over the menu, Jeremy leans back in his chair while clutching his side.

I eye his discomfort. "We can go back home if you need to rest."

He reaches for my hand. "No way. I'm fine." He kisses my knuckles.

The waiter greets us with salsa and chips a moment

later.

"What's next on the agenda?" I ask as I gulp down sweet tea.

"We're shopping for a crib."

"But... where will we put it? Isn't it too early?" I rub my belly.

"Ann, you'll be having that baby before you know it. And you don't even have a bed for him."

I run a finger over the condensation on my glass. "I'll get to it eventually. I don't want to rush it."

Because the next part of the process is scary and gross.

He touches my arm. "We can pick out everything on the list and have it delivered to the house. We can put it anywhere you want. Your room, your dad's, or the guest room."

Our order arrives before I can respond. It's not that I don't want to shop with my fiancé; it's just the more stuff we get, the more real the situation becomes. I dig into my enchilada and the cayenne seasoning pops on my tongue. It's been a long time since I've had something this spicy.

"That was delicious. How was your chicken fajitas?"

"Very tasty but too many bell peppers. I prefer more beef."

I bite back my comment about his meat-to-vegetable ratio.

We pay, then make our way up the escalator to the baby furniture. Jeremy's right. We should get what we need for Jack's imminent arrival. We spend the next three hours selecting and setting up delivery.

"I never realized they had this many choices for

babies."

"Babies are spoiled. Who's ever heard of *heated* wipes? It's for their butts. Does it really need to be warmed first?" He readjusts the bags he's holding. "Well, I think we have spent enough money. Are you ready to call it a day?"

"Not yet." I yank Jeremy to a bookstore. "It has been far too long since I've been inside one of these."

"Me too." Jeremy meanders with me but our interests tug us in different directions. "How about we meet at the cashier in an hour?"

I peck him on the cheek and dash to the romance section. "It smells like I remember it." I rub a spine.

As my words echo around me, they bring me back to that day in the Palace. I was so scared I entered the *wrong* room. My eyes mist over. That's when I first connected with Ryan. Life was simpler then. The quote I recited that day sings in my memory, which reminds me of the moment he came clanking into my bedroom wearing heels. I swipe my cheek. It's astonishing how scarcely any time passes, yet countless things change.

I clutch a few updated novels on small businesses, chickens, bees, and baby care before striding to the cashier thirty minutes later than I promised. Jeremy is nowhere to be seen. After I checkout, I make my way to the exit and crash into him.

"These are for you." He waves a bouquet of roses in my direction.

"They're beautiful." The petals tickle my nose. "They smell amazing."

"I'm glad you like them." He kisses my cheek. "I also bought baby-blue paint and brushes for Jack's room. I hope you don't mind."

"I've never painted a bedroom before, but I look forward to another first with you."

"We never had the funds at the compound to paint so this will be a first for me too, but the store clerk gave me a few how-to pamphlets."

We leave as darkness encompasses the parking lot. I stretch my back. "I cannot believe we spent a whole day shopping. I'm exhausted."

Jeremy massages my neck as we walk to the car. "I'm sorry it took so long."

"Jeremy, I haven't had this much fun in years. Thank you."

His blue eyes twinkle. "We'll have to make a habit of it." He helps me into my seat and comes around to the driver's side.

I relinquish the keys as my body sinks into the leather. "Yes, with a baby coming, we'll have loads of extra time to go on dates."

"We'll make it work." He squeezes my thigh. "And you're positive you *don't* want to get married before he arrives?"

"I have to fit into my feathered gown. So, yes, I'm sure."

His thumb caresses my wrist. "And when do you think we can move our relationship to the next level?"

My heart is in my throat. Is he talking about sex? Ryan was the only man I've ever been with. And that one time was painful, though I'm sure my lingering infection didn't help much. What if intercourse causes problems with Jack, like preterm labor?

Jeremy grasps my hand. "Talk to me. What's going on inside that pretty little head?"

"I'm not sure *when* I'll be ready for that."

"But you do want to, right?"

"Yes. Trust me, I do."

"Are you worried I'll hurt you?"

"Well, I've felt *it* against me a few times and I know it's not going to feel great."

His chuckle warms the air. "There are ways to make it feel good, even if you're intimidated by the size."

"I never said I was intimidated."

"Good. Because when you're ready, I'm going to make all your desires a reality."

"Really, because there's this one with a chicken..." I joke.

"*Realistic* fantasies." He rolls his eyes. "You and your flock."

By the time we return home, the moon is high in the dark sky while the stars sparkle like diamonds. We trudge through the house with our goodies in tow, then I plop on the couch and put my feet on the coffee table. "Shopping is draining."

"Especially when you're twenty-five pounds *heavier*." Jeremy puts the bags where they need to be. I grab a pillow and throw it at him, waiting until I hear the satisfying, "Ow." My fiancé drops the cushion on my head. "You dare hit a *wounded* man?"

"You made fun of a pregnant woman's weight."

He sits next to me. "We're cruel. Can you imagine what our children will be like?"

"Hopefully they will be wiser than we are."

"How many do you want?"

"I was thinking one girl and one boy."

"That sounds fair. Plus, this is a three-bedroom house, so they'd each have their own room."

"We could always add more rooms if we needed to."

"Are you saying you want more than two kids?"

"I'm saying… let's take it one step at a time. Pop this child out, then talk about another."

His fingertips draw circles on my belly. "Did Mom tell you she found a property near here?"

"I talk to your mom more than you do."

Sally calls every other day to check in and see how we're doing. I even get to talk to May. The rebels are receiving payments and land from the Palace and look forward to starting their new lives.

"Mom sounds happy," Jeremy murmurs.

"I agree."

"Did Tammy tell you she found her grandfather?"

Now that's someone I *rarely* speak to. "Is she excited to have her family nearby?"

He shrugs. "She's not sure she can trust him after everything that's happened."

"Can you blame her for being a little hesitant?"

"No. Not after what we've been through."

"It's getting late." I stand, but he puts a hand out to stop me. "Jeremy, I need to get the chickens up for the night so a coyote doesn't eat them."

He puffs out his chest. "Let me do it."

Normally, I assist him with corralling the feathered devils. Most of them go in the pen without a problem, but there're a select few that make you work for their well-being.

"Are you sure you can handle it?"

"Absolutely. I'll be back before you can say *mother-clucker*."

"Good luck." I settle into the cushions. "Call me if you need me." Twenty minutes later, Jeremy stomps in, covered in what I hope is dirt. I arch a brow at him. "Easy peasy?"

He grumbles incoherently as he stalks towards the bathroom. I lean on the doorframe as he sets his fashionable grey sweatpants on the counter and starts the shower. "You make it look easy."

"I've been around these girls all their lives. They'll learn to trust you too."

He wraps his arms around my waist. "Are you sure you want me here, even if I can't put the chickens up in under ten minutes?"

"Why? Are you getting cold feet?"

"If I said yes, would you join me in the shower and warm them up again?"

I push him towards the running hot water. "Rinse off. You smell like manure."

He removes his shirt but groans as he places a hand on his side. "You never realize how much you rely on your muscles until they hurt every time you move."

I frown at his bruised chest. "You're always getting into mischief."

Jeremy grabs my palm and kisses it, sending tingles to my toes. "And I never plan to stop."

Lost

Light slithers between the cracks in my blinds before smacking me in the face. I'm not a morning person, but with chickens, you have to wake up with the sun. That being said, today, they can wait five more minutes. I pull the sheet over my head. Jeremy mumbles before tugging me to his chest. Heat floods every body part, including the ones I didn't realize were still functioning.

"I'm getting up now," I screech.

He murmurs but I pry his bicep off me. "Wait!"

I stop in my tracks. Did I hurt him? "What's wrong?"

His icy eyes flutter open. "I'm taking in the sights and making sure I'm not dreaming."

"Jerk. I thought you were hurt."

"Yes, I'm painfully in love," he calls at my back as I scurry to the bathroom.

I adjust my new maternity clothes. Even though they're not fashionable, they are stretchy and comfortable.

As I drag my hair into a ponytail, Jeremy stumbles in, "What are you doing today?"

"I plan on getting ready for the beehives and tilling the garden."

"Isn't it too cold for bees?"

"I won't be receiving them for a while, but I can still set up their homes."

"And won't the ground be too hard to till?" He scratches his scruff.

"What would you have me do then?"

He wraps his arms around me. "Stay in bed with

me."

"I have *work* to do before the baby arrives."

"Why don't you add *me* to your to-do list."

"That reminds me. I have articles to bring to Richard." I stride to the kitchen.

As I push the start button on the coffee machine, Jeremy joins me. "*Why* did that remind you to see Richard."

"Because the last time I saw him, I was rescuing you."

He grumbles as he shoves his feet into his boots. I cringe as the back door bangs shut. I guess I got under his skin. When he brushes past me again, he deposits a handful of butt nuggets.

I slide his mug in front of him like a peace offering. "Do you want to come with me to see Richard and play big bad fiancé?"

Jeremy sips his coffee as he seems to consider my proposition. "I would love to put that man in his place."

"*Remember* he has been a huge help with getting us where we are now."

"Fine. I'll refrain from shooting him… out of the *kindness* of my heart."

I kiss his cheek. "That's all I'm asking."

He snatches my chin and meets my lips. His tongue demands entrance and I purr as he slips past my barriers and leaves me breathless.

"I'll make us some food, while you get started on those documents for Dick." Jeremy slaps my butt towards the living room.

I sashay for him, then plop on the sofa with my

227

laptop. I type up a few articles focusing on the retaliation brought on by the recent pardon and describing the unfair attacks on the guards and rebels. I email the drafts to Richard with a promise to meet him by lunchtime to review.

"Breakfast is on the table," Jeremy announces, pulling out my chair.

"French toast? Someone is getting fancy." I smirk at him. "And they don't taste half-bad." I sprinkle cinnamon on my bread. "Can we work on clearing out my dad's room? I'd like to paint before the furniture arrives."

"Someone is nesting." Jeremy arches a brow. "Are you feeling okay?" He nods to my belly.

"I'm feeling surprisingly energized today."

"I can definitely clear out your dad's room for you. Where do you want me to put everything?"

I bite my lip. "I'm not sure. Do we have space in the guest room for now?"

"I'll see what I can do."

"Just…" I push past the lump in my throat. "Don't get rid of anything, please."

Jeremy squeezes my hand until I meet his gaze. "Are you sure you don't want to leave it as is and use the guest room for the nursery?"

"I want the baby to be near my dad's presence." I sniffle. "That sounds dumb, but I want him to have a piece of his grandfather's memory, even if it is just a room."

"No need to explain."

After everything that's happened, I knew Jeremy would understand and be supportive.

My cell phone clucks, bringing me out of my momentary sadness. "Hello?"

"Good morning, Lady Ann. This is Tim, King Ryan's assistant." His voice still grates on my nerves.

"What do you want?" I grind out.

"The King is having a hard time locating some paperwork and he was wondering if you could assist him?"

"Doesn't his highness have an army of *goons* at his beck and call?"

I can almost see the satisfying scowl I'm certain I put on Tim's face. "He would like to speak to *you* about this matter."

Jeremy narrows his eyes in my direction. "Is everything okay?"

I pull the phone from my ear. "Ryan has lost some paperwork and needs my help."

"How convenient. We saw him the other day, and now he's calling you." Jeremy shakes his head.

"Would you like me to hang up on him?" I tease my fiancé.

"You do realize I'm still here," Tim grumbles. "And I can hear you."

I ignore the secretary and wait for Jeremy's response. "I guess we should play nice until after the government changeover." He rolls his eyes.

"You heard the man, Tim." I return to the call.

"Please hold while I transfer you to King Ryan," he replies curtly.

"Hello, Ann?" his majesty greets me. "I am sorry to bother you, but I cannot find the annual financial reports from last year. With everything that happened during the raid, they seem to have been misplaced. Plus, the computers were smashed during the attack and our back-up cloud only has half of what I need."

"I helped Christian organize those and he stored them in his filing cabinet."

"I can't seem to locate where Christian put them." I hear a thump over the line like Ryan kicked something.

Maybe this call is about more than business?

"Are you all right?" I ask him.

"Yes, I can't find the reports and I need them for a meeting."

"Stupid question, but I have to ask. Did you look in the filing cabinet?"

"Yes!"

"Ryan, I'm only trying to help."

"It would be more helpful if you told me a location I haven't checked yet."

I rub my temples. "Would you like me to come up there and help you look?" Ryan's acting like a child, and no amount of talking is going to change that. I need to smack some sense into him.

"No, no, I am sure I can... maybe... I do not know."

"If you need the paperwork immediately, send the helicopter. I can be there within the hour. And if you find the reports beforehand, please let me know."

"Thank you. I will look again. If I don't find them, I will see you soon." Then he hangs up.

"Why does he need you to assist him?" Jeremy arches a brow.

"Because his brother had a weird filing system. And

now that he's gone, Ryan can't find a financial report for a meeting."

"Doesn't he have a Palace full of minions to assist him?"

"That's what I said. But only a select few are allowed in the office, and even less are allowed in the King's personal domain."

"And you were one of those *chosen* individuals?" Jeremy stands to clear the table.

I trail him and place the dishes in the sink. "Well, I did work in the office and I was engaged to him."

"Do you have to go? We had the day planned out."

"I could call him back and say no, if you want. Or you can come with me and see that there's nothing to worry about."

"But I wasn't invited, nor am I a *chosen one*."

"You are my fiancé. I can get you in." I wink. "It'll be fun. We can ride in a helicopter and be fed amazing food from the Palace kitchen."

"I don't like being locked inside something I can't maneuver if things go south."

"I can demand he let us drive there."

"Then it'll take hours, and you said you wanted to get the nursery done as soon as possible."

He's got me there.

"How about you go while I move things around and paint."

"*How* about I help you clean the room before I leave?" I peck his cheek.

"Sounds good."

We sort through Dad's room, boxing up his clothes and papers. Jeremy hands me an old wedding card that was on the nightstand.

"Did you read it?" I ask.

"Yeah, sorry. I didn't realize it was a card for you and Ryan."

"Things have definitely changed since then."

"Things are still changing." Jeremy kisses me. "And for the *better*."

"You're right." I shove the card in my pocket to throw away later and wrap my arms around Jeremy's neck. "Call Vinny or Dan over to help you with the heavy-lifting. Remember to take it easy." There's a cordial knock on the front door, and I know it's the Palace to collect me to find the hidden documents for his royal pain-in-my-butt. "I'll be back as soon as humanly possible."

"Be safe." Jeremy guides me to the exit. "And if you need me, remember I'm only a text away."

"I will."

I pull my jacket tight and climb into the waiting helicopter parked in the front yard. It lifts into the air as soon as I'm buckled and we are on our way.

Once we arrive at the Palace, I'm surprised to see the Queen waiting. "Well, look who graced us with her presence." When I don't fall for the bait, she continues. "I swear every time I see you, you gain ten pounds."

"It's nice to see you too, your majesty."

Her heels click on the tile as we stride through the immaculate halls. "I told the King not to bother calling you."

"I appreciate that, but maybe next time, you should

try a little harder and really put your cleavage into it." I nod to her modest neckline. "Mary always won the boys' attention when half of her boobs were on display."

Cherie halts and pivots. "The quicker you get done with this fruitless errand, the sooner I can kick you out of my house."

The tension between us could be cut with a quill.

"Your husband called *me*, begging for *my* help." I plaster on my fake smile. "So lead me to him so I can return to my fiancé."

A maid scurries past us and Cherie clears her throat. "Right this way." Once we're out of earshot from all the servants, she whispers, "When are you going to follow through with your end of the bargain?"

"You mean announcing that Jeremy is the child's father?"

"Yes."

"Soon."

The Queen knocks on Ryan's office door and opens it. "Your friend is here, dear," she announces.

He waves her out without a word as he shuffles through a stack of papers. Cherie purses her lips, meets my gaze, then stomps out.

I tilt my head at the glass on his desk. "Are you drinking?"

"Yes."

"You had me fly out here to watch you drink?" I sneer.

"No, I need that file."

"You have a problem." I finger through the folders.

"Normally, Christian would have placed them in here."

"Don't you think I have looked there already!" Ryan downs his drink and slams it on the table.

"Have you checked the safe?"

"Yes, but go ahead and check again. I never changed his passcode." The King itches his beard. "Maybe your buddies stole it in the raid."

"No, they didn't."

"How would you know? You were lying on the floor when Max trashed the office."

Ouch. That was a low blow even for him.

I clench my fists. "Are you okay?"

"Why wouldn't I be?"

"Because you're not normally this big of a jerk." I shuffle through the contents of the safe. Then I shut it. "It's not there either."

"Thank you, Brainiac!"

"Hey, don't get mad at me!" I puff out my chest. "You chose to be in this situation, my King. You decided to ignore me so you could start the selection process and get married to Cherie." I poke him in the chest. "You've made your bed. Now sleep in it!"

"I hurt you," he whispers it like it's a question.

"Yes, you did!" I spit back.

"I *saved* you," he slurs. "I did my research, and I knew the Black Rose wouldn't harm you. I loved you enough to let you have your freedom." His palm rests on my belly. "I never wanted my child to grow up like me and my brother, with this cursed crown."

"I didn't need saving." I shove him. "You are *married* to a wonderful woman who loves you. You need to grow up, quit drinking, and stop making her regret her choices or you'll lose her like you lost me."

"Cherie told you she wasn't happy?"

"No, she's too much of a proper lady to say that out loud. But stop being so self-absorbed and take a second to look into her eyes. There's pain and suffering behind them." I aim to change the subject so I can get home. "Let's go to your room."

He shakes his head. "Excuse me? What did you say?"

"Sometimes, Christian would take his work to bed with him. Maybe he hid the folder in his room."

"Why didn't I think of that?" He smacks his forehead.

I shake the bottle of alcohol in his direction. "Because you're *drinking*. Ryan, you need to keep your head clear. Okay?" I toss the liquid in the trash can.

He opens his mouth to argue, but then changes tact. "How are you feeling?"

"Fat, but happy." I shrug, not wanting to get chatty while he's intoxicated. "Jeremy moved in, and we're well on our way to a new feathered beginning."

"That's nice."

"I felt the sincerity." I roll my eyes.

"I just... I mean..." Ryan stutters but shakes his head.

"What are you babbling about?"

"Ann, he's a spy, trained to manipulate people. Are you sure that's not what he's doing to you?" the King suggests, and my fist aches to meet his jaw. "Just be careful and make sure to remain vigilant." He puts a hand on the small of my back. "You should talk to the psychologist before you leave and get evaluated for Stockholm syndrome. It's not uncommon for a captive to develop positive attachments towards their kidnappers."

"Stop touching me." I smack his arm away. "Why is it so challenging for you to recognize that I'm *happy*? Is it because it's not with you or Christian?" I narrow my eyes at him. "I love Jeremy, whether you approve of us or not."

Ryan assesses my defensive stance and nods. "How about we check the room for that file so you can be on your way then?"

I wave him forward. "After you." He opens his bedroom door and lets me pass. I'm surprised to see not only Ryan's belongings adorning the walls but Christian's too. A mixture of art and architecture with a side of travel photos. "Interesting layout."

"Thanks. I didn't want to change the way he had it entirely, but I wanted to add a bit of myself too."

My fingertips glide over the dresser and pick up a framed photo of me and the boys at Christian's wedding. It was so long ago. Tears well in my eyes. But the past is that. *The past.*

I return the picture to its proper place. I look around the room for any signs of the documents. "Normally, if Christian were working late, the file would end up on his nightstand." My palm warms the surface in question. "But what if it fell off? Have you checked *under* the bed?"

"It's been months. Shouldn't the maids have cleaned under there by now?"

I cross my arms over my chest. "Well, there's no way my fat butt is bending down to check."

Ryan rolls his eyes but lowers himself to his hands and knees. "What the hell? I'm not sure how you do it." He waves a folder around. "The maids are getting an earful from me." He stands and fingers through the papers. "Yup, it is all here."

"That's great. Well, I should be getting back. We're painting my dad's room for the nursery."

The King tilts his head, as I turn to leave, and points at my butt. "What's *that*?"

"Did I sit in chicken poop again?"

"No, it's inside your pocket."

I tug out the wedding card from my dad. I hand it to Ryan. "A joke from heaven."

Ryan reads it. He pales and sits on the edge of his bed. "Wow."

"Jeremy found it while we were packing Dad's things up."

The King stares at the wall. "Your dad must really hate me right now. I screwed it all up."

I groan. I shouldn't be as nice as I'm being at the moment. I sit next to Ryan and place a hand on his leg. "You may not be dating me anymore, but you can grovel at my feet and beg to be my friend again. Remember, *no regrets*." I smirk at the slogan he churned up while we were in the safe room.

"If only it were that easy…" He rubs his face.

The adjoining door swings open and Cherie saunters in. "I thought I heard you." She pauses. "What is she doing in your bedroom without supervision?"

I snatch my palm from his thigh and leap off his bed. I don't even attempt to smooth things over. "Well, now that we've found the lost documents, I'm going to head home."

I make a quick exit. Before the door closes, a slew of shouting ensues. I cringe. These two should sit with the Palace shrink and hash things out. Hopefully they can mend their relationship; otherwise, altering the government will not only grant the people equal representation, but also allow Cherie to apply for a divorce.

New Coat of Paint

Once we land, I eagerly dash into Jeremy's waiting arms. He kisses the top of my head. "You look like you need a nap."

"You know how the Palace can be, with their demands and false pleasantries."

"Did they at least feed you as they manipulated you?"

"Between the flight and tension, my stomach would have thrown back their delicacies."

"I'm sorry the trip was a bust. Do you want to talk about it?"

"It wasn't a bust. I found the folder like the King asked."

"That's good." Jeremy guides me through the door.

"But Cherie and Ryan are fighting."

He shrugs. "That's what couples do."

"But it felt like Cherie was fighting and Ryan was giving up."

"I thought you didn't like her."

"I never said that."

"It's written all over your face." He pokes my forehead. "That wrinkle gives you away."

"Only because she has nothing nice to say to me."

"She did get me out of jail."

"By deceiving her husband."

"But her motives were understandable. She wanted to start a new life with her husband without another woman's child dangling over them."

I shake my head. "Let's agree to disagree for now. How is the nursery coming along?"

He guides me to my dad's old room, and the baby-blue walls bring tears to my eyes. Jeremy even touched up the baseboards. I hug myself. This is really happening.

"Dan and Vinny moved the furniture but couldn't stay long." He frowns at my wet lashes. "We can change the color if you want."

I sniffle. "It's beautiful."

"Then why are you crying?" His thumb brushes my cheek. "I thought you be so grateful you'd finally let me take this relationship all the way."

I laugh into his chest. "You think very highly of your painting abilities."

"Hey, it got you to smile. That's what matters."

"I can't believe we'll have a child running through the house soon."

"He'll crawl before he can run."

"After the pain of my mother's death, I swore I wouldn't put my child through something like that. I vowed I'd never have a kid, and it would only be me and my chickens, forever."

"You never wanted to get married?"

"Never."

"Then why sign up for the selection to become Christian's wife?"

"That wasn't in my folder?" I elbow him.

"I know your name was strategically placed on top of the list, but I assumed *you* wanted to be in the competition."

"My dad did it. He forged my signature on the documents, and when I was chosen, I kept it quiet because I didn't want him to get into trouble."

Jeremy's silent for a long minute. "I'm sorry."

I investigate his darkening gaze. "Why are you sorry?"

"My father forced me into this lifestyle. I never had the opportunity to choose what I wanted to do when I grew up and it sounds like your dad put you in a similar situation."

I consider his words. *Is that what happened?*

"My dad did what he did out of love. He wanted to encourage me to mingle and learn what it meant to love and be loved. He had no idea that such a simple act would bring me to this moment in time."

"And did he succeed in teaching you those things?" Jeremy asks.

"In a way, yes." I kiss him softly. "I met you, didn't I?"

"After various trials and errors."

"Isn't that how life works, *through* trial and error?"

"Or through pain and suffering," he grumbles.

We hold each other, lost in our reflections. My dad made many sacrifices to give me a life I love. Yes, he shouldn't have placed my name in the competition, but I learned more about myself and the crown than I ever thought possible. The good and bad. This makes me wonder about Ryan. He's been through so much, between losing his dad and his brother. Plus, he never wanted to be on the throne.

Could this be why he's lashing out at Cherie? Because it's easier to push her away, so he won't get hurt if she leaves? Just like my dad did to me, I could force the King into something he isn't ready for and hope for the best. Or I can let him make his own mistakes and learn along the way.

"So do you think the royal marriage is going up in flames?" Jeremy teases. "You said they were fighting."

"I hope not, because Cherie loves Ryan. She's given him chances to redeem himself, but I'm afraid this'll be the last straw if he can't pull his head out of his rear." I explain how my trip to the Palace was a disaster.

"Well, it's not your job to put those two together," Jeremy reminds me. "They must work things out on their own."

I stride to the kitchen and assemble a snack. They can *work things out* as I shove obstacles in their path.

I clear my throat. "How's your mom doing?"

Jeremy arches a brow at the topic change but plays along. "You mean other than babysitting Elizabeth and May?"

"Don't forget about Snowball too."

He leans against the counter. "I still can't believe she brought that primped menace to the compound."

I narrow my eyes. "*Menace?*"

"Come on. She's spoiled. You said it yourself. She doesn't belong at the compound."

"It's only for a month. She'll be fine. Plus, this trip will make her more grateful when she returns to a lavish life at the Palace."

"We'll see if you're right soon enough."

"I'm *always* right."

He smirks before redirecting the conversation. "Since

Mom's been busy playing host, she asked the group to vote on a new leader."

"Really?"

"She doesn't want to say it out loud, but she's getting older and wants a peaceful retirement home."

"But she's been there for so long."

"The Black Rose is disbanding, Ann. The rebels can find jobs, homes, and have normal lives again. The new leader will only have a temporary status."

"As long as Ryan keeps up with his side of the bargain," I add. "So, who'd they vote for? You?"

He wrinkles his nose. "I'd never take that position." Jeremy smirks. "But *Tammy* would."

I shove the rest of my food in my mouth to keep from laughing. Tammy will make a great leader to the remaining rebels. "Good thing it's only temporary."

"Did you get a chance to talk to Richard about your articles?"

I rub my temples, wanting to forget *that* headache. "Do you still want to go with me to see him?"

"Well, somebody should watch over you so you don't get into more trouble."

I poke his tender rib cage. When he groans and bends over, I respond, "I'm not sure *you* are up for the job."

"After everything I did for you today, you'd think you'd be nicer to me."

"Should we take my car or yours?"

"Mine." He grabs his keys and waves me out the door. "Walk in front of me, so you can't injure me further."

"You're a baby. That didn't hurt."

"I'll make sure I throw that back at you while you're in labor."

"You will not. That's different."

Jermey opens my door for me. "After you, my lady."

I settle into the seat. The sun glistens off the neighbor's mailbox and I frown at how quiet they are. "How're Dan and Sam doing?"

Jeremy buckles in and lets out a sigh. "Sam is still in pretty rough shape, but she's tough. And Dan is at her beck and call." He pulls onto the main road. "I bet she has a little bell and everything."

I roll down the window and embrace the cold breeze as it caresses my hair. "If your brother ends up in a maid outfit, it'll be the setting for a perfect romance story."

He grins. "We should write one."

"Our story is not *romantic*. It's hardly believable." I roll my eyes at the thought.

Jeremy squeezes my hand. "It's definitely *not* your average fairy tale, but it's quite the adventure." He kisses my knuckles, then releases me. "So, where are we going next?"

I input Richard's address into the GPS. "Let's see where the road takes us."

"As long as you are by my side, I'll go anywhere."

"Even the moon?"

"Yup."

"Well, for now, I only need you to take me to Richard's office."

As we drive, we discuss the process of a home birth

and the materials we'll have to collect for it. Jeremy is supportive but also shares his concerns about the possibility of needing to go to the hospital if things go pear-shaped.

"You heard the midwife. She said it's really rare to need medical intervention. But, if I have to go to the hospital, I will." I rub my belly. "I want Jack to be healthy."

Jeremy maneuvers the truck into a spot in the newspaper's parking lot. He side-eyes the building. "Are you sure about meeting the reporter right now?"

I suck in a steadying breath. "Yes."

We stride past the entrance and I smile at the receptionist.

"Good afternoon. I'm here to see Richard."

"Of course, Lady Ann, he's been expecting you." She waves us through.

I knock on his doorframe. "Sorry I'm late."

"It's not a problem." Richard stands but pauses as he arches a brow at Jeremy. "Am I allowed to hug her?"

Jeremy steps aside and mutters, "That better be *all* you do."

I allow Richard a brief embrace, then he leans on his desk. "Why do I get the feeling you are here to disappoint me, Ann?"

"Did you get the articles I sent you?"

"Yes, I did." He crosses his arms over his chest. "But what about our deal? I gave you the address so you could find the rebels, and I even aided in the rescue."

"Richard..." I shake my head. The baby's father's name is the only bargaining chip I have left. I can't give him the name until *after* Ryan announces the

245

government changeover.

"Why is it such a big deal? I mean, won't the truth come out eventually? It's no big secret. It's either your former fiancé King Christian, your old flame King Ryan, or a rebel that got *too* close."

Jeremy steps into the reporter's face, but I put my hand against his chest to stop him. I turn to Richard. "How long have we known each other?"

"Since grade school."

"And do you *trust* me?"

"Of course I do, but this..."

I lift a hand, stopping his protests. "Then trust me when I say it does not matter who the biological father is because I want this child to have a wonderful life, without looking over *his* shoulder."

"It's a *male*?" His eyes twinkle at the juicy tidbit.

"Yes, and I can give you his name too. I know it's not what we agreed on, but would it be a fair trade... for now?"

"You're right. It's not exactly what you promised me. I mean, I did run into an armed facility to retrieve you."

I dangle my ring in his face. "Would this soften the blow?"

He examines the jewelry. "Who's the lucky guy?"

I elbow Jeremy. "The *rebel*."

"Really? He's *not* your type."

"He's smart, cunning, and puts me first." I wink at my fiancé. "He's exactly my type."

Richard isn't convinced. "Can you *trust* him after everything that's happened?"

"What did you say?" Jeremy growls.

I shoo away his anger. "Richard, I trust Jeremy with my life."

The reporter assesses us for a long minute. He racks his hair with his fingers. Then nods. "Congratulations."

The response is forced, but at least he's attempting to be friendly. I'm not sure if it's because of his engrained manners or the fact that the rebel is two seconds away from clawing him in the face like an angry rooster.

Jeremy narrows his gaze as his jaw ticks. Richard offers a hand. The rebel snatches his wrist. "I hope there're *no* hard feelings, Dick."

Richard squeezes. "Ann may trust you now. But I'll be around when you *mess* up or get yourself killed in your line of work." He shrugs. "It's a matter of time."

My fiancé prepares to lunge but I calm him. "I'm very happy with my decision to spend the rest of my life with Jeremy." I clear my throat at my friend. "Richard, why don't you stop by the house in the next week or so."

"Are you that confident that he'll mess up so soon?"

"Richard," I warn as I rub my temples. "No. The nursery will be set up and I'll have some new equipment around the farm so there'll be plenty of things for you to report on."

"If you feed me, then you have a deal."

"As long as you keep your negativity at home, then you'll be welcome to stay for dinner."

"I'll do my best to behave." He returns to his leather chair. "If you aren't going to reveal the daddy as promised. Maybe I can guess from the baby's name?"

"You can certainly try." I smirk. "It's Jack." I grab

Jeremy's hand and stride out.

Once we get into the truck, Jeremy grumbles, "That guy is a jerk. I would love to *hate* him, but he has some balls."

"He's a good man."

"Who has his heart set on having *you*." He pulls onto the main road, and the trees pass by in a blur.

"Well, it's a good thing that my heart belongs to you."

When we arrive at the house, I eagerly plop into my recliner to remove my shoes. "What a day."

"I'll get the chickens wrangled up. Why don't you put your feet up and read, and I'll make you some coffee on my way back inside." He kisses me softly and massages my swollen ankles.

"That sounds wonderful. Make sure Whitey isn't hiding in the tree again."

"I'll even check the bushes. Do you want me to grab you a chick to pet while you relax?"

"Could you bring them all?"

He chuckles. "I'll also grab a towel, so they don't get your lap dirty."

"Can we diaper train them so they can sleep inside the house like Snowball?"

"Won't we have enough diapers to change?"

"Your mom and Karen will live close by. They can help."

I wiggle into the cushions with a paperback. I don't want the chicks to live in the house, but I wanted to see if Jeremy would deny me and demand that he gets dibs on the next house pet. He might think I forgot, but

I haven't. My soon-to-be husband will have his dog before I have my emotional support hen.

His lips linger on my forehead. "I love you. You can have whatever you want, if you do the task of popping the child out."

I giggle as his stubble tickles my face. "Deal."

Jeremy pulls his boots on and I smirk while wondering what I did to be worthy of this man's devotion.

Missing Piece

I slip out of bed to say good morning to the flock. I love that Jeremy helps around the farm, but I miss my alone time with my ladies. I rub my belly. And I should enjoy it while it lasts. My toe collides with a hard object, and I yelp. I rub the sleep from my eyes. There are boxes littering the living room.

Who knew baby stuff could take up so much space?

I maneuver around the changing table, only to smack my hip on the corner of the crib container. I kick it in retaliation, and instantly regret it. We need to build the furniture, so it's not sitting in the middle of the walkway. Why Jeremy thought it'd be a good idea to leave everything here is beyond me.

I smack my forehead. *Duh.* The poor guy is still recovering from his injuries, which means he instructed the delivery man to leave them past the front door until Vinny or Dan can assist him.

I start a pot of coffee and enjoy the familiar scent as it fills the softly lit kitchen, while the sun begins to make its presence known to the rest of the world. At least I was able to convince my fiancé to drink *my* favorite dark bean. He won't admit it, but it's better than the sludge he chose at the grocery store. It costs more but it's locally roasted and organic. Plus, Karen talked the owner into giving us a great deal when we discussed selling it at the café.

I slip my feet into my boots before I release the beasts from their confinement. They dash past me, then ruffle their feathers as the gusty breeze pushes them towards the warm pen. Some scurry back, while others brave the cold to scratch the yard for goodies. I sprinkle some freeze-dried mealworms into their dust bath area to encourage their treasure hunt. Once they settle into their routine, I examine the blue sky. It's the perfect day. There's no sign of rain or snow, and the air smells sweet with a hint of ice.

"I would have done that for you."

I smirk at my shirtless man, admiring how low his sweatpants hang. "Aren't you cold?"

He stretches, causing his pants to dip a little more. "Nope." Then he cringes and holds his side. "How long is this going to take to heal?"

"The process would be quicker if you'd stop trying to do everything you aren't supposed to do."

His grin makes me melt. "I like to break the rules with you." I roll my eyes, but my cheeks heat. "You better watch it, Willy," he adds while directing his glare at the rooster in question.

I giggle as the self-proclaimed ruler of the coop takes a running leap at Jeremy. My fiancé scoops up the ruffled chicken and shoves him into the crook of his arm. "I'm the *King* of this roost, and you'd better get used to it." My brows lift. "You are the Queen of the coop and my equal." He kisses my forehead.

I stroke Willy as I address Jeremy. "You sure know how to handle a cock."

His lip twitches. "I'd love to give you a more intimate demonstration of my abilities."

We turn our attention to Dicky as he attempts to free his buddy from Jeremy. "Here's your chance to show me you can handle *two* cocks at once." I bump my hip against his as I brush past him to return to the warmth of the kitchen.

His chuckle is muffled as I close the door and shake off my boots.

I glance at my text messages. I'm supposed to meet

Karen sometime this week to go over details for a last-minute event. It's a wedding reception for a client with deep pockets and a tight schedule. This'll be our first big project together and we want it to go perfectly. My phone vibrates in my palm and I answer quickly.

"Hi, Ann."

"Ryan?" I can't hide my disappointment.

"Is this a bad time?"

I pour my coffee and take a gulp. "No, I thought you were Karen. What can I help you with?"

"I know it's short notice, but I had an opening in my schedule and I was wondering if I could come by to visit Jack's grave today?"

"It's kind of busy around here." I tap my finger on my lip. "The boys are planning on putting together baby furniture. But maybe you could lend them some muscle while you are here."

"Jeremy doesn't have enough of that to go around?" Ryan taunts, but I hear the smirk behind it.

The man in question saunters in, flaunting every curve. "He has *more* than enough." I peek at the drawstrings of his pants. "But he's still healing after the raid."

"Are you talking about me?" My fiancé bristles. "Who is that?"

I twirl my hair, feigning innocence. "Just an old boyfriend."

Jeremy snatches my phone. "Who's this?" He narrows his eyes at me, but I'm already sauntering away with my mug.

I snuggle into my recliner and open my laptop. I'll let them figure out what they want to do. I type in the projection costs of the event and email them to Karen. I guess working in the office at the Palace did teach me a few useful things.

"Your work wife is calling." Jeremy leaves my phone on the side table. "And your ex is on his way with his wife to visit your dad's gravesite."

"Well, when you say it like that, it sounds a little ridiculous." I kick his butt with the tip of my foot.

"Because it is. Now, if you'll excuse me, I should put on some actual clothes, so his wife doesn't jump me and make this situation *more* awkward."

"I'm not scared to fight her. Even pregnant," I grumble.

"Karen's on the phone," he reminds me.

"Hey, girl." I slurp the last drop of my sanity from my glass. "Did you get my email?"

"Yes, but there's a problem."

I straighten and scroll through my notes. "Everything should be in order, but I'll triple-check."

"It's nothing on our end, Ann. It's the customer. She wants to have the reception *tonight*."

"What?" I reassess our inventory sheet. "It will take some work, but we have most of the equipment in storage, except for the custom cake because she never made the final decisions for that."

"I'll contact her, ask the bakery if they can manage a rush order, and get the crew to collect the items we need." She taps on her screen as she multitasks. "Can you meet me in a few hours to assist with the setup?"

"His highness and Cherie are coming over but I'm sure they don't need me to babysit them."

"Shoot. I was trying to volunteer Vinny and Dan

to help us, but they are on their way to your house to assemble baby furniture."

"I can reroute them if you want?"

"No, they are excited about this. Especially Vinny. He thinks he's superior because he has experience with children," she scoffs. "Little does he remember, Christian gifted us all our furniture and we never had to assemble anything."

I smirk at the memory. "I almost forgot."

"Apparently he did too," she grumbles.

"If you're going to the café and Vinny is here, who's staying with the twins?"

"The nanny, so I can devote my full attention to party preparation and Vinny can still get his weekly bro time."

"Are you sure this is worth all the hassle? Maybe we should back out."

"Trust me, Ann. This will be the talk of the town when we are done with it. I promise."

"But… it's a lot of work and so little time."

"Do you doubt our abilities?"

"No?"

Her laughter eases my anxiety. "We got this. Oh! I have a call coming in from the bakery. Let me go. I'll see you soon. Kisses!" She hangs up before I can reply to her weird send-off. She always keeps me on my toes. I don't know how Vinny handles her 24/7.

"I hope you're dressed." Vinny pops his head around the corner.

"The door was unlocked so we let ourselves in." Dan waves from behind him.

"About damn time," Jeremy grumbles as he adjusts his tactical pants. "We've got a lot of work to do."

"Don't boss us around, Mr. Alpha. Save that bedroom talk for your lady." Vinny shoulder-checks Jeremy before kneeling by the first box with a knife. "Remember... we are here as your *guests,* to help *you.*"

"What's got your panties in a wad?" My fiancé hugs his brother, then helps Vinny untangle bubble wrap from a piece of hardware.

"Karen is freaking out with everything going on and she's acting like a dictator."

"She seemed chill and confident on the phone with me," I interject.

All three men blink at me, as if they forgot I was sitting in the same room.

"Shouldn't you be primping for your meeting with his highness?" Vinny asks.

Jeremy whacks the soon-to-be-dead man with the instruction manual. "Why would she primp for him?"

"Don't hit me," Vinny growls.

Dan throws his palms out to separate them. "It was paper, Vinny." He pivots to his brother. "Can we channel our energy into something more productive?"

The doorbell chimes. I hurry to answer it before World War III breaks out, because we ought to have the crib done *before* Jack's arrival. The entrance swings open and flowers are shoved in my face. I cough the sudden fragrance out of my throat.

"Cherie," Ryan warns.

"What? You asked me to hold them, but now that we are here, I'm giving them to her," she barks.

I guess they haven't made up yet.

255

I sidestep to let them pass. "You guys might want to come inside before people see you fighting."

"There's no one of importance out here anyway," Cherie snaps, but brushes past me.

Once she's out of earshot, I lean into Ryan. "Did you *force* her to come here?"

He rubs the back of his neck. "I wanted to spend time with her outside the Palace walls."

I smack his arm. "You should bring her to the beach or lake, not to your ex-girlfriend's house."

Cherie stands at the picturesque window overlooking the backyard. She's not wearing her normal fancy attire, but a long black skirt and a floral top with a scarf wrapped around her delicate neck. Even if she's snippy, her body language is more relaxed than before.

I nudge his highness towards his wife. "Fix this," I whisper.

"How?" he hisses.

I shove the floral arrangement into his chest and pivot to the Queen. "Cherie, I can give you a tour of the property if you want." Her shoulder lifts but she remains singularly focused. "Ryan, you can visit the headstone whenever you are ready."

"Great idea." He nods to the guards he brought, and they exit.

I join Cherie. I admire the layout of the farm with its grassy fields and tall trees. *How does she see this land?*

I sneak a peek and notice she's not interested in the scenery, only the slouched figure trudging along the beaten path towards the rear of the property. Once he's out of view, she tilts her head towards me. "I heard you were starting your own business."

"Karen and I bought a local café from a widowed father who lost his wife. He needs the money to take care of his young child." I shrug. "And Christian always overpaid me."

Her lip twitches. "He may have been firm, but he was very *generous* to those he loved."

I rub my arms. "But not so kind to those he considered to be his enemy." I side-eye Jeremy as he twists a screwdriver.

She follows my gaze and nods. "Are you looking for investors to assist with the financial burden?"

She has my full attention. "Why do you ask?"

"Well, as you may know, my father loves small businesses with a sappy tale like yours. So if you need an investor, I might be able to put in a good word for you."

"I'll keep that in mind."

"Have you made a business plan?"

What is she up to? Is she really trying to help?

"Yes."

"Have you taken your recent fame into consideration?"

"My *fame*?"

"People view you as Saint Ann. You are a celebrity, and they will come from all over to buy your products because they are from *you*."

"Really? Isn't that exploitation?"

"How? They get what they want, and you get more profits to support yourself, employees, and investors. Plus, if you go digital, you can sell online and ship to individuals who aren't local but want to support your cause."

"I didn't think about that."

"It's a suggestion." She pivots to watch her husband as he kneels at the graves, and the sadness returns to her pretty face.

After everything that's happened, I feel I need to explain to her what transpired between the King and me. "When Ryan and I thought we were going to be crushed under the rubble during the Palace raid, we slept together. It was a split-second decision that was made when we were going through our own mental and physical turmoil." I sigh, allowing the truth to escape. "Once we were rescued and we found out Christian was dying, that grief tore us to shreds and we went our separate ways. What we did in that safe room was a mistake." She meets my gaze and I hold it. "Believe me when I say he and I are *over* and I'm very sorry that we hurt you. You didn't deserve that."

Tears swim in her eyes. "I love him so much it's painful." She releases a shuddering breath. "I don't know if I can get through to him. I feel like I'm constantly trying to force him to love me."

"I know we've both seen our share of heartbreak, especially at the hands of the monarchy. That's why this government changeover is so important. With this transformation, Ryan can do whatever he wants and be whatever he desires. Then he can focus on what's really important... *you*."

"He doesn't want me."

"If you truly believed that, you wouldn't be fighting for your marriage."

Cherie touches my elbow. "Thank you for the encouragement."

I squeeze her hand. "I'm *not* your enemy. Heck, we could even be friends if you'd pull that stick out of your butt." She rolls her eyes. "So, it's stuck up there? Bummer."

The front door opens and the man in question enters. "What's stuck?" Ryan joins us.

"Nothing." Cherie assesses her husband's red-rimmed eyes. "If you'll excuse me, I'm going to use the restroom." She gracefully bypasses our group.

"That toilet might need two *flushes* for you, Queenie!" Jeremy shouts at her back. The guys laugh as red creeps up her majesty's ears. The door slams shut, and they cackle louder. "I'm not sure the royal rear can handle the downgrade to single-ply."

I chuck a manual at the instigator's head and he refocuses on the final box.

"What were you and Cherie talking about?" Ryan asks as he kneels to assist the other men.

"She's interested in investing in the café."

"That sounds like Cherie. She loves to help others. It's one of the reasons I fell in love with her."

"I'm starting to see that side of her too."

He tugs plastic wrap off the crib rail. "I'm glad. You two could be friends. You actually have a lot in common."

"Ann suggested the same thing." Her highness flutters into our conversation.

"I recommended something else too but was shot down." I smirk at my new pal.

"Are you ready to leave?" She elegantly ignores my comment. "We have a teleconference in about an hour and I want to adjust my casual attire."

"Why? You look beautiful," the King declares.

She tugs on her skirt. "They'll expect me in a dress."

"Well, your King says otherwise."

"Okay, Romeo, help us lift this," Jeremy gripes.

Ryan follows the trio down the hall. When he returns, he points to the fireplace with mischief written all over his smug face. "I can't believe it was a year ago, in this very spot, that you and Dan slept together."

The room grows deathly quiet. I peek at the brothers. Dan's eyes are wide while Jeremy gives him a dark glare.

I pinch Ryan's arm. "Why are you causing trouble? That isn't the whole story. Dan was helping me with blizzard preparations until he was snowed in. Then the power went out and we literally *slept* in front of the fireplace."

"Wasn't that the time Ryan stole the Palace helicopter? Right before the flu epidemic?" Cherie tilts her head at her husband. "Like his brother, he has major *jealousy* issues. Don't you?" She elbows him in the stomach, making him expel a puff of air. "It's time to go. Say your farewells, dear."

"Can I show you their nursery first?" Ryan recovers. "It's giving me ideas for ours." He tugs her towards the room.

"*Our* nursery?" she inquires. "I'm not pregnant."

"Well, eventually, you might be." He clears his throat. "I've always thought we'd have at least two or three because you love children. I even made sketches of some of my layout ideas." He rustles around in his pocket and hands her his phone. "See?"

Cherie's lip quivers as she zooms in. "You are drawing again?"

"Yes, but I like how they have the crib positioned against the wall by the window." He points. "What do you think? I know how you love natural light."

She wraps her arms around him. "It's perfect."

He embraces his wife and kisses her hair.

"Now, we're only missing one more very important item to make the room complete," Jeremy announces.

I scan the space with its cherrywood changing table, spacious dresser, crib, padded rocking chair, plush rugs, nightlights, and stocked closet. "What piece are we missing?"

"Little Jack."

Death by Napkins

"Weren't you supposed to leave twenty minutes ago?" Jeremy yells from the living room.

"Women take forever to get ready for everything," Vinny announces.

I hear the men clink beers and chuckle. I snatch my purse and dash past the trio as they sip their well-earned drinks and watch wrestling.

"I'm running late because his highness took forever to leave, then I had to pick up all the leftover Styrofoam from *your* mess," I snip. "I'll see you guys later. Please don't forget that Karen is bringing the kids over for dinner, so don't start a boxing match while I'm away and destroy the house."

"That was one time." Vinny smirks. "And we replaced the lamp we broke."

"Well, how about not breaking anything this time?" I peck Jeremy on the cheek. "Bye." He tugs me closer and devours my mouth—the acidic beer taste makes me gag. I shove him away. "Gross."

"It's only one drink."

"It's enough to make me feel queasy." I wrinkle my nose.

"Text me when you're on your way home, so I can get the house ready for the kids and prep for the meal." Jeremy smacks my butt. "Now hurry up so you can return to me."

"You could come with me," I purr.

"No way!" Vinny barks. "This is the only kid-free time I get all week."

"You can stay as long as you want. You don't need Jeremy to hold your hand."

Vinny snatches Jeremy's wrist. "What if I do?"

Jeremy tugs his arm free before turning to me. "Don't work too hard."

"I'll try not to." I jingle my keys. "Bye, boys."

"Took you long enough," Karen huffs out.

"I'm sorry. This pregnancy brain is killer. I left my keys in my pocket and forgot they were in there when I went to the bathroom. So when I bent down to go, they fell out."

"In the..."

"Yup. In the toilet."

"Disgusting."

"Tell me about it. Then I spent fifteen minutes sanitizing them. I'm sorry." I hug her.

"You're excused *this time*."

"And when your kids flush weird things down the toilet, I'll let you have a few *get out of trouble* passes too."

She laughs and guides me to the café. "Thanks."

"Did anyone get upset when you closed early?"

"No, we offered them twenty percent off their next purchase for the inconvenience."

"Wow, that's generous."

"Trust me, I'm charging the client enough to cover

those costs and more."

"You never told me who's paying for all this. Even the paperwork has her listed as *rich lady*."

"Karen." We both pivot as Justin jogs over. "I left the sound system and microphone in the back for you." The mechanic smiles at me. "Well, look who finally showed up to help."

I hug him. "Thank you for letting us borrow your stereo."

"Don't mention it," a gruff voice hollers from the mechanic shop. "I need to get back there before Dad loses it. I'll see y'all later." Justin dips his head in farewell, then rushes out.

My eyes widen as I look around the immaculate space. The café is always clean, but this is above and beyond. There's not a speck of dust on the light fixtures and the floor is sparkling. Even the windows have been scrubbed, allowing the natural light to brighten the interior.

"What do you think?"

"It's incredible."

Karen shrugs. "I put my Palace training to good use." She tugs at my wrist. "I rearranged the furniture to allow for a better flow. We'll set up the food on this table. The cake will be on a stand and we'll wheel it out for the reveal."

"So the cake will be done in time?"

"I hope so." She holds up a hand. "I have my best man on it. If he can't do it, no one can."

"What do you need me to do?"

She leads me to a chair. "These black roses need to be clipped and placed in this vase. Then you have to add an LED light on the bottom, here. And the finishing touch…" She places a clear dome lid over the vase, sealing the light and flower inside. "See?"

"It's gorgeous." I finger the petals that symbolize so much.

"Then, after assembling these centerpieces, you can work on the napkins. They want them folded so they look like tiny books." She points to the step-by-step instructions.

"I never knew you could do that with a napkin. That's very clever. I'm actually looking forward to creating these."

"Good, because it'll take you a few hours to complete."

I scan the materials. "I'll need to pee every hour so it might take longer."

Karen laughs. "I forgot how fun the last trimester is."

"How are the kids doing?"

"Olivia likes to beat up Carter, then cries when he retaliates," she groans. "If they're like this now, I'm not looking forward to the terrible twos when everyone says they're at their worst." Her cell phone rings. "I need to take this. Let me know if you need anything."

Karen dashes down the hall while juggling her folder and phone. I smirk. Even though she's running around like a chicken with her head cut off, she's happy. It's that sparkle in her eyes and the excitement in her words that tells me as much. It's also the same way I feel about my hens. I click a picture of the sample Karen made and text it to Jeremy, telling him I want them for my wedding whenever we get around to it. Then I get to work.

The flowers aren't difficult. But these napkins keep

flopping around and losing their shape. I never want to mess with linens again. A few hours later, I'm about done.

"Hey, girl." Karen saunters in. "Those look amazing." She beams at the vases. "And these..." She smirks at the napkins.

"I'm fixing them," I grumble. "They're more delicate than the plants."

"I would stay and assist you, but Vinny needs me."

"Anything serious?"

"No. He took over for the nanny and the kids ganged up on him. Olivia knocked over a shelf and Carter peed all over him." Her lip twitches. "And he can't shower until I relieve him of his parental duties."

"What else needs to be done before the client arrives?"

"Just these sad linens."

"They'll look like books by the time the guests arrive," I huff as Karen walks to the front door. "Oh, are we still on for dinner tonight? We can always reschedule if you don't think Vinny will be groomed in time."

"I'll make sure he's ready to go. Do you need us to bring over any sides or drinks?"

"Nope." I shoot a reminder text to Jeremy to preheat the oven for the lasagna. "We have everything at the house."

"I'm looking forward to relaxing after all of this." Karen waves her hands around the café.

I take in our masterpiece. "It reminds me of a storybook wedding."

"Thank you for your help."

266

"We make a pretty good team." I grin, and she runs over and hugs my neck. "Love you, sis."

"Love you too."

"I'll see you soon." She waves before closing the door.

I scour the internet for videos, attempting to fix my mistake. By the time I need to leave, the napkins closely resemble open pages. Hopefully everyone's happy with them, because I'm done.

I send a message to my fiancé, letting him know I'm on my way home, and clean my work area so the staff can finish the rest of the preparations for tonight.

Maybe I should grab an extra head of lettuce from the produce fridge so I can assemble a quick salad to go with dinner?

I'm sure the restaurant can spare one. I usually end up bringing home a bunch at the end of the week, because the quality is only good enough for animal consumption and chickens love to peck them and gobble the insects the deteriorating vegetable attracts.

I push open the door and freeze. "Jock?"

He pivots to face me. "Lady Ann, it's wonderful to see you."

I tilt my head at the towering work of art demanding his attention. "Is that chocolate cake?"

"My famous, special dark-fudge cake." He readjusts the third tier. "What do you think?"

"It smells heavenly."

He nods to the scraps by the stove. "Have a taste. I won't tell anyone."

A shiver runs up my spine. I feel like I'm a naughty child, eating dessert before dinner. I shove a chunk in my mouth and moan. The flavors create a symphony of sweetness.

"Is there too much cocoa?"

"You can never have too much cocoa." I plop another sliver in my mouth. "I'm going to have to hire you to make my wedding cake. This is amazing."

"It would be an honor to create that for you and Jeremy." A spoon scrapes a bowl. "This is between the layers."

I sample the syrup. "Oh. Is that strawberry?"

"Yes, fresh from the greenhouse."

"That's going to really complement the dessert. I hope the customer appreciates all of your hard work."

"They will."

Before he can elaborate, there's a tap on the front door. I stride over with Jock in tow. "I thought Karen told the staff to park in back and use the employee entrance?"

I tug open the door and my jaw drops. There's a man in a pristine suit. He removes his hat and bows. "Lady Ann, I have arrived to escort you to your next great adventure." He waves his palm to the horse-drawn carriage.

"They are beautiful." My hand grazes the beasts as they stand proudly. The closest one shakes his mane and paws the ground. "Who set this up?"

"Your fiancé."

My neck snaps back to the man. "Jeremy did this?"

He counters with a question of his own as he opens the carriage door. "Are you willing to take the next step with him?"

My brain can't compute what's going on. "But Karen and the kids are coming over for lasagna," I blurt out. "Oh, I forgot the lettuce!" I turn back to the restaurant.

"Why don't you see what's in store for you, and *if* you need lettuce, give me a call and I'll bring it to you." Jock assists me inside the carriage. "Do you want me to ride with you?"

I glance to the man in the suit, then back to Jock. "Would you? I'm feeling a bit overwhelmed."

He settles in beside me and squeezes my hand. "Don't forget to enjoy the ride. Your fiancé did all of this for you," he repeats, and the reminder soothes my frayed nerves.

The driver cracks the reins and the carriage jerks forward. Hooves pitter-patter on the gravel and the sound makes me giddy.

Where are they leading me?

The sleeping fruit trees wave in the wind, encouraging us to continue our journey, while livestock lift their heads as they chew their hay. Some even stroll in the direction we are traveling as if they're as curious about our final destination as I am. The country landscape twinkles as the sun descends, the tip almost kissing the horizon. The beasts slow before they glide into my driveway, and I gasp. The house is decorated with twinkling golden lights.

"Jock? What are you doing here?" Karen arches a brow as she helps me step down.

"Ann was a little hesitant to travel with a stranger. But she's better now." The chef winks in my direction.

"Don't worry, ma'am, I'll take him back to the café." The driver tips his hat before he coaxes the horses to trot forward.

My mouth can't form words and my legs are shaking. "When did you do all of this?"

Karen guides me through the entrance. It's booming with activity. "Everyone has been working tirelessly since you left this morning. Dan's rebel team is building a gazebo, Jeremy and May are gathering the flock, Jock is designing your cake, Vinny is setting up the chairs, and Elizabeth is paying for everything. Now, come on. It's time to make you into a goddess, so when you walk down the aisle, your man will beg you to share your body with him."

"Elizabeth and Sally are here?"

"Yes, we made sure everyone important in your life is present." She fluffs my hair. "Are you surprised?"

My lip trembles. "Yes, I'm waiting to wake up from this fantasy. Ouch!" I rub my arm. "What was that for?"

"To remind you this is real." She walks me to my room. "Close your eyes and let me work through this mess. We have to get you ready for your rebel hunk."

I do as she says. I can't believe everyone worked together to do this for me. And right under my nose! Heck, I even made the centerpieces and cloth napkins. I laugh to myself. When we were planning this event, Karen always asked for my opinion, and now I know why.

"Where are the kids?"

"Sally is helping the nanny keep them in line until Vinny and I can sit with them at the wedding."

"I'm glad you brought them."

"Just remember you said that when they're crying or chasing the chickens." Karen sets the brush down. "Okay, now that your hair is manageable, let's see if the dress fits."

I cringe at my belly. Karen tugs a gown out of my closet and I squeal. "That's the feather dress I picked out."

"Your man helped us with measurements. Apparently, you sleep so soundly he was able to get a tape measure around you. Plus, at the baby shower, we played *guess the circumference* of your stomach."

"How long have you guys been planning this?"

"A little while." She helps me with the fabric. "That was the easy part. Now let's see if the zipper will go up." It tightens but glides in place without a problem.

I admire the soft material in the mirror. Even with my protruding baby bump, it's still the perfect outfit for the occasion. I adjust my cleavage. "I think Jeremy got my cup size wrong."

"Or he wanted to see more of it." Her lips twitch. "He has the patience of a saint. I can't believe you guys haven't done it yet."

"After the mess I got in with Ryan, I wasn't taking any chances." I smooth the skirt. "I hope Jeremy is better than the Prince," I blurt out, and my face turns scarlet.

"Now that's the kind of girl talk I'm looking forward to. After you pop the child out, we are going to have a girls' weekend to chat about men." She dangles a pair of wispy earrings in front of me. "Here's something borrowed. I wore them when Vinny and I eloped, and I know they'll bring you luck. But I want them back for my daughter's big day." She clips tiny blue diamonds to my dark hair. "And here's something blue."

I angle my head until the light dances across the gems. "What's left?"

She jiggles a cosmetic bag in front of me. "Do you

271

want to go all natural?"

"You can add some lipstick." I pucker up for her.

She applies a thin layer. "And we made the dress a little shorter, which gives you the option to wear flats or go barefoot."

"I can go barefoot?"

"Elizabeth ordered space heaters so the ground won't be too cold." She laughs. "And it's *your* special day."

I curl my toes. "Let's go naked."

Karen kneels while shaking a bottle of royal-blue polish. "Then I'm painting these piggies."

"Thank you."

"Don't thank me yet. We still have work to do, and you still need something *new*. Which May volunteered to grab. So prepare yourself."

"We better hurry. My bladder will only last one, maybe two hours tops, before I'll need you to help me out of this dress."

Karen scrambles around. "And we need to get the wedding started before it gets dark."

"A ceremony at night sounds magical. Especially with all the lights hanging around the house."

After Karen curls my hair, there's a tap on the open door. We both turn to see Jeremy in a pressed black suit. He looks stunning.

"I told you it's bad luck to see the bride in her dress."

"And I explained that I don't give a f—"

"Karen, you've made me into a blushing bride. Why don't you get ready to be my matron of honor?"

"Then who'll sit with the kids?"

"Sam," Jeremy declares. "Because Vinny and Dan are my groomsmen."

"Why didn't I know about this?"

"Because I don't have to explain myself to you," he reminds her with a smirk.

She pivots to me and rolls her eyes. "I'm ignoring him until further notice. I'm honored to stand by your side today and for the rest of our lives." She hugs me. "I'll see you out there." Then my bestie shoulder-checks my fiancé on her way out.

"She's a charmer," he grumbles at her back. She flips him the bird, then shuts the door. When he meets my gaze again, he fidgets with his sleeve. "Listen. I know this is a lot for you, and at first, I thought you'd love the surprise but now I'm having second thoughts. Not about marrying you, but the fact that we didn't coordinate everything together." He straightens his posture. "So, if you want me to send everyone home and do your dream wedding properly, all you have to do is ask."

I readjust his tie. The color really makes his icy eyes pop. "This is the sweetest thing anyone has ever done for me. You gathered my closest friends, tricked me into designing my own reception, and even measured me while I slept."

"The last part was fun."

I wrap my arms around his neck. "I love you. I want to marry you today in front of all our friends."

"And flock."

I smirk. "Yes, and our flock."

His lips brush mine. "Then let's get this party started."

We hold hands and stride to the back door. There's a small group gathered in front of us. "I'll be the handsome one at the end of the path." He kisses my palm. "See you soon." Jeremy leaves me in the doorway while May steps forward with an object roughly wrapped in newspaper. I carefully tear the edges aside and smile at the homemade gift.

"I've been collecting feathers as the chickens *molted*. I may have *accidentally* plucked some too." She taps a few. "And these are *split feathers* that I found. I glued them together to make you a crown."

I place the mixture of plumage on the top of my head. "How does it look, May?"

Her face brightens and she squeezes me. "I'm so glad it fits!"

"Me too." I kiss the top of her head.

"May, here's your bucket." Elizabeth hands it to the girl. "Remember, you're Ann's flower girl, okay."

"Technically, she's my *feather* girl." I wink.

May skips outside with Scarlett close behind on a lead. Once their feet hit the grass, the red hen pecks for bugs while she waddles with her owner.

"Elizabeth, thank you."

She rubs my arms. "No, thank you. You've opened my eyes to so many things. I owe you a great deal."

"You owe me nothing." I hug her.

"I tied them to her feet like you asked." Sally passes Snowball to Elizabeth.

I gawk at the hen's lacey blue dress. It's intricate yet simple. Even her toes are painted to match. I finger her leg and tilt my head. "Are these our wedding bands?"

"Yes, Snowball wanted to contribute so she's your

ring bearer." Elizabeth strokes the sweet girl. "And I'm officiating the ceremony. It'll be the country's first legal marriage involving a member of the Black Rose."

"I never thought of that," I whisper.

"Don't worry, I know how you dislike having the press on your property," Elizabeth adds. "So I only invited your friend from school. The one who helped you in the raid."

"Richard's here?"

"Yes, and I warned him to be on his *best* behavior. Plus, he's to submit the article to you for review before he can publish it." She pauses as soft music starts to strum in the breeze. "That's my cue." She kisses my cheek. "Good luck, dear. You look beautiful."

Elizabeth sets Snowball down and they elegantly parade towards the small crowd. I spot Tammy sitting near Brad, with Olivia and Carter nestled between them. Richard is snapping photos from the side, and somehow they corralled the entire flock—the chickens are eagerly searching for crumbs as they maneuver around other guests.

A sniffle causes me to turn to Sally. She dabs her cheeks. "All those years ago, I never imagined I'd actually unite our families. I mean, your mom and I joked about it but that's all it was—something to giggle about as we watched our children grow."

"I wish they were here," I whisper.

"Me too, sweetie." Sally clears her throat. "Jeremy wanted you to have a one-of-a-kind bouquet."

"Aw," I coo as she hands me a tall basket with the chirping chicks huddled inside. "They really shouldn't be away from their heat bulb this long."

Sally strokes their fluff. "They have warmer feathers

growing in. Plus, we positioned heaters around the area to keep everyone toasty."

"They even have blue bowties." I rub my cheek over their tiny heads.

"I should find my seat."

"Wait." I grab her elbow. "Can you walk me down the aisle?"

"I'm no substitute for Jack or AnnaBelle."

I rest my palm over her chest. "But they are living inside here, and soon, you'll legally be my mother-in-law."

Her lip quivers. "If that's what you want, nothing would make me happier."

I clutch our feathered children and tuck my arm through Sally's. "Lead the way."

The grass tickles my feet as we follow the path leading to Jeremy. May does an impressive job as flower girl. Most of the ground is dotted with black, white, and speckled plumage. Jeremy's gaze shimmers when he notices his mom is a part of the precession, and I wonder if he's thinking about his father. Dan swipes at his cheek before patting his brother on the shoulder and whispering something that has them both chuckling.

"They're observing the main event too." Sally nods to the headstones. "We made sure they were close to the action." She squeezes my wrist, then passes me to her son. "I love you both. I'm so proud of everyone." She scans the group. "I'm grateful to be here with you all."

Jeremy and Dan embrace their mom, then she holds my bouquet and sits in the front row. Snowball chirps and demands our attention while Jeremy clasps my hands and kisses my knuckles. "It's not too late to run."

I glance at the setting sun as it glimmers behind my closest friends before meeting my soon-to-be husband's stunning blue eyes. I close my lids to let everything soak in. I'm getting married and it doesn't scare me. I feel safe and loved.

A breeze twirls over my ankles and the feathers that were caught in its vertex brush my legs as a shadowy voice whispers, *"You were destined to soar beyond these walls, not be caged within them."* And I recognize Christian's husky tone mixed with his musky scent.

My eyes pop open. But it's Jeremy who's standing in front of me, waiting for my answer. I peck him on the cheek. "Let's soar into our next adventure." I place his palms on my belly and Jack snuggles into the new warmth. *"Together."*

Better Together

Even in my wildest dreams, I never would have imagined this. I snuggle into my husband as the horse-drawn carriage trots down the gravel road. The wedding went by in a blur with many happy tears running past my cheeks. It was perfect.

Jeremy's fingertips dance over my arm. "I swore I'd never do this again."

"What? Ride in a carriage?"

"No, *tie the knot*." His thumb lifts my chin. "You reminded me that true love is worth *fighting* for."

"I am pretty amazing."

His lips brush mine. "You really are."

"You're not so bad yourself."

The horses slide to a stop as they reach our destination. The café is booming with music and friends. With the number of cars parked in the lot and grass, I'd say we are overcapacity.

My husband follows my gaze. "We wanted the wedding to be intimate, but the reception to be the party of a lifetime." He grins. "Are you ready for the night of your life?"

"Absolutely."

He tugs me inside and we are bombarded with cheers and confetti. I hug hundreds of people. All of whom have touched my life in some way, and I'm glad they could share this occasion with us. The music is mostly country with a few fun songs in the mix, like the Chicken Dance. Buffet-style trays line the wall with more food than I thought possible. They went all out with barbecue favorites and Palace picks, which include my coveted macaroons.

"I made sure they had the red velvet ones." Elizabeth nods to my plate.

I settle beside her in a quiet corner. "Did you eat anything?"

"I tried some pulled pork and baked beans."

"And?"

"I think your competitors better watch out, because this restaurant is loaded with flavor and could take over the town."

"That's very kind of you." I nibble on my sweets as I watch Karen and Vinny laugh before clinking their beers together. "Everyone looks happy," I whisper, thinking of all those who couldn't be in attendance.

"They do, don't they?"

"Are you okay?"

For a minute, I think she didn't hear me. Then I pivot to see a tear escape. Elizabeth swipes it before it falls to the floor. "After you walked down the aisle, I swear I heard..." She shakes her head. "I'm just tired."

I rub her worn hand. "What did you hear?"

"You'll think I've lost my mind."

"Try me."

She glances at May as the little girl snatches a cookie while speaking enthusiastically with Sally. "Over the past few weeks, I've been kicking myself over my choices. Did I leave the Palace when my son needed me the most? Was I running from the problems I caused and making him clean up his mother's mess?" She rubs her temple. "Did I fail Christian too? Was I so hard on him that he felt like he had to rule with an iron fist?"

"Elizabeth, your boys love you with all of their hearts."

"I've made many mistakes. I'm far from perfect."

"No one expects perfection from you."

She snorts. "Yes, they do. They always have, always will."

The disdain radiating from her shocks me. *How long has she felt this way? And now that the blinders have been removed, what will she do?*

"Only you get to choose what your future will look like," I remind her.

Elizabeth's lip twitches. "You've really grown, Ann. I'm proud of the woman you've chosen to become."

"I've had many amazing role models. And I know your sons would say the same thing about you." I tap my shoulder to hers.

"I *heard* him, Ann. Christian. He spoke clear as day before the ceremony. He told me he was watching over us. Those simple whispered words…" Her voice wavers. "I miss him." She swipes her cheek. "I know it sounds crazy…"

"I heard him too." When she meets my gaze, I add, "I think he approves of my marriage." I smirk. "Even in the afterlife, he's inserting his opinions."

We share a laugh and the pressures of our past flutter into the air before tugging us closer together.

"What's funny?" May skips to our corner.

"Bossy but loving men." I wink.

May wrinkles her nose before squeezing between me and Elizabeth. Her feet sway. "Did Elizabeth tell you she's going to be my new mommy?"

"What? Really?"

Elizabeth strokes the girl's hair. "Now that the

280

Black Rose members are pardoned, the orphans can be adopted by loving families. I submitted my request for May, and I'm confident it'll be approved."

The little girl smiles, the chocolate on her face only highlighting her natural beauty. "I can't wait to have my own flock of chickens." She nods to Snowball and Scarlett as they snuggle in a box in the corner of the room. Their eyes are closed and their breathing is steady as the party goes on around them. It seems they, too, have signed a peace treaty. Or maybe they know the mingling of families can only mean one thing — more treats if they behave and play their cards right. Between Elizabeth and May, those spoiled hens will be fat and happy for life.

"I'm surprised Sally didn't fight you for May," I blurt out.

"She has her hands full with all of the recent information from the Palace and wants time to plot her next step."

"Plus, I know Sally sees how you've bonded with this little brat." I ruffle May's hair. She giggles, then takes off into the crowd. "Were the other children able to find homes too?"

"Yes, most of them are being claimed by other ex-rebels."

"What about the compound?"

"Tammy and her partner are maintaining it, and it'll function as a safe haven for those who require a longer transitional period."

"Excuse me, ladies." Karen slides over. "Ann, it's time to reveal the cake Jock made for that annoying last-minute customer," she teases Elizabeth.

"The weather was perfect *today* and I didn't want to

waste this opportunity. Plus, they predict snow next week so you really should be thanking me." Elizabeth rises and walks with us to the unveiling.

"There you are." My husband wraps an arm around my waist.

The partygoers cheer as Jock wheels out the three-tiered masterpiece. When I saw it earlier, it was bare, but now it's marbled with intricate swirls of black, royal blue, and white. Everyone is in awe as they get a closer look. Multi-colored chocolate feathers flutter over the sides in soft wisps. They glitter and shine as if the sun's light is reflecting off them. My gaze stumbles on the item decorating the top. It's a white hen, dressed in a flowing gown that mimics my own, alongside a black rooster in a suit.

"Do you like it?" Jock questions us.

I'm at a loss for words. Jeremy offers a hand to the aging chef. "I couldn't have imagined a better dessert for the occasion. Thanks, man."

Jock tugs my husband into a hug and pats his back. "Welcome to the family."

Everyone claps, and when Jeremy pulls away, tears dance in his eyes. *Now look who's speechless?*

"Okay, let's see how this baby tastes," Karen encourages.

Heavenly. That's the only way to describe how my taste buds explode. The cake is light and fluffy but not too sweet, even with the frosting and strawberry center. When I return for my third slice, I see I'm not the only one who's overindulging.

"There won't be many leftovers." Karen warms my side. "But don't worry. I saved a chunk for your one-year wedding anniversary."

I elbow her. "You're sure we'll last that long?"

She side-eyes our husbands as they arm wrestle. Grunts echo around us. Sweat drips onto the floor. "If you two don't work out, I'm sure they'll comfort each other with the sweets."

Jeremy slams Vinny's knuckles into the table. A screaming match ensues, then they unbutton their cuffs, roll up their sleeves, and begin another round.

"Are you ready for your honeymoon?"

"I'm ready to sleep for a whole week."

My bestie laughs. "Before or after a trip to Pound Town?"

I roll my eyes at her joke.

"Don't worry, your man planned a relaxing staycation for you guys at the farm. You'll have couples massages, pedicures, manicures, and anything else your heart desires but in the comfort of your own home with your feathered companions."

"That sounds peaceful."

"The calm before the storm." She pokes my abdomen. "The midwife will be stopping in to check on Jack too."

"I could have lived without that appointment," I grumble.

"And…" She nods to the mountain of presents. "I made sure to give you plenty of lingerie and sexy-time toys." She holds up a hand. "In case you two decide to break through your cobwebs."

"Ew." I smack her. "There's no dust down there."

"Are you saying he's at least touched you?" She latches on to the juicy gossip.

283

"I beat him fair and square." The man in question wraps an arm around my shoulder, effectively putting an end to my bestie's inquisition. "I'll always be better than him."

"You smell like you worked hard for that." I grimace at his slick skin.

He taps his father's wristwatch. "It's already past midnight."

"Are you afraid I'll turn into a cinder girl?"

He chuckles. "Even if you did, I'd still have you."

"And did the carriage turn into a pumpkin and the horses into mice?"

"I wouldn't know. They left hours ago."

"Did you know chickens eat mice?" I yawn.

"Really?" He winces. "That's gross."

"Frogs too."

"That's it. We aren't eating eggs anymore in case that somehow transfers to the yolk."

We gather our things and say our goodbyes. Even Richard is still hanging around with his camera draped over his neck. Once we load into the truck, I relax in my seat. Today was hands down the best day of my life, but my social battery is drained.

Soon, we park in the driveway and turn off the car. The silence is amazing after all the crowds. "Do you want me to run you a bubble bath? Mom sent over some lavender oil. I can add some to the water," Jeremey asks.

"That sounds marvelous."

"Dan already took care of the chickens and will be tending to them for the next week, so all you have to worry about is chilling. You can read, watch movies, or sleep all you want."

"And what will you do?"

His lips brush my knuckles. "Stand by your side."

"Thank you again for all of this."

"I had tons of help. You, my wife, are very loved in this community."

"And now I get to share that love with you, my partner in crime." I slip out of the vehicle and Jeremy scoops me in his arms bridal-style before carrying me over the threshold.

"Welcome home, Mrs. Sumptor."

"It's good to be back, Mr. Sumptor."

Jeremy dips his chin and devours my mouth, not holding anything back. Telling me how he feels through this heated exchange. When he pulls away, I'm left breathless with desire.

"You know, our bedroom has an enormous bathtub."

He arches a brow. "Do you think it's big enough for two?"

"There's only one way to find out."

He quickens his pace as he carries me to the bathroom with a newfound pep in his step, and I giggle at his excitement. But I also value it. He's been patient with me. He's waited a long time, making sure I felt loved and cared for first and foremost while putting his own needs on the back burner.

Now we finally get to test the waters, to see if the wait was worth it.

Gifts

The first official day of our married life starts later than normal. We both passed out after multiple rounds of lovemaking, and now it's past noon.

"How do you feel?" Jeremy strokes my arm. "I didn't hurt you, did I?"

"Everything was perfect." I kiss his lips. "Thank you."

"No, no. Thank *you*." He nibbles my ear.

My phone clucks and I tap it. "Yes, Tammy?"

"Sally wanted me to drop off your wedding gifts. Are you two *done* yet?"

"Charming," I snip out. "We'll be out in a minute."

"Hurry up. I don't have all day."

I hang up and slap Jeremy's butt. "Tammy is at the door with gifts."

"But I only want this gift." He nuzzles my belly.

"Come on. We both need to stretch our legs and eat something."

He yawns as I shimmy out of the bed. We get dressed, then meet Miss Whiney-Butt.

"What took you so long?" she grumbles as she pushes through. "Some of these things are heavy." She shoves past us with an armful of wrapped presents. "Where do you want them?"

"The coffee table is fine," I yell over my shoulder as I stride to the SUV to collect more.

After every package is laid out, I flop on the couch with Tammy while Jeremy makes coffee.

"Elizabeth mentioned something about you having a

partner." I elbow her. "Are you and Brad a couple?"

She fidgets with a giant bow. "Brad has been my closest companion since Jeremy moved out. He was by my side when the Palace informed us that my dad was held captive in a prison camp. Held my hand as my grandfather introduced himself to me. I value his devotion and support during these trying times."

This news about her dad is shocking, but I aim to keep her in good spirits. "Is Brad also keeping your bed warm at night?"

"You're crude." She rolls her eyes, but there's a twinkle in them. "If I must define it, then we're boyfriend and girlfriend."

Jeremy sets mugs in front of us. "Not intimate friends?" He winks my way. "What do you want for breakfast, wife? Bacon, sausage, eggs, toast, or maybe some biscuits and gravy?"

"Yes." I smirk.

He chuckles and kisses my cheek. "I'll get started on it. Are you staying, Tam?" He ruffles her hair as he passes.

She smacks his back. "Brad's at the training facility with Vinny for another hour, so if you can cook as fast as you talk, then, yes, I am."

Once Jeremy turns the corner, Tammy and I sip our steamy cups. "Do you want to talk about it?"

"About which part? My cowardly grandfather, who left his own daughter to be slaughtered by the King's hands? Or my dad, who's been raised from the dead?"

I rub her arm. "Whatever you need to get off your chest."

She clutches her cup and leans into the cushions. "After the Palace pardoned the rebels, all of the containment facilities started to close down. Those places tortured innocent people..."

She's quiet for a moment and I nod. "But your dad survived and that's what's important."

"The enforcers used him. They made him apply his medical training to patch up prisoners so that they could interrogate them over a period of *days*."

"But he's gained his freedom and he'll be home before you know it," I soothe her.

"I'm afraid of how different he'll be."

"When do you get to see him?"

"I'm not sure. He was in pretty bad shape. According to the reports, he was malnourished and living in his own filth. So he's in the hospital, regaining his strength and probably some of his sanity too."

"I'm sorry." I hand her a tissue.

She pats her eyes. "Hey, I got my dad back and that's what matters, right? Wouldn't you give anything to have a second chance with Jack?"

I can only nod. I miss my father. But at the same time, I wouldn't want him to suffer like Luke.

"While you guys chat, why don't you snack on some meat." Jeremy sets a plate of bacon in front of us.

"Can we unwrap some presents?" Tammy shakes a square box.

My husband shrugs. "I don't care."

She claws the paper like it's Christmas morning. I meet Jeremy's eyes. He wants to wipe the frown off Tammy's face. Another present tumbles from the pile. *Mission accomplished.*

After we settle down for the day, Jeremy lights the logs in the fireplace. Then he tucks me into the crease of his arm. "Now I can officially say *we* did it in this exact spot."

I punch his chest. "Really?"

He kisses the top of my head. "What was your favorite gift? It's the waffle maker, isn't it?"

"Which one? We received three."

"The chicken-shaped one."

I laugh. "I like that gift but it's not the best."

"You're right. Technically, I'm the best present."

"You think very highly of yourself."

"Well, you did choose me. That makes me the luckiest man on earth." He grins.

"Cheesy."

"No, it's romantic."

"You're just trying to get in my pants," I counter.

"Again?" His fingers dip into my waistband but I swat him away.

I grab a shadow box. "This is my favorite gift." I tap the glass. "This is the stuffed animal and note my dad snuck into my bag before I was whisked to the Palace. And now it'll hang on the wall to remind me of all I've been through."

"It's everything that started you off on this crazy journey." Jeremy clears his throat before he reads the note out loud:

Ann,

I can't imagine how hard this must be for you, because for me, it's like a piece of my soul is being torn out. After your mother died, you had a lot of roles to fill. And you did an amazing job. But it is time for you to fly the coop—see, I can be funny too. You need to see what the world has to offer you and you to it. I feel I have held you back for far too long, Ann, my dear, so spread your wings. I know you will soar to some amazing heights. Remember I love you and only want the best for you. Please give this an honest try.

All my hugs,

Dad

As my father's words of wisdom echo around us, my lip quivers. I stare into the crackling embers of the fire, and I swear his baritone voice says, "It's time to fly."

Buns in the Oven

The days of lounging around and sprawling out under the covers pass too quickly and we begin our preparation to become parents. We schedule infant and first aid classes, plus tour the local hospital in case the home birth doesn't work out. It all happens in a blur.

We turn the guest room into a multipurpose office space. There's everything I need to work from home. I even set up an online scheduling system for clients to book photo shoots. I still consider myself an amateur photographer, but you have to start somewhere, and I've always loved cameras.

I scan the walls of the house. Every frame tells a story and evokes emotion. It's as if they capture the best parts of our lives and our hardest times.

A clang from the sunroom causes me to jump. I follow the grunts and lean on the open door. I'm still getting used to having a weight room in the house. I know physical fitness is important to my husband, but it's loud and smelly in here. Even with the windows open. Sweat glistens over Jeremy's abs before slithering past his waistband. I lick my lips, remembering some of the many things he's taught me during our staycation. I guess I can endure this hardship for him.

"The Palace called while you were in the office." He pats his face with a towel. "They are requesting our presence at the meeting with the Black Rose."

"Why do they need us? Tammy is the leader now."

"Because everyone on both sides trusts you." He glances over. "Plus, you started this, so you might as well see it through."

"I'm tired. My feet are swollen. Can't I just do a video chat?"

"I'd feel better if we're physically there, just in case." He tugs on his shirt, ending my peep show.

"But what about the chickens?"

"Dan will look after them." He kisses my neck. "I'm going to shower, then we can leave." My gaze drifts over his back until it lands on his rear. "Are you going to continue to drool in the corner, or follow me and watch the water show?"

"We should take my car. The seat reclines more."

Jeremy pulls onto the highway. "Your car is not bulletproof."

"And neither am I." I suck in a breath as my stomach tightens.

"Should we call Shelby again?"

"No, she said they're *false* labor pains. She also mentioned that I'll know when the real ones start."

"Maybe the doctors at the Palace can check you out too?"

"You are fussing over nothing. I'm fine."

"And you're cranky."

"Excuse me? How about you try being pregnant!" I point at him. Jeremy bites his lip and his dimple appears. I narrow my eyes. "Do you have something else to say to me, husband?"

His palm warms my thigh. "I think you might be

grouchy because Shelby put a stop to our nighttime exercises."

I slap his hand aside. "Concentrate on driving."

"You are beautiful, Ann, and soon we will be holding our baby boy. Then you can have as much alone time with me as you want."

"Except for the fact that we'll have an infant in the house." I yawn. "I'm closing my eyes. Wake me up when we get there."

When we arrive, Jeremy helps me out of the truck. The Palace was once full of surprises for me. I was enthusiastic to see what was inside. Now, I want nothing more than to return to the comfort of my farmhouse with my partner and feathered companions. I've found where I belong and couldn't be happier to live out my days there.

"Good morning, Lady Ann," a guard welcomes me. "The King is in the office."

We stride in that direction, but I pause at an open door. I detour and step inside one of my favorite spots. Bright light glitters through the tall windows. The familiar smell of old books causes a rush of endorphins to pump through my system. My finger tickles the spine of the closest novel.

"We should put your library in the office." Jeremy warms my back. "You can have your own little reading nook."

"Do you think it'll fit?"

He nibbles my ear as he whispers, "I'll make it fit."

"My books will probably be safer in there, at least until Jack is older."

"I'll make sure it gets done when we return *home*." That word fluttering between us warms my heart.

"This is where my journey began," I whisper to the endless shelves of literature. "With one wrong turn and a case of mistaken identity." I take Jeremy's hand and pull him to the staircase. "Let's get this meeting over with."

The second I open the conference room door, I'm bombarded with hugs from Tammy, Brad, Sally, and Elizabeth.

"Sally? I thought you were spending some time with Luke?"

"He wanted to be alone." She hands me a binder. "I found this at our old house in the attic."

I flip through the contents and gasp. "This is Mom's handwriting."

"These are some of her recipes she shared with me."

"Even her bread recipe..." My mind floods with memories.

"Now you can share those moments with your little one." Sally rubs my belly.

"Sorry to keep everyone waiting," the King announces as he and Cherie enter. "Let's get started."

"Over the last month, the rebels have begun merging with society, but most of them have been met by opposition," Sally begins.

"For their protection, I've employed more soldiers to aid in the transition," Ryan soothes.

"And when are we going to vote on governmental change?" Tammy demands.

"That's not on the agenda for today's discussion," Cherie *tsks* her tongue.

"The people should make that choice. The sooner the better. Especially while everything is still fresh in their minds," Tammy starts.

"We will consider that option at another date," Ryan commands.

"But that's why we're *here*, to get the process started," she pushes.

"We are coming together to negotiate the *possibilities*, not to finalize anything," he insists. "Isn't freedom enough for now?"

What has the Palace been doing since we left? Did they even bother to consider a change?

"I think a good compromise would be to *schedule* a time to vote for the modification," I interject. "Do you agree?"

Tammy groans. "If that is all *he* is willing to do, then, yes, I'll accept those terms. For now."

Ryan scratches his beard and leans into Cherie. They whisper before nodding.

"Thank you," I breathe out, grateful I don't have to play Mommy anymore between the groups.

Cherie squeezes her husband's hand and smiles. The twinkle in her eyes matches his. I'm glad they are working together.

"You are all welcome to join us for lunch in the dining room." The Queen rises to her feet.

"We appreciate the offer, but we don't want to stay any longer than we must. Especially considering your hospitality during our last visit. Thank you, King Ryan, for your time." Tammy straightens her shirt. She pivots to Jeremy and me. "Don't be strangers, you two."

"That goes both ways, Tam." Jeremy hugs her.

"Yes, it does." She brushes past us and out the door like there's a fire on her heels.

"Are you sure you don't want to take over for her?" Ryan whines. "She is bossy and prickly."

I smirk. "Tammy is the perfect person to keep the Royals in their place."

Sally taps on her phone and sighs. "I'm heading out too." She kisses my cheek and rubs my arm. "I'll be over this weekend, and we can catch up."

"Can we bake some bread?"

"Yes, and I'll bring over some nail polish and facial cream. We'll make it a girl's relaxation weekend." Sally grins while my husband clears his throat. "You and Dan are more than welcome to join in. But we'll be talking about things you might not want to discuss." She winks at me. "Karen and Sam can come too if you want."

I squeeze her hand. "Can I have you all to myself?"

Her lip quivers but she nods. "Whatever you want, *sweetheart.*"

Instead of the normal pang of fear I used to feel whenever I heard the pet name Max gave me, my heart warms. "Thanks, Mom."

Jeremy joins us. "Have a safe trip home."

Sally waves to the group and walks out. It's just the married couples left in the conference room now. So much has happened between us. The air is electrified with unspoken words.

"Where's Elizabeth?" I question.

"She stayed back with May until they can find homes for all of the children. Then they are coming back to the Palace."

"Are they bringing all of the chickens?"

"No, only a few. The rest are staying at the compound."

"I see."

The awkward silence returns.

Cherie clears her throat. "It is such a lovely day. Why don't we take a stroll through the gardens before lunch?" She nods to me. "Ann can stretch her legs a bit and visit the Palace flock."

"That's a great idea." I tug my husband outside, and the others follow.

The wind is chilly, but it cools our heated frames. The hens are excited when Ryan offers them crumbs from a bag in his pocket. I watch as he kneels and strokes them. He's changed since we dated, but not everything is different. He's built an icy barrier around his heart to keep from getting hurt again. Cherie maintains her distance, but appears to admire his actions from afar.

"Although we have our differences, we want to be present in Jack's life," the Queen says.

"Why?" Jeremy crosses his arms over his chest.

"Don't worry. We won't be a nuisance," she continues. "It's just that..." She worries her lip. "This child is *special*, and we want to make sure he lives a happy and *free* life." Her hidden implications are clear. Ryan's not going to claim Jack as his own, but he still cares about his offspring and wants to be reassured that the child is loved.

"Then his highness might want to reconsider how he speaks and acts," Jeremy warns. "Because I won't tolerate *my* child being constantly surrounded by bickering and negativity."

I rub my husband's back. "I agree. We want to provide a healthy atmosphere for him."

Ryan wipes his hands on his pants and straightens to

his full height. He offers his palm. "I'll attempt to be on my best behavior."

My husband returns the gesture. "You won't come over unannounced or be alone with my wife or son, unless you discuss it with us first."

"I agree to your terms."

I bump Cherie with my shoulder. "It's nice to see the *kids* getting along."

Her lip twitches. "How long do you think they'll maintain this peace?"

"An hour? Two tops."

"We can hear you," Ryan growls.

"When do you think you'll add another baby to your family." I grin at Cherie as I continue to poke at Ryan's immaturity.

"In about eight months."

Did I hear her right?

Ryan scoops her in his arms and twirls. "Are you serious?"

Her laughter is contagious. She wraps her arms around his neck. "I was trying to wait until I was a few months along. But, yes, I'm pregnant."

The chickens dash out, squawking their distress while they maneuver around the couple, until the King stops and kisses his breathless wife.

"That'll keep them off our backs for a while." Jeremy tugs me to his side.

"And push them to get rid of the monarchy, so their child isn't oppressed by the weight of the crown." I lean my head on his chest. "The great circle of life."

The King and Queen tumble to the ground in a

frenzy of limbs. I cringe and Jeremy covers my eyes. "I say we skip lunch and get out of here as quickly as we can."

"That's the best idea you've had yet."

He guides me to the truck. I take one last look at the towering building and wonder what will become of it when the government changes.

Will all the servants be fired? Will Ryan and Cherie keep the Palace in the family and continue to live here?

"Do you want to grab a cup of coffee in the city?"

I meet my husband's gaze. "No, let's go home."

Feathered Finale

"See? I told you I'd fit all your books in here." Jeremy puffs out his chest like a proud rooster.

My grin spreads as my fingertip glides over the spines. Each one offering an escape to a faraway place, a new adventure. My eyes meet my husband's. And yet, no matter the options, all I want is to be here with him.

"Thank you."

He twirls his level in the air. "I can be pretty handy when I want to be."

"What time is everyone coming over?"

"Why? Are you already trying to push me away?" he teases.

"It was just a question."

When we got back from the Palace, we decided to turn this weekend into a last-minute guys and girls retreat. Jeremy, Dan, and Vinny are going fishing and camping in the woods. While Karen, Sam, and Sally are chilling with me at the house. I know I wanted it to be just me and my mother-in-law at first, but Karen talked me into this last *childless* get-together.

"Vinny's dropping the kids off at their grandparents' house and the others are driving in from work." He kisses my forehead. "Are you sure you're going to be okay without your pickle jar opener?"

"It's only for the weekend."

"Will you miss me?"

My lips brush his. "How could I *not* miss my pickle man?"

"I left Shelby's number on the fridge for the girls in case they need to call her—why are you looking at me

300

like that?"

"Because you're worrying about everything. Why can't you relax and enjoy some time with your brother and best friend?"

"I'll always worry about you." Jeremy tugs me against his chest. "You're my wife, so get used to it."

"Hey. We're coming in. You better not be naked," Vinny announces.

"I guess we should start locking the door. That way, outsiders can't barge inside." Jeremy slaps his friend on the back. "Have you ever heard of *knocking*?"

"I brought junk food and adult movies," Karen sings.

"I thought I was bringing the snacks?" Sam enters with a few cartons of ice cream and Dan in tow.

"The more the merrier." I organize the goodies in the kitchen.

"Sorry we're late," Sally calls from the entrance. The room grows quiet as a tall man stands beside her. She clears her throat. "Luke asked if he could tag along. I hope that's okay."

From what my mother-in-law explained, she and Luke go way back. He was the first rebel to introduce himself and basically saved her life after the enforcers abused her. Then, after Sally divorced her husband, she and Luke dated. Before the raid, there was even talk of him asking her to marry him. But he was captured and everyone thought he was dead.

Surprise! It looks like they thought wrong.

Dan's the first to step forward and pull Luke in for a hug. "It's good to see you, man. How was the drive?"

"Not too bad."

"Good," Dan answers. "The girls put the snacks

301

in the kitchen. Do you need help carrying anything inside?"

"No, I'll grab our bags." Luke pivots and makes his way back to the car.

Once he's outside, Jeremy grumbles, "You should have warned me he was coming."

"Jeremy, please. He's trying to return to a normal life. A camping trip with people he's familiar with is the perfect opportunity to reconnect with him."

"He should be spending time with his daughter," he hisses. "I don't want to *reconnect* with him, Mother. Not after what he did…"

Sally lifts her chin. "If you don't want him to come along, then *you* can tell him. But if you're mature enough to give him a chance, then keep your mouth shut. He's gone through a lot and yet *never* revealed our location. Never risked the compound's safety to save his own neck."

"Maybe not, but he executed my unborn child." Jeremy snatches his backpack. "I'll be in the truck when everyone's ready to leave." He kisses my cheek. "I love you."

I squeeze his hand. "Try to enjoy yourself. I love you too."

He stomps past the crowd without another word. A minute later, Luke enters with his hands full.

"Thank you." Sally grabs a few of the bags from him and sets them on the counter. "The boys are ready to go, whenever you are."

Luke nods. "He's not happy, is he? I knew this was a bad idea."

My gaze travels over the former rebel's scar-riddled frame. *What did those guards do to him?*

302

"Jeremy will be fine. You know how he can get." Sally waves off his concern.

Dan comes to her aid. "After we roast marshmallows, all will be forgotten. You'll see."

Once the men are off doing their own thing, the real party begins. We turn up the music as we paint each other's nails, talk about boys, and munch on sweets.

"Is Dan still in the doghouse?" Karen taps Sam's shoulder. "You guys have gone through a lot."

Sam shrugs. "We're working on our relationship."

"Has the D-word been thrown around?" my bestie questions.

"No, we aren't going to get a divorce." Sam sighs. "We need to rebuild our trust."

"I'm sorry for what happened," Sally admits. "But my son does love you and wants to spend his life with you."

"I know he does." Sam stares at her feet while wiggling her hot-pink toes.

"What about you and that silver fox?" Karen jabs at Sally.

"We go way back." Sally blushes. "I'm not sure if he wants to start anything serious."

"But do you?" she pries.

"I admit not a day went by that I didn't think about Luke. I missed him. But now that he's back, he's not the man I remembered."

I nod as I think about Ryan and how he's changed. Heck, even I've become someone completely different after the events of the last few years.

"I'm glad you two are building a strong friendship."

I pat her arm. "Just see what happens after that. There's no rush."

"You're right."

"Let's put on a movie and order a pizza." Sam waves her phone around. "I say stuffed crust with everything on it."

"And extra meat." Karen giggles. We laugh and settle into the couch cushions. Their company is a breath of fresh air. I'm glad I can spend time with my girls. Feathered and human.

I jolt upright. I'm drenched in sweat and holding my stomach.

"You fell asleep while watching the movie." Sally wipes my brow. "Are you feeling okay?"

"It's probably false labor pains," I huff out.

Karen passes me a glass of water. "Should we call the midwife?"

"No. I'm sure it'll pass."

The three girls share a look.

"I'm calling Jeremy," Sally announces.

"No, let him enjoy his trip." I cringe as the pain twists to my back.

My mother-in-law taps on her cell. "They are packing up now."

"But..."

"Ann, your husband wants to be here with you. Let him," Karen soothes. "He loves you and has been texting us *every* hour checking in. He can't relax anyway."

I smirk. "That sounds like him."

Although Jeremy was an hour away, it takes him less than twenty minutes to return.

"Ann?" My husband breezes to my side and kisses my knuckles. "Did you call Shelby?"

"Yes, she's wrapping up with another patient and will be here soon," Sally answers for me.

I smile at my mother-in-law. My girls have been at my beck and call. Getting me ice to munch on, water to drink, and offering back massages to ease my discomfort. I squeak as the pressure builds with another contraction.

"Do you want me to check her cervix?" Luke asks Jeremy. "To see if she's dilated?"

"Absolutely not," my husband snarls. "Stay away from her."

"I'm just trying to help. I have training in this process."

"The *midwife* will be here soon," Jeremy snips.

Sally clears her throat. "Maybe we should leave."

I clutch her wrist. "But I need my mom."

Her expression softens as she rubs my arm. "Are you sure?"

"Yes." I push through another wave of pain.

"This place is a little crowded," Sam announces. "And I don't want a front-row seat to Jack's arrival. Dan and I are going to go next door, but if you need anything, let us know."

I nod and wave them off—it's about all I can do right now—while Karen swipes my forehead with a rag. "How are you feeling?"

"Like I'm going to implode," I bite out. "My back hurts. Help me walk this out."

Jeremy wraps his arm around my waist and lifts me off the couch. I stride to the back door and Sally helps me shrug on my coat. I take a deep breath as I step outside into the cool evening air. When I look up, I can make out my parents' headstone in the distance. I send a quick prayer, asking them to guide me through this.

I take another step and the chickens peck by my feet, hoping to get a treat. Karen catches Henrietta and brings her to me. I stroke her soft plumage. For a moment, I forget I'm in labor. It's just me, surrounded by my friends and hens. Until that peace is broken and I lean over as another pain shoots through my frame and liquid drips between my legs.

I meet Jeremy's shocked expression. "I think the baby's coming."

Karen and Sally dash into the house to get the bedroom ready for the home birth.

"Please, let me check how far along she is," Luke pleads. "That way, we can prepare for what's next."

My husband bites the inside of his cheek. "What do you think, Ann?"

"I want Jack to be healthy."

"Give me a second chance. I won't let you down," the former rebel pleads.

All eyes are on my husband as he battles his inner turmoil. "You better not."

Once I'm settled, Luke snaps on gloves. "Take a deep breath. I'll be as quick as I can."

I wish I could say it felt awkward having a stranger between my legs, but at this point, I'm in so much pain I don't even question it because I want to hold my son.

Suddenly, Karen bursts inside the room with Shelby on her heels. "Is everyone ready to meet Jack?" the midwife sings. "Because he's on his way."

Jeremy holds my hand and talks me through breathing exercises, while Sally stands by my side, wipes my brow, and hums a familiar tune my mother used to sing to me when I was little.

"Okay, it's time to push," Shelby instructs.

True to her word, Karen assists as my catcher. Vinny is nowhere to be seen. I'm guessing he's standing guard in the hallway or throwing up in the bathroom. Luke passes instruments to Shelby and runs errands whenever he is asked.

The rest of the night and early morning hours are devoted to encouraging Jack to make his appearance. When the pain consumes me, and I'm about to give up on this *all-natural* crap, my newborn's scream rips through the haze. Everyone is silent as we take in the miracle. Tears of joy and exhaustion roll down my cheeks. Shelby lays the baby on my chest, and I hold him tight until he stops screeching. He buries his little nose into my skin as Jeremy moves a shaky hand to Jack and strokes his cheek.

"Hey, son," he whispers.

Sally rubs the infant's back. "You are one lucky guy to have such an amazing mother and father." Then she lifts her eyes to meet our gazes. "Congratulations."

Shelby passes scissors to Jeremy. "Time to cut the umbilical cord, Dad."

Jeremy completes his task with ease before Karen helps clean Jack, then wraps the infant in a soft blanket. She kisses his forehead. "He's perfect, Ann."

"Thank you, everyone, for your love and support. I couldn't have done it without you." I snuggle closer to my son before glancing around my parents' old bedroom. I'm surrounded by their spirit and my friends, both new and old. Collectively, we'll raise this child to have a bright future. One bursting with love, laughter, kindness, and of course his own feathered dreams.

Epilogue

"Jack?" I call from the back door.

I step aside and Jeremy holds out his arms. "Where's our big birthday boy?"

Jack runs over, his dirty blonde hair blown back by the wind.

"Didn't Mom ask you to check on the hens? Where're their eggs?"

"In my pocket."

Jeremy's booming laughter bounces off the walls. "Jack, go change your pants."

I ruffle Jack's messy locks. "Hurry before Aunt Karen, Uncle Vinny, and your cousins arrive."

He examines the yellow spots decorating his jeans. "Oh man!" He stomps past us.

"Take off your shoes!" I shout as he tracks mud into the kitchen. "He never listens. Just like *someone* else I know."

Jeremy gently pushes me against the wall with his body. "Have I told you lately how much I love you?"

"Not since last night."

He kisses my neck. "My mistake."

I arch my back as tingles rack my frame. "We have company coming over any minute. The answer is no." I put space between us. "I mean it." I wag my finger. "Six feet away at all times."

His blue eyes sparkle with mischief. "I'll wear you down by the end of the night." He winks and steps towards me.

"Jeremy..."

Jack runs into his father's leg. "Did Gammy give it to you?"

"Who said I brought you anything?"

The two walk out of the kitchen. "Because you promised me you'd ask her and you always keep your word."

My husband tugs a tiny knife out of his pocket. "Remember, this was my dad's so be extra careful with it, okay?"

"Awesome."

"He's only six. Are you sure a knife is an appropriate gift?"

"Why wouldn't it be?"

"Mom!" a female voice screeches from outside.

My neck snaps to the yard again. "Jack, where's your sister?"

He shrugs as he fiddles with the knife's handle. "Playing with the chickens."

"Marie?" I stride through the lush grass and find my four-year-old yelling at a feathery butt. "I'm telling Mommy on you, Clucker." When she sees me, the girl's hazel eyes light up. "She's stuck in the bush! I told her it was almost bedtime, but she won't listen."

I reach in, past the poison ivy and spider webs, until my fingertips ruffle the spoiled brat's rear end, and then tug. The feathered menace screeches, and her wings scratch my cheeks, but I hold her under my arm.

"Don't worry, honey, I got her."

"You're a hero, Mom!" Marie skips by my side. I toss the hen into the pen. "Are Uncle Ryan and Aunt Cherie here yet?"

"Not yet, honey."

"Do you think they'll bring me something too?"

"It's your brother's birthday party." I glide my hand through her chestnut hair, breaking up her braid.

"Yes, but they never forget me."

I help her inside. "Why don't you wash your hands? It looks like you may have touched some chicken poop."

"Do I have to?" my little tomboy grumbles.

"Yes." I guide her to the sink.

I grin as Karen's family arrives carrying presents, cake, and balloons several minutes later. "Sorry we're late. Someone couldn't find their shoes."

"Vinny, you really need to stop losing your shoes," I tease as I hug my niece and nephew.

The kids giggle, but Vinny rolls his eyes as he sets the cake on the table. "That's very funny—it was *one* time."

"Sure, it was."

As everyone settles in, Jack starts a game of tag that soon gets too rowdy, and the kids take it to the back field. The adults use this opportunity to relax as we watch them out the window.

Karen sighs as the children roll around in the grass. Then she pivots to Jeremy. "Hey, you."

He arches a brow. "What?"

"Are you going to score tonight?" She winks in my direction.

"Karen, shut it," I warn.

Vinny grins at his wife. "I want in on this bet." He

pulls out some bills. "I say Ann can hold back."

"You're not gambling on my sex life." I sip my wine.

"My money is on Jeremy. He's a magician with that mouth of his." Karen fans her face.

I spit out my drink while Jeremy wraps an arm around my neck. "I *am* pretty good," he agrees.

The doorbell rings and I eagerly leave the conversation. I swing the door open and smile at the trio. "Thank goodness. Some *proper* human beings. Please come in before I lose it."

Ryan arches a brow. "What are you losing?"

"Her clothes!" Jeremy shouts.

"Ignore him." I embrace the little angel standing between her parents.

"Daddy said these are your favorite." She hands me a bouquet of roses. "I clipped them from the garden."

"That's very thoughtful. Thank you. The other kids are out back but be careful. Jack has already changed his pants once today."

"I thought you potty-trained him years ago?" Cherie asks.

"For some reason, he decided carrying eggs in his pocket was safer than a basket." I sigh.

"He's clumsy just like his mother." Ryan snorts.

"I am *not*."

"Really? Tell me, have you worn any heels lately or been around any falling hammers?"

"I'm changing the subject now." I lead the group towards Jack.

"Christina, try not to get your dress dirty." Cherie

grimaces as their daughter joins the dog pile in the grass.

I smirk as the kids wrestle, knowing dirt should be the least of a mother's worries, while Ryan rubs Cherie's back. "She'll be fine. Plus, we have that surprise for the birthday boy that should keep her out of the dirt."

"Does Christina enjoy traveling?" I ask the pair.

"Now that she's old enough to accompany us, she's ecstatic." Cherie beams. "She's discovering different cultures and countries firsthand."

"She'll be a formidable ambassador someday," Ryan adds. "It's easier than ruling as queen, and far less dangerous," he whispers the last part to himself.

"She's lucky to have you both leading the way to a brighter future." I elbow him. "I've heard that international trade has never been more accessible."

"You should see some of the silks we obtained last week," Cherie gushes. "I've never felt anything like it— *and* it's durable and affordable."

"You'll have to set it aside for me to look at when we come over for Christina's birthday."

Even though the monarchy has been revamped, Ryan and Cherie still live at the Palace. But now we actually look forward to visiting. The home's more peaceful without the heavy weight of ruling resting on the couple's shoulders.

"Hello!" Elizabeth and May wave at us. "My, oh, my. They grow up fast." Elizabeth's eyes tear up as she takes in the playing children.

We watch as the unstoppable team laughs and catches up with their own flock of misfits.

"Jack, look who's here," I call out.

313

Jack's blue eyes sparkle with recognition. "Uncle Ryan! I missed you!" He hugs him tight.

"I missed you too, buddy. Are you helping Mom around here like I asked?"

Jack grins while lifting and presenting his pointer finger. There's an angry red dot at the tip. "I helped her with the bees this morning."

Ryan kisses the mark. "Sorry, little man. Those bees can really be a pain, huh?"

"Yeah, but Mom put cream on it and made it feel better."

"She's *almost* the best mom in the whole world, huh?" Ryan wraps an arm around his wife.

Jack nods. "Except at bedtime."

"Yeah, I bet."

"What did you guys get me?" My son smiles expectantly.

"Jack Christian Sumptor," I scold. "That's rude."

Ryan waves off my concern. "Come and see, little man."

Jack grabs Ryan's and Cherie's hands and they lead him to the front yard. The other kids follow suit.

"You did it!"

Ryan tugs open the trailer. "We brought four horses for one special boy."

My mouth drops open. "You did what?"

Ryan laughs as the children pet the beasts. "Calm down. I *rented* them. They'll go back to their respective homes tonight."

"You almost gave me a heart attack."

314

"You can afford them, you know. Your and Karen's business is booming."

"That isn't the problem. I do not have the *time* for any more animals."

On cue, Jeremy's massive German Shepherd follows his master. Before the dog passes us, he shoves his nose in Cherie's business and she yelps.

"I've told you a hundred times. Baby Girl won't hurt you. She's saying *hi*," Jeremy says as he lifts Jack onto the horse and secures a riding helmet.

"And I asked *you* to keep the mutt inside the house when we visit," Cherie sneers.

"Why? She's better behaved than you are. Plus, your daughter loves her." Jeremy throws a thumb behind him as the dog licks the little girl's face.

"Christina! Do you know what that thing has licked?" Cherie all but faints.

I rub my palms over the dog's back. "Come on, Baby Girl, why don't we go inside and find you a treat?"

"Mom! Look at me!" Jack calls from atop his mighty steed.

I wave at him as he clutches the horn of the saddle. Even though his eyes are wide with fear, that sparkle behind them reminds me he's Jeremy's child and an adrenaline junkie. As I guide the dog inside the house, the other adults assist their bunch onto the horses. Baby Girl's soft patters echo in the quiet kitchen. I grab a beef bone with swirls of marrow from the freezer and drool drips from her mouth as she sits.

"While the royal pains-in-my-butt are here, you will lie down in the sunroom with your treat. Deal?" I hold out my palm until she agrees by placing her paw on me. "Good girl." I stride to the sunroom and toss the goodie inside before shutting the door. I wait until she happily curls up in her doggie bed and licks the frozen morsel.

As much as I thought I disliked dogs, this one changed my mind. She's well-behaved, affectionate, and protects the children with her life. Jeremy chose the perfect multipurpose farm buddy. And she follows him everywhere. As if she's imprinted on his soul.

"Gammy and Grampy are here!" Marie shouts.

Sally sets her massive stack of gifts on the overcrowded present tower. "Sorry we're late. My tutoring session ran over at the library. But my students can finally work through fractions without pulling their hair out, so it was worth it."

"Can you take me to the library, Gammy?"

"What about your brother's birthday party?"

"I don't like horses. They smell funny."

"Is there an activity we can do together inside the house?"

The girl twirls, her pigtails dancing with the movement. "Could we bake something?" She clutches Luke's arm. "Grampy can help too!"

Sally kisses the child's cheek. "Let me wash up and we can find something to do while the others ride the stinky mammals."

I laugh as the trio raids the cabinets for ingredients. "Is Suzanne coming?" I ask Sally.

"She had to stay behind to clean up, after craft time turned into a glittery war zone. But she and Justin shouldn't be too far behind."

My heart warms at the thought of the family of four joining our entourage. We've grown close to them, especially after the kids were born. The veteran parents know all the good locations to visit to keep our rugrats' growing minds busy. Plus, with Justin working in the same plaza as the café, he's never far away when I need his help.

"Are Heather and Kyle able to drop in?" Sally inquires.

"They have a function at the university but promise to stop by if it's not too late."

The professors that I aided at the charity ball stayed in contact with me. Every year, just as Christian promised, I travel to the school and offer our generous donations while flocking as many deep pockets as I can to the event.

Knowing Marie is in good hands, I join the others on the front porch. I settle in on the swing with Jeremy and he wraps his arm around me. The kids spend a few hours riding the horses before the sun begins to kiss the horizon. The owner loads the beasts back into the trailer and we watch as the dust kicks up as they leave.

"Carter, look at this!" Jack pokes something with a stick.

"Cool!" Carter joins him.

"Daddy!" Olivia runs to Vinny. "The boys are playing in a poop pile."

Vinny jogs to the troublemakers. They grumble but leave the horse patty alone.

I pat Jeremy's thigh. "Good luck cleaning *that* up."

"Ryan brought them over. He should clean it." Jeremy shoots a glare to the man in question.

"Hey, I brought them here for Jack. The least you can do is dispose of their waste."

"As I recall, it's good fertilizer," Cherie interjects. "Ann can utilize it for her fruit trees."

The grumbles cease and the opposing parties retire to their corners, while the children dash inside the house, tracking everything with them in the soles of their boots.

Jeremy kisses the top of my head. "Are you happy?"

"I am."

"She'll be even happier tonight." Karen wiggles her brows.

Cherie clears her throat. "I'm going inside for some refreshments."

I share a giggle with my bestie, then we join everyone in the house. The kids play in Jack's room, while the adults scatter in the living room.

"Patience is everything. Without it, we're lumps of dough," Sally's voice sings from the kitchen.

I peek and see Marie resting in her grandmother's lap, staring into the oven while Luke scrubs the bowls in the sink.

"Look how tall it's getting." The little girl bounces on her feet.

"Yes, with the right ingredients and instructions, we too can rise to the greatness we were designed to achieve." Even though she's whispering to my daughter, Sally meets my gaze and holds it.

I smile and nod, knowing all too well what she means.

At the end of the day, Karen and Vinny carry out two sleeping, sugar-stained kids. Gammy and Grampy tuck in a yawning Jack and sleep-deprived Marie before reading them a bedtime story about a beast and his beauty. The children's eyes remain closed, even after the door is cracked, and Jeremy and I say our goodbyes to the other partygoers.

"I'm going to take out the trash," I tell my husband. As I walk outside, Dan and Sam pull into their driveway. I wave.

"How was the party?" Dan asks as he helps his wife exit the vehicle.

"Loud, messy, and fun. How was work?" I hug the duo.

"It's something to do." Sam shrugs.

"How do you like your new position?"

"I get bored easily sitting in an office chair, but it's nice being closer to Dan."

He kisses her neck. "It's weird having the wife close to me 24/7. But a *good* weird. And she works hard to keep me in line."

"It really is a full-time job," she teases as she rubs her swollen belly. "Plus, it's less physical than security."

"And you can always return to your career after the baby arrives."

"I don't know. I kind of like the flexible hours and

alone time at the desk."

"Whatever you want, I'll support you." Dan massages her shoulders before turning to me. "We'll stop by tomorrow and wish Jack a happy birthday."

"Good, because we saved you some cake and horse manure for your flower garden." I laugh at their frowns. "Or you can just take the sweets."

I close the front door and let out a breath. Being a parent is hard work. I look around at the semi-cleaned house before gliding a fingertip over the new frames on the walls. Life moves faster with children. It feels like I just gave birth to them yesterday.

I jump as Jeremy warms my backside. He wraps his arms around my waist before slipping his hands into my front pockets while his lips trail soft kisses over my neck, lingering at the base of my ear.

"Are you ready for bed?"

I playfully push off his chest. "Who said *you* are winning the bet?"

He grins into my gaze. "What do you mean? I've already *won*."

My husband scoops me up into his arms before carrying me to our bedroom. No matter how many times he does this, I always feel giddy at the gesture.

And we lived happily ever after...

The end

Letter to the Reader

Dearest Reader,

Words can't begin to express my gratitude. This journey has been full of turmoil and hard choices, but you've remained by my side. Through the selection process, when King Mark showed his true colors, and as I mourned the loss of so many loved ones.

Thank you.

Even though my adventure has been tough, I've gained so much. My husband, children, and new besties like you. And for all that I've been blessed enough to receive, I had to endure numerous hardships leading up to this very moment.

Enclosed are a few pictures of our family. Normally, we'd be barefoot and in overalls (or, in the kids' cases, running around naked). It's gifts like these that I cherish. When time freezes and love shines through a moment in time so we never forget.

The flock also sends their love. I'm trying to convince Dan to pen Snowball's adventures, but he feels the task is beneath his abilities. That being said, I bet once Sam has their child, he'll change his mind. Children do that to you. I still look back at how naive I was during my stay at the Palace before I had Jack. One day, I'll explain to him how his journey started, but I'll worry about that later. For now, I'm going to soak in every wonderful moment with my family. And I hope you will too.

All my love,

Ann Sumptor

Thank You

Thank you for reading *Final Flock*. Could you please leave a quick **review** on Amazon and Goodreads? Reviews are so important, and I would greatly appreciate it. Just scan the QR code in the next section. And don't forget to follow me on my socials and sign up for my newsletter to learn when my next book signing will be. Plus, as a bonus, you'll receive Ann's wedding night scene.

Also, a big thank you to my hubby and kids. You guys inspire me (and my stories) every single day. My love for you has no bounds.

A super-sized hug goes out to all my alpha, beta, and ARC peeps. You are amazing! Thank you for taking the time to make this story fantastic. Especially my marvelous word witch editor, Kat Pagan, who has to deal with my word repetitions and comma splices. Frankie, for your alpha read-through, stellar formatting, beta reading, and calling me out with your incredible advice. Also, Alicia, Jennifer, Heather, and Ami for being my VIP readers and providing recommendations on how to make the story better. And who could forget the best digital designer a girl could ask for! Thank you, Rae Lumpkins, for your hard work and dedication. Your masterpieces brought the *Feathered Dreams* world alive. From the five covers to the snowball sketches, the series wouldn't be the same without you.

Additional Titles by the Author

Feathered Dreams, completed series (a rags-to-riches, clean romance):

Join Ann and be swept into a world of swoon-worthy characters, glittering gowns, and unrelenting intrigue.

Ann is beginning to see how naïve she has been, though by no fault of her own. Farming side by side with her father, away from the drama of the outside world, is what she has always loved most. But now that she is at the Palace, she is forced to focus on other people and their daily struggles. In the midst of her personal growth, she starts to realize how cruel the world can be. Will she shy away and run back to the familiarity of her old life? Or can she share her unique sense of compassion and fierce loyalty to help those in need?

Feathered Dreams (Book 1)

Plucked (Book 2)

Molting (Book 3)

Split Feather (Book 4)

Final Flock (Book 5)

Wolves of Cold Creek, standalones within a series (18+, paranormal romance):

The Cold Creek packs are loyal—while bursting with mouthwatering, unclaimed shifters—all just waiting for their mates. Why not drop in and enjoy the picturesque views by day and scorching fires at night? Don't be shy. They don't bite... hard.

Scarlett's Tail

Sky's Tail

Lily's Tail TBA

Cooking Up Disaster (slow-burn romance):

Step into the Decadent Cup and grab something hot! In the small town of Jasper, this café offers handcrafted coffee and killer banana nut muffins while stirring up the most unlikely couples. Read their journeys as they cook up disaster and create new blends of mischief. Season 1 with Blake and Amy: Ep 1-69. Season 2 with Kay and Jason: Ep 69+.

(Episodes available now only on Kindle Vella.)

About the Author

Brittany Putzer was born and raised in Central Florida, so the need for sunshine (and coffee) is imbedded in her DNA.

Growing up, she turned to books to escape, because it was easier to pretend to be a wizard, vampire, or damsel in distress.

She hopes her stories help readers remember how strong they really are... if only they keep moving and fighting the good fight.

Scan to chat with Brittany on social media, **review** her books, get signed paperbacks, check out her merchandise, meet her at conventions, and join her newsletter for freebies and sneak peeks.

Want a glimpse of Ann's steamy wedding night? Sign up for my newsletter and I'll send it to you for FREE. This is an 18+ chapter that depicts how the couple consummates their marriage.